THE PASSAGE

Emily Slate Mystery Thriller
Book 16

ALEX SIGMORE

Dark Woods Press

THE PASSAGE: EMILY SLATE MYSTERY THRILLER BOOK 16

1st Edition

Print ISBN 978-1-957536-79-8

Description

Where the highway ends, the nightmare begins.

Reassigned to a quiet field office in Albuquerque after a mysterious data breach, FBI agent Emily Slate is restless. But when a young woman's body is found in the New Mexico desert, she's thrust into a case that feels far more dangerous than it seems. With only her partner Zara for backup, Emily quickly realizes that this wasn't a random killing—but instead is part of something much bigger.

As they dig deeper, Emily and Zara uncover a twisted conspiracy of treachery and betrayal, a plot that stretches across the barren desert and threatens to claim more lives. Racing against time, they must unravel the deadly scheme before the killer strikes again—and before they become the next targets.

In the vast emptiness of the desert, danger is closer than it appears.

Prologue

"I TOLD you half a dozen times already. It's not a big deal." Gregory sat behind the wheel, his focus divided between the dark road ahead of him and the fact his wife wouldn't drop the subject since they'd left Albuquerque. This was supposed to be a *relaxing* vacation, after all. But she'd been determined to start it off like they started every trip with an argument.

"I just don't understand why you didn't tell me *before* you made the appointment. We could have gone together."

Gregory shot her the side-eye. "It wasn't a date. You didn't need to be there." Ah, shit. He hadn't meant for it to come out like that. And yep, there she went, shutting down like always. Great. Perfect start to their trip.

"What did you do, Dad?" Gregory glanced in the rearview at his eight-year-old son sitting in the backseat. His eyes were wide, probing.

"I thought you were tired," Gregory whispered. *That* should have been the tone he took with Bev.

"The seat's lumpy," Ben said. "I can't get to sleep."

Bev turned around in her seat. "Here, let me fluff your pillow. It's a long drive to Phoenix. You don't want to be tired when we see Grandma and Grandpa, do you?"

"No," Ben replied.

"I know it's not as nice as your bed," Gregory said. "But it's just for a few hours. Then we'll be there and you and Molly can play all day, okay?"

"Okay," his son replied, lying back down. Playing with his parents' beagle had been all Ben had talked about for the past week. Bev turned back around in her seat, but she didn't look at her husband. The two of them stayed silent for the next twenty minutes as he drove, the darkness stretching out before him. At this time of night, there were barely any cars on the highway, only the occasional truck that passed on the other side. Behind them was another pair of headlights in the distance, but they had to be at least a mile back.

He wished they could have gotten out of Albuquerque sooner, but he'd taken longer at his appointment than he'd thought, and Bev hadn't finished packing by the time he returned home. Then Ben had made a fuss about dinner. Somehow he'd gotten it into his head that any kind of fast-food was going to kill him one day, which meant he no longer touched it. So they'd had to fix him something, delaying things even further. All of which meant it was two hours past schedule before they were finally on the road. At this rate, they wouldn't hit Phoenix until noon tomorrow, and that was if they drove all the way through. He was tired enough from a full day at work, but the two Red Bulls he'd pounded before getting in the car should be enough to get him through the next few hours. If he got tired after that, he'd pull over.

"I just don't see how we're supposed to be a team if you hide things from me," Bev finally said, her voice hushed so she wouldn't wake Ben, who had finally fallen asleep.

"Jesus, Bev, you're acting like I went out and bought a car or something," he said, his voice equally quiet. "The whole point of the meeting was security for you and Ben."

"It just doesn't feel like it when you don't tell me, is all I'm saying."

He wanted to slam his head against the wheel. Why was she being so obstinate? Just because he went out and set up a will without telling her. It wasn't like he'd been planning on it for months. They'd had someone come around that morning at work advertising the service, and it sounded like a good idea to him. After the nightmare Aunt Shelley went through after Uncle Roman died, he figured it was the best thing for his young family. That way, if anything ever happened to him, there would be no confusion where what few assets he had would go.

"Remember what the therapist said? You need to include me when you make decisions like that," she added.

Gregory rolled his eyes. Right. The *therapist*. The one she'd forced him to see. He'd done that for her, hadn't he? What did he have to do to prove himself to her?

"Fine, as soon as we get back, I'll take you right over there. You have to sign the forms anyway," he said. "Happy?"

"Not if you're going to keep shutting me out," she replied. She placed her hand on his arm. "I just want to be part of the decision process. I mean, why not wait until after the trip?"

"Well, you never know," he replied. "The way the salesgirl made it sound, I thought before the trip was better. She started reading off all these statistics about car crashes and—"

"Okay, stop," his wife said, holding up her hands. "I don't need to hear the odds of us dying in a fiery crash." She took a breath. "But maybe if you'd called me, I could have told you it was something that could wait until we got back. We're only going to be gone for a few days."

"I know," he replied.

"You're always so impulsive," she said.

"Yep, that's me," he replied sarcastically. "Impulsive Gregory, as always."

His wife huffed. "You know what I mean."

The car descended into silence once again. They'd been arguing more lately, *despite* the therapy sessions. Maybe that was because therapy was forcing Gregory to open wounds he'd long thought closed. That was one reason he didn't like it. Why bring all this stuff from the past back up when it's over and done with? Why not let sleeping dogs lie?

But no, they had to pick at the scab, tear it away and start the bleeding process all over again. He took a deep breath. This was going to be a long ride, and he didn't want to fight the entire way. Instead he checked the rearview mirror, only to see the car that had been far behind them only moments ago was a lot closer.

"Huh."

"What?" Bev asked.

"Nothing. Just… that car must be doing about ninety to have caught up with us this quick."

His wife turned around in her seat to look past the packed bags that filled the space behind their sleeping son. The vehicle behind them couldn't have been more than a few hundred yards back.

"I think you're right," she said. "They're coming up fast."

Despite his best efforts, Gregory felt something like anxiety deep within his chest. When he argued that he'd set up a meeting with the will sales associate, it had been mostly to prove a point. And to deflect from the fact the saleswoman had been drop dead *gorgeous.* Not that he thought anything could ever happen between the two of them; but if he was going to get a will, he'd much rather have purchased it from her rather than some old fogey. Had that influenced his decision? Maybe. But he wasn't going to apologize for it.

He also wasn't going to admit it to his wife.

Though, as he watched the headlights bear down on them, all of that slipped from his mind as it went into survival mode. Should he speed up? Pull over? They were out here in the middle of nowhere. What if the person behind them had fallen asleep at the wheel and was about to ram into them doing seventy-plus?

His grip tightened on the wheel.

"Greg?" his wife said, grabbing hold of his arm. But his attention was laser-focused on the vehicle, which looked like a sports car of some kind. It was coming up so fast. He pressed on the accelerator, pushing the speedometer past eighty and still the car was bearing down on them.

"Just pull over," his wife insisted.

"What if it's one of those things?" he asked, sweat forming on his brow.

"What things?"

"Where they get you to pull over and rob you? Or worse?" The car had pulled right up on their bumper. It hadn't slammed into them, which meant the driver hadn't fallen asleep. But that didn't make Gregory feel any better. The car behind them both flashed its lights and honked its horn.

"What's going on?" Ben asked from the backseat.

"Nothing, honey. Go back to sleep," Bev said.

It was clear he wouldn't be able to outrun them. Not in a twelve-year-old SUV that hadn't had its oil changed in twelve months.

"Just go around," Gregory muttered. *Please.* His heart was hammering in his chest now. What would he do if they forced him off the road? He didn't have a gun or anything else that could be a weapon, except maybe a tire iron.

Finally, the car swerved around him into the other lane. As it drove up beside him, he couldn't help but look over. A pair of boys—men, really—sat in the front seat, shooting Gregory the finger and laughing. Their dark red Camaro pulled ahead of Gregory and slammed on the brakes, causing him to do the same.

"Dad!"

"Ohmygod," Bev said at the same time their son yelled. For a brief second, Gregory thought he hadn't been able to stop in time and would slam into the back of the car. The seatbelt was digging into his chest, threatening to rip him in half. A second later, the Camaro then peeled off, speeding out into the distance ahead of them.

Gregory looked down at the speedometer. He was barely doing forty, but his heart felt like it was going a thousand miles per hour.

"Daddy, what was that?" Ben asked.

"Just a couple of assholes," he replied.

"*Greg!*" his wife shouted.

"Sorry," he replied. But it was true. Just a few joyriders out late, doing what teens always did. It had been the same when Greg had been a kid. Though he'd never done anything as dangerous as brake-check cars on the highway.

He took a few deep breaths as the taillights of the Camaro disappeared into the distance. His hands were still shaking. As soon as he saw a rest stop, he would pull over, get a hold of himself.

He turned to Bev, who was tending to Ben in the back. "You okay?"

"Yeah, just a little rattled," she said. In the back, his son was sitting straight up, any semblance of sleep lost to him.

"Hey, bud, why don't you pull out your Switch?" Gregory suggested. His wife shot him a glare. "Just for a few minutes."

"Really?" he asked.

"Greg," Bev said.

"I'm going to pull over at the next stop anyway," he said. "He's not going back to sleep. Might as well keep him busy." His wife was notorious among all their friends about limiting "screen time", but they'd all just had a harrowing experience and the last thing Greg wanted was for their son to dwell on it any longer than necessary. Playing the game would get his mind off things.

Fifteen minutes later, they finally saw the first gas station in what had to have been a good forty-five minutes, its bright red and orange lights contrasting against the pitch black sky.

"Finally," Gregory said. He'd calmed down since the incident, but he was eager to get out of the car for a minute and walk around. Try to burn off some of this extra energy.

But as he was pulling into the parking lot, he noticed a dark red Camaro sitting at one of the gas pumps.

"Damnit," he said.

"Language," Ben said from the back, though his attention was focused more on the game. He'd gotten into the habit of calling either of them out when they cursed in front of him.

"Let's just go to the next one," Bev said.

"That might not be for another hour," he replied. "I'm not going to let them terrorize us into leaving."

"Weren't you the one just talking about risk?" his wife said. "That something might happen at any moment?" All it took was one look to realize she was right. The sales pitch from the pretty saleswoman earlier in the day rang through his mind. *You could never be too careful.* What if they were armed? He couldn't put his family at risk, no matter how remote that possibility seemed.

"Look, just pull around back until they leave, okay?"

Gregory sighed, then nodded. He pulled past the pumps for the smaller vehicles and around the back of the station, putting the car in park. He'd wait another five minutes before driving back around to check again. As he sat there, rubbing his forehead, the only sound in the vehicle was the soft music coming from Ben's video game. A second later, the telltale music chimed that marked the end of one level and the beginning of the next.

"Ok, Ben, time to put it away," Bev said.

"Already?" he protested.

"Already. We're going to use the restroom in a minute and then we need to get back on the road."

Their son sighed. "Okay." Greg looked at the clock on the dash. It had been four minutes. They were probably gone, right?

"Dad?"

"Yeah?" he answered.

"What's that?"

"Hm?" Gregory turned around, but his son was staring out the window. As he was sitting on the same side of the car as Greg, he turned to see what his son was staring at.

All at once, his stomach dropped and all thoughts of the Camaro disappeared.

Sticking out from behind the dumpster were a pair of human legs. He realized how much they looked like the saleswomen from earlier today. Except these legs were in fishnets, not pantyhose.

"What are you doing?" his wife asked as he got out of the car.

But he didn't answer. He had to see for himself.

As Gregory came around the corner of the dumpster he blanched, then ran to the other side and promptly threw up.

Chapter One

THIS PLACE FEELS LIKE DEATH.

Maybe it's the vast emptiness of it all, or maybe it's the fact that I keep running into skeletons out here. Don't get me wrong, this place has its own kind of beauty. Drive five minutes outside the city and I can see more stars than I ever knew existed. Or when I'm on a hike with Zara and I can't help but stop to admire the local fauna. It's beautiful, but deadly. Life is tough out here, and everything has adapted. Which means it's all a little sturdier; a little sharper. And no matter what I do, I can't seem to get mortality out of my head whenever I stare out into the endless nothingness of the desert.

The wind whips at my face as I drive down the empty road, looking for our target. Beside me, Zara is singing at the top of her lungs, though most of her voice is lost to the breeze as she's got all four windows of the SUV down. In the month we've been here, I've used more moisturizer than I have in an entire year just trying to keep my skin from drying out. That's another thing about this place; the dry air will suck all the moisture out of anything. Half the days when I wake up I feel like a mummy recently risen from the dead.

For whatever reason, this place hasn't affected Zara like it has me. Maybe it's because she doesn't have a house she just purchased with her boyfriend and two dogs at home. Or maybe she's just tougher than I am. Over the past month, while I've been navel-gazing, she's remained as constant as ever. This place hasn't gotten to her yet. Maybe it never will. But it's driven me to the brink. Not being able to see Liam or the pups has really done a number on my psyche, and I haven't felt like myself these past two weeks. I've been part of long assignments before, but this is different. This time, I'm not in control. Someone else is.

Zara smacks my arm playfully, bringing me back.

"Em! C'mon!"

I sigh and inwardly roll my eyes before joining her. For some reason, she can't just leave me to myself; she insists I sing along with her. But I'm not in a singing mood. I move my mouth to placate her; not a sound coming out. There's no way she'd be able to hear me anyway, given I can barely hear *her* because of the wind buffeting the vehicle. As soon as she dropped all the windows I had to tie my hair back to keep it from whipping about my face like a medusa.

"Hey, like you mean it!" She smacks my arm again.

"Ok, jeez," I yell and finally start belting out the tune: some nineties pop song I vaguely remember growing up.

"I know all your tricks, *Agent Dunn*," she chides again before joining me. The two of us sing-slash-yell at the top of our lungs as the drab landscape passes us by. I have to admit, it feels good and as I finally put my all into the words I somehow know by heart, I feel all the anger and anxiety at our current situation flow through me like a dam that's been broken.

Forty-one days. That's how long we've been sequestered in New Mexico. Ever since a breach was discovered in the FBI that seemed to target me and five other random agents. I was pulled from all my assignments, had to say goodbye to Liam and my dogs and sent out into the middle of the fucking desert to work out of the New Mexico field office. Apparently, it was the only way I could continue working for the FBI. But further complications meant both Zara, and I had to adopt aliases, something my boss wasn't too happy about. They wanted to throw me into protection, keep me holed up in some house in the middle of the woods somewhere until they worked this whole thing out. But that wasn't about to happen. Thankfully, with Zara's skills, we convinced SSA Caruthers we could make it work with no one being the wiser. But the bigger problem is the Bureau has no idea why we are being targeted. It's not my first time adopting a new name, but it *is* my first time going undercover in my own organization. Except this time, it isn't to sniff out a rat or to help the investigation; instead, it's to keep me safe while they figure out what's going on.

I assume, but can't say for sure, the other five agents have been put in some kind of protective custody—or at least sequestered from view for the time being. Maybe some of them could wrangle themselves into a temporary position out of a satellite office somewhere like Zara and I have, or maybe they're happy to be relegated to the shadows for the time being. There's no way for me to know because I don't know who they are. Rule number one since the discovery of the breach has been to wall off information as much as possible. Right now, the right hand of the FBI doesn't know what the left is doing, and vice versa.

So this is the deal. Zara and I work under assumed names, complete with backstories Zara constructed—and we get to keep working for the FBI while the investigation proceeds. However, one stipulation is that we are to be assigned only low-level cases, in order to keep a low profile in the Bureau. Which is how we find ourselves driving deep into the New Mexico desert looking for some random turnoff on a dirt road.

"Should be about—" Zara yells over the wind, but her words are lost.

"What?"

"A HUNDRED FEET!"

I slow the car, allowing the wind to let up. Before she can say anything else, I see it ahead, a small turnoff from the highway, dirt tracks leading to and away from it. A small mile marker post is the only sign that we know where we are. Well, that and Zara's satellite feed.

I turn on the road, slowing the SUV so the bumpy track won't tear the transmission from the vehicle. Now that the wind isn't blowing so hard, I turn the music down so I can actually talk to my partner.

"How long on this stretch?"

"About five hundred feet, then there should be another turnoff," she replies, staring at the laptop on her lap. Her legs are crossed even though somehow she's kept her seatbelt on. But she's hunched over the computer, much like she is when we're in one of our apartments back in Albuquerque. Zara is the definition of relentless, and ever since we arrived, she's been doing her best to figure out who is targeting me and the other agents, but so far, she's had little luck. It doesn't help that she's been frozen out of the usually vast resources she's used to, so she's been hamstrung from the beginning. Any searching she might do could end up attracting unwanted attention. And until the Bureau has a handle on whatever is happening, I don't see either of us regaining access soon.

Ahead of us I see the fork in the dirt, marked only by dried natural drainage ditches on each side. I stay to the right and after another twelve minutes, we find ourselves at a makeshift parking lot in the dust where six other vehicles are parked, including two local patrol vehicles. An officer stands in front of one of the vehicles and raises a hand to us as we pull alongside his truck.

"I hate this part," I mutter as I cut the engine.

"Just think of it as a play," Zara replies. I give her a look that says I'm not amused before stepping out of the vehicle, my alias already in hand.

"Agent Claire Dunn, FBI," I tell the officer, barely flashing my new ID. "This is my partner, Agent Fiona Laidlaw. We're your backup."

The officer nods. "Thank you for coming. Have to admit, I was surprised to get a call from the local FBI office. But I'm not about to turn away another two pairs of eyes. We're short on staff because of a big train incident down in Sierra, and this is a matter of some urgency."

I survey the area and can spot a couple of dots of people in the distance. "How many do you have on site so far?"

"About thirty. Was really hoping y'all would have a helicopter we could use."

"Sorry, it's in the shop," Zara says. "Typical grid pattern?"

He nods. "Yep. We got over six hundred square miles to search out here and we've barely broken the surface. Ideally, I'd like to find her before nightfall."

I check my watch. It's closing in on eleven A.M. Which means the hottest part of the day is still ahead of us. We heard the call come over the monitor in the office—missing hiker that didn't check in yesterday. Which means she's still out here somewhere. Normally it isn't even something the FBI would be involved with, but after some pleading with our new boss, SSA Strong, he finally relented and let us offer our help in the search. It was either that or continue to sit around the office and do menial paperwork like we have for the past four weeks. The only reason he probably approved the request was so he wouldn't have to listen to me moan and complain any longer.

The truth is, I don't care *what* the case is. I've been so antsy to get out of the office that I'll go pull a cat out of a tree if I have to. Just as long as it's *something*.

The officer hands me a map of the area. He's already marked through a small portion of it with a red felt pen.

"Here's what we've managed so far. Teams Verde and Indigo are here and here. Figured y'all could coordinate this section."

"Sounds like a plan," I say, gathering the map and folding it in my pocket. I already have a good idea of the geography out here—it's flat, open and desolate. If she's still alive, then she's probably under a rock cropping or other natural shade area, trying to stay out of the sun. The only problem with that is snakes and other venomous creatures like to use that shade, too. "What's your frequency?"

"Uh," he looks down at the radio strapped to his hip. "Seven hundred hertz."

I hold out my hand. "Thanks officer—"

"Arras," he replies, taking it and giving it a hearty shake.

"We'll be in touch," Zara says, heading back to the SUV to grab the radios. Arras nods, then gets in his truck and heads out into the desert, driving away from the teams of people in the distance. I grab a coverall hat and a large bottle of water before removing my blazer and tossing it in the back of the SUV.

"See, that wasn't so hard," Zara says.

I purse my lips as I lock the vehicle. "C'mon. We're wasting daylight."

Chapter Two

"Em," Zara says, pulling my attention from the map Arras gave us this morning. Using the volunteers on hand, we've covered approximately a sixth of the entire area, which is impressive given how much open space there is out here. But unfortunately there's been no sign of the missing hiker—yet. I'm not giving up hope even though I already know what Zara is going to say. We've only got another thirty minutes until sunset, which means we'll need to round up the volunteers. The last thing we need is to lose someone else out there tonight. Combined with the local officers, we have almost a hundred people searching different areas of the desert. We could use at least another hundred, but that brings its own challenges. The more people we have searching means the more people we need to keep track of, to make sure are staying hydrated, and to monitor. I check my empty water bottle, knowing full well I haven't had nearly enough water today, and I can feel it in my joints. That, and my back is completely soaked.

"Yeah," I say, flipping the map back over. "Let's call them back in. We'll have to start again first thing in the morning. Preferably before sunrise so we can beat some of this heat."

"Agreed," she says and gets on the radio to relay the orders to the team leads. "I just hate giving up knowing she's out there somewhere."

"Me too," I reply. "But we can't search in the dark. We're just as likely to get lost as we are to stumble upon her." Still, there's a deep ache in my stomach, like I've eaten something sour. One night out in the desert is survivable, two is stretching things. Unless our hiker is very good at survival, I don't put her chances very high. And every hour we wait makes it that much more likely we'll find a corpse instead of a very thirsty woman.

As the teams return to the parking lot, I check with each of them to make sure they didn't see something that could have been significant. Even though they have been given specific instructions to report *anything*, sometimes people don't realize what they're looking at. A discarded bottle cap, a handprint on a glassy rock… sometimes the signs are right in front of us and we don't even know it.

"Wait a second," I say, looking over the list of volunteers Arras gave us this morning. "Look at this." I hand the list to Zara as she furrows her brow.

As her gaze meets mine, I know we're thinking the same thing. I pull out my radio again. "Team lead six, report your position."

"About twenty feet from the parking lot," the man replies.

"How many people were on your team this morning when you began searching?" I ask.

"Fifteen, why?"

"Because we just checked *sixteen* bodies through here," I say.

"That can't be right," he replies. "I checked them myself when we went out this morning and again when we took a break for lunch."

"Hang on," I say, but Zara is already way ahead of me,

speaking with each of the volunteers headed for their respective cars.

"Agent Dunn," she calls from the location of a blue Subaru sitting in the corner of the "lot." The same blue Subaru that belongs to our *missing* person. I trot over to her standing beside a dazed-looking woman with a set of keys in her hand. "I think we can call off the search."

"You've got to be shitting me," I say, looking the woman over. Her dark hair is matted, but I figured that was from spending the day out in the desert searching. "What's your name?"

"Angelica," she replies. "Is something wrong?"

"Angelica Dumfries, correct?" I ask. She nods. I grimace and get on the radio again. "*All teams, this is Magenta Lead. Be advised, subject has been located. I repeat, the subject has been found. Stand down all search efforts and return to your designated rally points. Confirm receipt.*" While each of the team leaders check in, I look our missing person over. Her hair is a lot longer than the reference photo we'd been given. That and she looks generally emaciated, like she hasn't been eating well lately. "Where did you come from?"

"Um, I was over by Huxton Canyon," she says. "You know, just… relaxing. I heard somebody shouting someone's name, so I figured someone must be lost. I couldn't really make out what they were saying, but I figured I'd help too."

"Yeah, they were shouting *your* name," Zara says. "You've been missing for over twenty-four hours."

"Wait…" the woman says. It's easy to see her eyes are glassy. "What day is it?"

"It's Monday the seventh," I reply.

"It's *Monday*?" she asks. "Crap, I missed work."

I sigh as I receive the last of the confirmations. I turn it off before facing Ms. Dumfries again. "Do you realize there has been a massive manhunt looking for you for the past sixteen hours? You joined your own search party."

"I did?" she asks before grinning. "That's pretty funny."

"It's not *funny*," I say. "You have wasted hours of government resources, not to mention put other people's lives at risk. We have volunteers from three counties out here looking for you."

"I'm sorry," she says. "I was just looking to get away for the weekend. You know, head out to the desert and just… *relax*."

Yeah, I know what she means. It seems to be a popular pastime here to go out where there are no people around and partake in various *substances*. I'd have to do a drug test for sure, and I wouldn't be surprised if Ms. Dumfries was on something strong. Much stronger than marijuana anyway.

"What do you want to do?" Zara asks.

I sigh. She can't drive in her condition, she's still coming down from whatever she took out in the desert. Not to mention we'll need to get the locals involved again. I switch my radio back on and call Arras before returning my attention to Zara. "Observation until she clears whatever is in her system. Then we cut her loose."

"Wait, what does that mean?" Dumfries asks.

"It means a night in the drunk tank," I reply.

"*Jail?* I can't go to jail, I haven't done anything wrong," she protests, stepping back from the car. But Zara is right behind her and gently urges her back into place.

"Trust me, you're getting off easily," I say. "I should charge you with a misdemeanor and order you to repay what this cost, but I'm not going to do that. But the next time you head out into the desert for a little personal time, make sure you at least tell someone where you're going. Or keep your phone charged."

"Oh," she says. "Right. I guess… I guess I wasn't thinking anyone would be looking."

"Maybe more people care about you than you think," I say as Arras pulls up in his patrol car.

After about fifteen minutes of explaining the situation and making sure the rest of the volunteers are all accounted for, Arras leaves with Dumfries in the back of his squad car. She gives us a little smile as he drives off. And while I should feel better, I don't. Dumfries was never in any real danger; she lost track of time because she was careless. And we wasted a full day out in the desert searching for someone who wasn't really missing. It's a microcosm of this entire last month. We're here, we're "working," and yet we're not actually *doing* anything. I'm not moving the needle. All I'm doing is spinning my wheels. And it's infuriating.

"C'mon Agent *Dunn*," Zara says, putting her arm around my shoulder. "Let's get back home. I've got a bottle of Pinot with my name on it."

"It's not home," I say, opening the door to the SUV. The heat of the day has made it like an oven inside and I keep the doors open for a minute to let the car cool down.

"I know," she says, sympathy in her eyes. "But for now, it's the best we've got."

Two hours and a long, cool shower later I'm sitting in my apartment in the comfiest sweats I own, a glass of whiskey and a bottle of water sitting on the table in front of me. There's a knock at my door, startling me out of the trance I don't realize I'm in.

"Evening," Zara says, her signature grin spread across her lips. In one hand is a bottle of Pinot Noir and in the other a singular wine glass. I step to the side and she comes in, setting her glass beside mine on the table. "Don't tell me you got started without me."

"Haven't taken a sip," I reply, though I had meant to. I'd meant to down one before she even came over but I just… didn't. I don't know why.

"Good," she says. "We can drink to a job well done together." With one hand she unscrews the cap from the bottle of wine and pours herself a generous glass. "Gotta keep it fancy, you know, for appearances."

"I wouldn't care if you drank it out of a trough," I say, taking a seat on the couch and pulling my legs up under me. My "apartment" is little more than a one-bedroom studio in a small complex on the east side of town. Zara snagged us units next to each other in this block, which is convenient considering she's the only person I interact with. Tonight is my night to host. And while her apartment is completely decked out in décor she believes is fitting for her "alter-ego," I've not so much as hung a single picture and my clothes remain in my suitcase—at least, the ones I haven't worn yet. I don't see the point. I hadn't expected to be here this long and every day that passes is just another failure on the FBI's part to figure out what's going on here.

In some ways, this place reminds me a lot of my apartment after Matt. But at least there I had Timber. Here when I come home, it's just… empty.

"Here, do the thing," Zara says, holding up her glass.

"Seriously?" I ask.

"C'mon… do it. Dooo ittt."

I sigh and pick up my glass. "Congratulations on cracking the case, Agent *Laidlaw*."

She clinks her glass with mine. "Why, thank you Agent *Dunn*. Congratulations yourself." We both take a ceremonious sip, but I barely even taste mine before returning it to the table. "I think your new persona fits you."

I scoff. "It's no different from my regular persona."

"Oh, yes it is," she replies. "The brooding, mysterious Agent Claire Dunn, whose background is shrouded in mystery. Who never interacts with her fellow agents unless she's required to."

"You make that sound like a bad thing, *Laidlaw*," I say,

taking another drink and this time actually tasting the liquor. "Real inconspicuous by the way."

She puts her glass down. "Ok, first, it's awesome. It's like I'm *laying* down the *law* wherever I go. Criminals cower at my feet when they hear my name aloud. And second, I think it's English. I got it off some movie credits I saw once."

For the first time all day I actually produce a smile.

"You have to give us a little credit," she says. "We *did* find her."

"Yeah, by accident," I say.

She purses her lips and sets her glass back on the table. "Okay. Out with it."

I look up. "What?"

"Whatever is gnawing at you. I'm not going to sit here all night and watch you wallow in self-pity. So let's get it over with so we can watch a movie or something."

I glance over my shoulder at the flowers wilting on the kitchen counter. They're the only color in the room. A gift from Zara a week ago after complaining my place resembled a hotel room. Since then, I've been pretending they were from Liam. As a condition of this "arrangement" I haven't been able to talk to him regularly, in the event communications channels are being monitored. In order to have any communication at all, I purchase a "burner" phone, which can be used for a maximum of five minutes. Then I'm required to wait seventy-two hours before I can call again. This situation isn't doing either of us any good.

"It's fine," I say. "I'm fine."

"You can't lie to me, remember?" she says, getting up.

"Where are you going?"

"I'm not staying here if you're going to mope all night," she says. "Cthulhu is calling my name." I assume that's some new video game she's been working on in the few spare hours she's not investigating the breach.

"Wait," I say, getting up as well. "I'm sorry. It's just this whole thing with Dumfries today. It's just so *stupid*."

"Look at it this way: that's another person out in the wilderness we don't have to worry about," she replies before leveling her gaze at me. "Look. I know this isn't ideal. Neither of us wants to be here. But why not try to make the best of it. Who knows? Caruthers and Janice could figure out what's going on tomorrow and we could be on a plane home by the end of the week."

I give her a derisive snort. "Yeah, and I'm about to win the lottery."

"Statistically it *is* possible," she says. "However unlikely." Thankfully she returns to the side chair with no further pleading from me.

"Today was the first day in a month I actually felt a tiny bit like my old self," I say, resuming my seat on the couch. "Like I was actually working. And then when we 'found' her, it was like it was all stripped away again. Just another punch in the gut telling me we're not really FBI agents out here. At best we're beat cops. At worst, parking attendants."

"C'mon Em, you know that's not true," Zara replies. "We've been working backup on a lot of higher profile cases. What about that thing Agent Dent was investigating? We did a lot of background research on that one."

"For all the good it did. They shuttered the case. I guess I'm just not used to so much desk time." I sigh.

"That's true," she says. "It comes a lot more naturally to me, I suppose."

"I just don't know how much longer I can do this," I finally say.

"What? New Mexico?"

"All of it," I reply. "The alias, the tiny office, the desert. At this rate, we're never going to figure out who is behind the breach and why. And I'm not about to spend the rest of my life out here."

"What are you saying?" she asks.

I take another swig of the glass, emptying it and setting it back down on the table. "I think…I'm going to talk to Agent Strong tomorrow. And if he's not willing to put us on a genuine case, I'm going to hand in my resignation."

Chapter Three

WHOEVER SAID the cure for a hangover was greasy foods was full of shit. My head has been pounding ever since I woke up severely dehydrated and despite multiple attempts at rectifying the situation, I feel like I've been run over by a tank.

Still, I'm resolved to go through with my plan. To say Zara was shocked was an understatement, but what I realized last night in a half-inebriated fog is that all this time I haven't been willing to give myself permission to quit. I've never quit anything in my life before. It was something pounded into me from a young age; you can't succeed if you quit. And despite everything that's happened in my career, I've never given up hope and I've never stopped working towards my goals. And all of that was going swimmingly until I was promoted to SSA. I think that's where the trouble began. Because that wasn't the position for me. I didn't enjoy overseeing the operations from the office and I didn't enjoy bossing my peers around. I didn't want all the responsibility.

And that's when the crack formed.

Maybe I didn't realize it at the time, but I think something began growing in my brain that maybe this career wasn't the right one for me after all. I've spent so much time and effort to get where I am only to realize that this is the end of the road. I will be a field agent for the rest of my career here—which was and is absolutely by choice.

But this situation… this is unsustainable. I can't keep pretending to be Agent Claire Dunn and hope that someone at the Bureau eventually figures out what's going on. I have to *do* something. And I think I finally realized last night that I needed to give myself permission to quit.

But that doesn't mean I plan on working in retail, or, God forbid, an office job. I have a certain set of skills that could be very useful to several organizations, primarily the CIA. They'd be thrilled to have someone of my age and experience on their team, though it would mean most likely leaving the US. I don't know how that would work with Liam. But it can't be any worse than the situation I'm in now.

Zara tried to talk me out of it, but my mind is made up. If this situation doesn't change, and I mean today, then I'm calling it. I'll notify Caruthers from here. Maybe if I'm no longer an agent, I can at least get my life back. Maybe whoever is targeting me and the other agents is hoping to get some classified data out of me. If I'm removed from the system entirely, my value to them drops to zero.

At least, that was my thinking last night. I don't know who it was, but someone said that you should make a decision twice: once drunk and once sober. And if you come to the same conclusion both times, then that's the direction you should take.

It was easy enough to reach this conclusion last night. And when I woke up this morning, I felt even better about it. In fact, the more I think about it, the more right it feels. Maybe I'll regret it in a month or two, but at least I'll be back home. And with any luck, I'll be on my way to a new career.

I approach my boss's door, giving it a quick knock before sticking my head in.

"Agent Dunn, come in," SSA Reginald Strong says. He's a

thin man with an even thinner moustache with a penchant for wearing suspenders and dark green striped ties. I've known Strong for a solid month now and I can say for certain he's a straight-shooter. He doesn't put up with any bullshit and doesn't like inefficiency. He and I are alike in that respect.

"Good morning," I say, fully resolved to go through with my plan. Why does this feel so right?

"Your timing couldn't be better," he says, still not looking up from his monitor. "I was about to call you."

I furrow my brow. "Call me, sir?"

"Here, look at this." He turns his monitor around and on the screen is a case file that's just been opened. On the main part of the screen is the image of a young woman who goes by the name Annabelle Witter, with a home address in Sanders, Arizona. The picture shows a smiling young woman with dark hair that's cut short, though it looks like a photo from a high school yearbook.

"Annabelle Witter?" I ask. "What about her?"

"Her body was found last night beside a dumpster about twenty miles outside of town," he replies, deadpan. "Thankfully she still had her ID on her so we're not looking at a Jane Doe."

"Oh," I reply. "I'm assuming we have this because of foul play."

"We can guarantee it," he says. "Though I wouldn't be surprised if drugs were involved somewhere." He turns the monitor back around and begins typing away at the computer. "I want you and Laidlaw to work on this one. The locals are dealing with something of a jurisdiction issue, and I don't want something like this falling through the cracks."

It takes a moment for his words to sink in. "I'm sorry, you want *me* to work the case?"

He nods. "You two did a bang-up job yesterday with that missing hiker."

"But sir, it was just—"

He holds up a hand. "If you hadn't been there, it would have been days before the locals figured out there wasn't even anyone to search for, which would have only wasted more resources and manpower. You two are good, capable agents. What I can't seem to figure out is why when you transferred to this office, I was advised to keep you on desk duty."

I don't have an answer for him. I can't tell him who I really am without risking the security of the ongoing operation. But Strong isn't stupid. He knows something is going on.

"I took a risk yesterday, mostly on a hunch. And it paid off. I'd like to see what you and Laidlaw are really capable of," he says. "Whatever you did to get you on the shit list holds no interest with me. We need all the good agents we can get in this office."

I take a breath, not sure how to handle this. "Sir, you really don't need to do that," I finally say, looking for some way to protect my cover while reassuring him everything is above board here.

He sits back in his chair. "I don't get it, Dunn. Yesterday you come in here practically *begging* me to give you a nothing case but when I have something substantial for you, you don't want it. Why?"

"It's not that I don't want it, sir," I say, looking at the ground. "It's just..." My breath catches in my throat. Wasn't this exactly what I was just complaining to Zara about? That we weren't making a difference? And here is an actual case, being handed to me on a platter and I'm refusing it? What's wrong with me?

"I'm sorry sir, of course I'd—we'd be happy to take the case."

He eyes me carefully. "You're sure? I can give it to Dent if it's too much for you. And if it is, I need you to tell me now." He opens up a drawer and pulls out a file with my cover name on it. "I know you haven't worked a murder case before, but

I've seen a fire in your eyes since you got here. I think you can do it."

Yeah, no murders here. "Thank you, sir. I appreciate the vote of confidence."

"Fantastic," he says. "I've upgraded your security clearance, you should have access to everything on your terminals. Please relay my confidences to Agent Laidlaw as well. I want regular updates on your progress."

"Yes, sir," I say, though it's without any enthusiasm. I thank him again and head back to my desk, feeling deflated. What the hell just happened? I was on the verge of quitting and now I have a real case to work. As I return to my desk, Zara is typing quickly on her phone, but shoves it in her pocket as soon as she sees me approaching.

"So?" Zara asks, as I return to my desk. "Do I have to handcuff you to your desk so you don't actually go through with it, or did you already tell him?" I know she's pissed. And for good reason. She spent half the night trying to convince me to change my mind. And I got here early so she couldn't run interference.

I take a seat, almost in a daze. "We have a case."

"What?"

I look up. "He gave us a case. A murder. It should be coming through—"

Her hands fly over her keyboard before I can even finish the sentence. In less than a second her face is inches from the monitor, no doubt reading the same information Strong just showed me.

"Holy shit, Em—*err*, Claire. How did you do this?"

"It just kind of… happened," I say. "He said he was impressed with our performance yesterday."

She cackles. "See? Even *fate* is on my side. Suck it, Dunn."

"Yeah," I say. "Fantastic." Before going into Strong's office I had been feeling a sense of elation at the fact I was about to leave all of this behind me. It was freeing in a way. Like I had swiped all the obstacles from my path and I'd be home to see Liam and the dogs soon.

But now our position here will only be prolonged by this case. It's not that I'm not grateful, I'm ecstatic that I finally have something *real* to do; that I can finally do something meaningful. Still, it's hard. I had been looking forward to going home. And now that won't be happening.

"Oh, quit bellyaching. You got what you want." She pauses. "Do you think he knew?" Zara asks, leaning forward to whisper to me. As she does, Agent Dent passes our desks, her dark hair streaked with silver strands tied in a tight bun. I don't miss the quick glance she gives us but she's gone a moment later.

"Knew what?" I whisper back.

"That you were about to quit," she says. "Maybe he saw it coming and was trying to head you off."

"How would he know?" I ask. "I only made the decision last night."

She shrugs. "Yeah, I guess you're right." Though, now that she's brought it up, I can't help but think about the convenient timing of this assignment. Does Strong know more than he's letting on? Does he know who Zara and I really are? And if so, is he under orders to keep that information to himself? With how fractured the Bureau is after the breach, I have no way of knowing that. But it's worth keeping in the back of my mind.

"It says here the body has already been transported to the morgue?"

"Yep," I say, feeling some of that familiar vigor return to my veins. "C'mon. I'm driving."

Chapter Four

THE BERNALILLO COUNTY morgue is a one-level building near downtown Albuquerque on the edge of downtown. Like a lot of the buildings out here, it was designed in the Spanish style, complete with ceramic roof and stucco walls. There are even a series of archways out front that create a makeshift "porch" on the front of the building. Of course, the delivery of the bodies goes through the back, but to anyone passing by, this building looks like any other. It's not designed to stand out, which is probably the point.

Of course, Zara and I haven't been here before, other than perhaps driving by occasionally. But once we're inside, we're able to find our way to the Medical Examiner's office easily. It's not partitioned off from the examination area, but is separated by only a small divider. As we come into the morgue itself, a man in thick glasses with a shock of white hair glances up. He's balding on top, but his hair is long around the rest of his head, almost sticking out around the sides and the back. It gives him the look of a mad-scientist and I have to refrain from making the comment to Zara as we enter.

"Yes?" he asks, looking over the monitor of his computer.

"Steven Hendricks? Agents Dunn and Laidlaw," I say. "We're here about Annabelle Witter." I hold up my badge.

"The DOA," he says, standing. "I was just working on my report. She came in overnight so I had a chance to take a look early this morning." He rounds his station and breezes past us, heading for the drawers on the side of the room.

"You've already finished the examination?" I ask.

"I don't like to waste my time, Agent Dunn," he says. "Unclaimed hours of the day can not be regained."

I shoot a glance to Zara who gives me a small quirk of her mouth. "What was the cause of death?"

"Asphyxiation is the most likely culprit," he replies. "Given the state of her windpipe."

"She was strangled," Zara says.

He goes to one drawer and unlocks the handle, pulling it open. "Take a look for yourselves." He yanks the sheet covering the body back to reveal Annabelle Witter, her body pale and bloodless. Thankfully, her eyes are closed because Hendricks pulled that sheet with the dramatic flair of a magician, revealing his latest trick. I bend down for a closer look, though it's clear from the residual bruising around her neck that she was strangled. I can even see individual finger marks embedded into the skin.

"Whoever did this wanted to make sure she wasn't faking it."

"It takes approximately thirty-three pounds of pressure to crush a human windpipe," the medical examiner says. "I would estimate from these marks forty to fifty pounds of pressure was applied. Unfortunately, there were no fingerprints. I expect the assailant used latex or nitrile gloves."

I give the body a once-over, looking for anything else out of the ordinary. Other than the Y-shaped incision along her sternum, nothing stands out. "What else?"

"Not much on the body," he says. "No material under the fingernails, though given the state of her bloodstream, that isn't a surprise. I separated and identified two different substances. Heroin, for one. And it's not conclusive, but I believe the other substance is methamphetamine. But I'll need a toxicologist to confirm."

"Stomach?" Zara asks.

"Nothing but carbs, most likely the culprit being multiple bags of potato chips. She hadn't had a proper meal in at least sixteen hours."

"You're thinking she was too drugged to even know what was happening?" I ask.

"That would be my professional opinion. It's a common occurrence for lot lizards."

I turn to him, narrowing my eyes. "*I'm sorry?*"

Hendricks motions to her. "That's how we refer to them. It's a dangerous line of work, if you can even call it that."

"This is a human being we're talking about here," I say. "A *victim*."

"Who prostituted herself out to men for money," he replies. "Hardly a noble profession."

"Hey," Zara says. "Maybe she didn't have the best opportunities in life. Maybe she had a turn of bad luck. You said yourself she had little in her stomach. She might have been doing whatever she needed to survive."

"I'm sure she could have found another job. The local fast-food restaurants are always hiring."

"And most of them don't pay a living wage," I reply, swallowing my anger. Arguing with the medical examiner isn't going to get us what we need. "Was there any sign of sexual trauma?"

"Difficult to tell," he says. "Given how often she was *engaged*, I can't say for sure one way or another." The way he talks turns my stomach. It's like he doesn't even consider her a person.

"What about semen in the body? Or any DNA that didn't belong to her."

"Clean," he replies. "At least she had the good sense to insist they wear condoms."

That's it. "*Look*, I don't care what your personal feelings are about her situation, we still require you to do your job."

"Which I have done, *agent*." He returns to his desk. "Unlike some people, I actually care about the quality of my work. You will find my report to be more than comprehensive."

"Good," I say, pulling a business card with the name *Agent Claire Dunn* emblazoned on it, along with my contact information. "Email me a copy as soon as it's completed."

"Of course. Good day, Agents," he says and goes back to his work without another word. I presume that means we're dismissed. But instead of heading out, I return to Annabelle's body and take a minute to inspect her further before replacing the sheet over her body. I catch him throwing glances our way as I do, but I don't let it bother me. Finally, after I feel like I've irked him enough, we leave.

"He's *fun*," Zara says under her breath as we head back to the car.

"I just hope we don't have to come back here," I say. Out of all the medical examiners I've worked with, he has to be one of the vilest. "Unfortunately he's probably right about Annabelle's activities prior to her death." According to what little information we have on the woman, she disappeared from Arizona about six months ago, reported missing by her mother. She was only three years out of high school and had been in the middle of beautician school when she just up and left. I wouldn't officially classify her as a runaway since she was legally an adult, but the behavior is similar. And unfortunately, most girls who run away without a plan end up in compromised situations.

"Gloves and maybe a condom," Zara says. "Someone didn't want to get caught."

"No, but they left her with her ID," I say as we get back

into the SUV. "Which means he was either in a hurry or didn't care about anyone learning who she was."

"What's your feeling about it?"

"I'm not sure," I say. "Could be either. I'd prefer the first situation, though. If he was in a hurry, maybe he slipped up somewhere. If he didn't care—that makes him much more dangerous."

"I thought you might say that," she says. "Site?"

I nod. "Site."

Chapter Five

"OKAY, we're not doing this again," I say as I roll up all four windows of the SUV at once and turn the music volume down about ten notches. Quickly I flip the window lock switch on the driver's side of the car as Zara moves to roll her window back down.

"Spoilsport," she huffs, crossing her arms.

"My hair can only take so much," I reply. "And I'd really rather not spend another hour trying to detangle it again."

"*That's* why you always insist on driving, isn't it?" she says, poking me in the shoulder. "It's always about control with you."

"It's not control," I say. "It's *choice.*"

"Pssh. Whatever." She pulls out her phone looking at a recent notification before putting it away again.

"What's going on?" I ask.

"Nothing," she says.

"It's not nothing. That was a text from someone. And I'm pretty sure it wasn't anyone from the office."

She sighs. "Well, I guess since you won't let me blast *Spice Up Your Life* and you're not quitting anymore I might as well tell you. I reached out to a few contacts outside the Bureau to help us with our little problem."

"Z! You can't be doing that! We're under strict orders—"

"Relax," she says, waving me off. "They're contacts from my days when I was in intelligence. They only know me by an alias, and they don't know I'm in the Bureau. But I figured since we're not getting any answers from HQ, I needed to bring in the big guns."

"You haven't been talking to Theo, have you?"

"Of course not," she scoffs. "Theo wouldn't be charging me this much."

"How much are you paying them? And where are you getting the money?"

"It's not important," she replies.

I can't believe what I'm hearing. We're supposed to be on complete lockdown here, and Zara has been secretly doing research this entire time? "How can you say that? It's *incredibly* important. Z, if you're unofficially funding illegal operations with Bureau resources that's classified as a *felony*. We could both go to prison, without trial, for the rest of our lives. I can't believe—"

"Em," she says, her voice soft. "It's okay. I'm not breaking the law. I have some extra… funds… that I've saved up for stuff like this."

"Funds from what? You're not supposed to be accessing your bank back home. Someone could be monitoring."

"Don't worry. It's from an account here, after we moved. I haven't even touched my accounts back home," she says, but doesn't answer the original question.

Her silence isn't making me feel better. "Where's the money coming from, Z?"

She sighs. "Maybe I took a few… feet pics."

"*Feet* pics?"

"Yeah, you know. For the internet."

I pull the car to the side of the road and kill the engine, turning my entire body to face her. "*What?*"

She rolls her eyes, followed by her neck, producing a cracking sound somewhere deep within. "I took some pictures of my feet and uploaded them onto this site called *Footsie*, okay?"

To say I'm gobsmacked would be an understatement. "Why?"

"Because, believe it or not, people pay good money to see a nice-looking foot. And if you haven't noticed, I have some of the best." She gives me a satisfied smile.

"You're telling me you're making money on the side by selling pictures of your feet to strangers on the internet?"

"Yep," she says, pulling out her phone and bringing up a collage of images. All of them are of feet in different poses, locations and some even have accessories, showing them off.

"Are all these yours?"

"Sure are," she says proudly. "So far I've cleared just under six grand."

"*Six thousand dollars?*" I nearly choke. "How long have you been doing this?"

"Since we got here," she replies. She gestures to the empty road ahead of us. "I've been bored, okay? There's nothing to do here. And you've been so mopey lately I needed an outlet. I just found one that makes some money. Money we can use to help our cause." She shoots me a sly grin.

"Do people ever see your face?" I ask.

"Oh, hell no," she says. "I scrub the images of anything that could be identifiable. Both in the image itself and in the digital marker. People out there are crazy." She makes a little circular motion with one finger beside her head.

"Yeah, people like you," I say. "Jesus. Six thousand dollars. I think I went into the wrong profession."

"Hey, if you want me to set you up with an account I have a referral link. If you get a hundred subscribers, I'll get a nice little bonus. Plus, you have really delicate feet. Wanna see if we could double our money?"

"I am *not* selling pictures of my feet or anything else on the internet!" I nearly shout. But when I see the grin on her face, I can't help but laugh at the absurdity of it all. "You're insane, you know that?"

She shrugs. "You do what you gotta do to get by. Doesn't really matter, anyway. I'm killing the contracts tomorrow. Apparently, no one has any information about an FBI breach. And given these guys work in all kinds of clandestine circles, it's kind of odd."

"They haven't found *anything*?" I ask.

"Nothing worth mentioning. There's some minor chatter about it, but mostly people wondering who could be behind it. No one is claiming responsibility, much less explaining *why*." She shoots me a glance. "I… uh… I also tried to find the names of the other five agents."

I slide my eyes to the side without turning my head. "And?"

"Nothing yet. But I thought maybe if I could find out who they were, we could figure out why the six of you have been targeted. There has to be a common link between you."

"No there doesn't," I say. "We don't know who is behind this. It could be completely random for all we know."

"Em, how often is something like this completely random? Were the letters from your aunt random? Was *The Organization* random?"

"No," I admit.

"Exactly my point! Someone has taken you off the playing field. You and five other agents. You know as well as I do we're not going to get a straight answer from Washington. Which means we need to figure this out for ourselves. *I* need to figure this out. It's why I'm here."

"It's not why you're here," I say. "The reason Caruthers

kept us together is because he knows you'll see anything coming a mile away."

"In other words, I'm a bodyguard."

"Well—"

"Em, believe it or not, but you're not the only one who doesn't do well sitting on her ass all day. Some of us just express it in different ways. I'm not going to stand around while someone targets you for who knows what. The best way we can combat this thing, whatever it is, is to get ahead of it. I just had to become a lady of the night to do it."

I give her a playful shove. "You could have told me, you know."

"I wanted to make sure it was going to work first. But hey, at least now we have a little spending money, right?"

A chuckle escapes my lips. "Yeah, let's drive out to Vegas and test our luck." I start the car again and pull back on the empty road. "*Footsie.* Unbelievable."

"I mean it's not even that scandalous," she reiterates. "You'd think I was stripping in front of the camera, but nope. Just good old-fashioned photos. Weird, right?"

"I guess there's something for everyone out there," I say, though I'm thinking more about what she's been doing with that money than how she got it. "I know you're trying to help. But what if trying to get ahead of this thing draws it to us instead?" I ask.

She cracks her knuckles all at once. "That's where my skills come in handy. Because when they make their move, I'm going to make sure there is a light on them so bright you can see it from space."

"So then… I'm the bait."

She gives me a finger gun. "Exactly. But c'mon. You trust me, right?"

I shake my head, incredulous at my best friend. It pains me to admit I'm feeling a lot better than I was this morning. Having a case to focus on has galvanized me, given me a direction I've been sorely lacking the past four weeks. But really it's Zara. Intentionally or not, she keeps me grounded.

She turns the music back up and starts bopping along to the song again as the gas station ahead finally comes into view. They weren't kidding. It really *is* way out here. It's been a solid thirty minutes since I saw the last one. "The Speedy Stop," I say, reading the big sign.

As I pull up a Bernalillo County patrol car sits in one of the gas station's spaces. But otherwise, the place looks normal. Tractor-trailers are pulled off to the side to refuel, a few other vehicles are parked either at the gas pumps or right in front of the station, and there is a family with two young kids sitting at one of the plastic tables underneath the overhang beside the station. From the looks of it, there's a fast-food kiosk of sorts inside.

"Busy day," Zara says.

"Probably normal for out there given how few stops there are," I say. I pull beside the patrol car and kill the engine. "Ready?"

"For some real action? Yes, please," she replies.

We both step out into the dry air, the heat of the day already beating down on us. Within seconds I'm sweating through my suit. We head inside where we find the owner of the patrol vehicle standing near the check-out counter, which is a large oval in the middle of the store. To our right along the back, is the fast-food counter with bright blue digital menus above the counter advertising all of the available options for the day. Two people stand in line waiting to order while a third is off to the side with a drink in hand, waiting. There's only one other person in the building, and they're in the shop section, looking through the chips and candies.

"You must be the Feds," the officer says. He has a large Styrofoam cup in hand and sips from the straw as he eyes us up and down. The man behind the counter glances up, but his eyes shoot straight back down again. The name on the cop's tag says Ridout.

"Agents Dunn and Laidlaw," I say, showing my badge.

"Good," Officer Ridout replies. "Now I can finally get out of here."

"Hang on," I say as the man heads for the door. "What can you tell us? Haven't you done any preliminary work?"

Ridout turns, looking us up and down again. "Sure I have. I did all the preliminary work. Spent nine solid hours on it before my boss informed me you were coming to take over." He grins, showing a row of crooked teeth. "I'm sure you'll want to start from scratch. Never know what we might have missed." It's obvious he's not happy with giving up the case, but that's not my problem. I'm not about to let some asshole jerk me around just because he's having a bad day.

"How about you stay and cooperate and I won't file a notice with your department that you were unhelpful and combative? Sound good?"

He grimaces before sucking on the straw again, the slurping noise practically echoing through the store. He tosses the cup in the nearest can then heads back to the counter. "This is Frank Crest. He was on duty last night. Called it in to us. He didn't see anything. Also, there are no cameras back there, so they didn't see anything either. I canvassed the area, no witnesses. And that's it. Happy?"

"No," I say. "Show me where she was found."

Ridout grits his teeth but makes a motion with his head for us to follow him back outside. We do, walking all the way around the building to the back where the dumpsters are located. Back behind the station hills and mesas rise out of the desert in the distance. It's as clear of a day as it can get out here, and I can easily see all the details of the mountains.

There are four dumpsters behind the station, all set up in a row about thirty feet off the building, creating almost an alleyway between them and the station.

"Here it is," Ridout says, motioning to the area between the middle two dumpsters that's been taped off with yellow caution tape. Small yellow markers lay on the ground where presumably Annabelle's body once lay.

I duck under the tape and bend down, looking at the grease-stained concrete. There's no blood to be found anywhere, but given Annabelle's condition, I wasn't expecting any. I bend down a little further so I can peer under one of the dumpsters. Something small—probably a lizard—scurries away as I get closer.

"What are you doing?" Ridout asks.

"Investigating," I shoot back.

Ridout groans. "Look, no one saw anything. There was no evidence left on the scene and I already spoke to Hendricks. No evidence left on the body. There's nothing to do here. It's a cold case."

"It hasn't even been twenty-four hours," Zara says. "Why are you so eager to give up?"

"Because I have twelve other cases that actually *have* evidence and since this isn't my case anymore I really don't feel like wasting my time here. Maybe you two don't get it, maybe you haven't been around long enough. But when you come across a case like this, you learn that there is nothing you nor anyone else can do. So you might as well save yourselves the time."

"I'll take that under advisement," I say, wishing I could rattle off the litany of cases I've worked that have started very similar to this one. Maybe they weren't open and shut and maybe we had to do a bit of work to figure out what was going on, but no case is ever just immediately cold. I don't care *what* the circumstances are. As I bend down a little further, something catches my eye.

"Hey *Fiona*," I say. "Hand me an evidence bag and a pair of gloves, will you?"

"Sure," Zara replies, ducking under the tape and producing both from her jacket pocket. "Find something?"

I snap on one of the gloves and reach under the dumpster, carefully picking up the object that looks like it rolled underneath. When I stand back up, a gold keychain glitters in my hand. On the front is an overly enthusiastic cartoon mouse pointing to a castle, courtesy of one of the biggest entertainment companies in the world. "Miss this on your investigation?"

"That could belong to anyone, could have been here for weeks," Ridout replies.

"Or it could have belonged to Annabelle, or the person who killed her." I deposit the keychain into the bag Zara has open for me. She seals it and marks it with her pen. "What else did you conveniently miss out here?"

"I don't have to stand here and take this," Ridout says. "Best of luck with your investigation, *Agents*." He turns and huffs off, headed back around the station.

As soon as he's out of earshot, I turn to Zara. "What do you think?"

"He's right. It could belong to anyone. Some tourist could have thrown it away for all we know."

"Still, I want forensics to take a look. Maybe we can get a print." I take a few more minutes to examine the scene. Other than a few pieces of errant trash blowing across the concrete, Ridout is right. There's not much here. I check the building's corners. No cameras, just like he said. However, there is an access door that can be used by employees. It doesn't have a handle on this side I assume for security reasons.

"C'mon. Let's see if what footage they do have can provide anything useful." The keychain is a long shot, even so, Ridout missed it. Maybe we'll get lucky and it'll belong to our assailant.

As we head back around the station I'm surprised to still see

Ridout's car sitting in the same spot. However there is another vehicle on the scene, a pickup truck with a logo on the side which says *Reservation Police*. It's parked near the edge of the station's lot, though I don't see the driver anywhere. As we're heading for the doors, a man in a tan uniform with a black tie and a wide-brimmed hat pushes through from the other side, heading straight for the truck. He doesn't so much as give Zara or me a look. A moment later, Ridout is right behind him, muttering under his breath as he heads for his own vehicle.

"Hey," I say, causing him to turn back. "Who is that?"

"By all means," Ridout nearly shouts. "Let me be your guide to everything!" He opens the door to his car, shooting us one last glare before getting in. "Have a nice day." I'm about to shout a retort but he slams the door and revs his engine before pulling away.

I turn to see the other officer standing near his truck, watching the interaction. As soon as Ridout has left, he gets in his truck as well and begins heading in the opposite direction.

"What is it with people today?" I ask Zara. "Did everyone have a glass of liquid asshole this morning or what?"

"Maybe it's the heat," she suggests. "Or the dry air. Sucked all the moisture from their brains."

She's probably not far off. I head back into the station to confront the clerk, Mr. Crest. "What was that about just a minute ago?"

He's checking out the customer we saw earlier, who looks eager to leave.

"Oh," Crest says. "That's Andersen. Bernalillo County and the Reservation don't get along too well. Jurisdiction issues, I assume. They was arguing about what you folks are here for."

"The body?" I ask. The customer gets his change and heads quickly past us, his head down.

"Yeah," Crest replies. "'pparenly Reservation thinks this is something they should take care of. But Officer Ridout informed him that it was your case now. At least, I think that's what I heard. Is that right?"

I nod. "Yes. I need you to show us your footage from last night."

"But the cameras don't point back there," he replies. "Ridout already looked."

"I want to see it anyway," I say. "Just in case."

He shrugs. "Sure. Whatever you need." He locks up the cash register before coming around the island to meet us. "It's in the back."

We follow him to the opposite side of the station from where the fast-food place is located, through a cracked door that says *Employees only*. Another smaller man sits inside, an empty salad container in front of him and a cigarette hanging out of his mouth as he plays on his phone.

"Daryl, can you watch the front for me? I need to show these officers the footage from last night."

The man looks up, putting out the cigarette. "Sure Frank." He gives us a quick nod and heads back out to watch the station.

"How's your security here?" I ask Mr. Crest as he heads to the only desk in the back which is a mess of papers, invoices, shipping notices and bills. A computer sits somewhere among everything.

"You mean how many times we been robbed?" he asks, taking a seat and waking up the computer.

"That's one way to put it," Zara says.

"I keep a shotgun under the counter," he replies. "That count?"

"Is it registered?"

"'course," he replies, his face lit up by the screen. "Locals know not to mess around here. Occasionally we get the passer-by who thinks we look like an easy score. Remote location, nobody around. But I have yet to give up a dime to a robber. Ridout can attest to that."

"You've known him a long time?" I ask.

"Sure. Tommy works this area a lot. Known him for years." He types on the keyboard. "You want to see the same thing I showed him?"

"I want to see all the footage from yesterday, starting at six A.M. all the way through the night."

He looks over the monitor. "Why?"

"Just pull it up," Zara says. "Unless you want us to do it for you."

"No need to get feisty, just curious is all," he says. He types a few seconds longer before standing up. "There you go. We got six cameras, four in the store and two outside in the front. Feeds are already up." Zara takes the seat as Crest works his way out from behind the desk. "Is there anything else you need?"

"I'll come get you if we do," I say. He heads out as Zara searches through the footage.

"This is going to take a minute, Em."

"That's ok," I say. "Despite what Ridout thinks, there's something here. We just need to find it."

Chapter Six

We spend a solid two hours looking through the feeds for anything that might be relevant. It's slow going since we don't know exactly what we're looking for. But we need to cover our bases, and honestly, my conversation with Officer Ridout has lit a fire under my ass to find *something*, if for no other reason than to throw it back in his face. I'm not usually a vindictive person, but I make an exception for assholes.

Zara and I take turns on the footage, looking at every person who comes into the store throughout the day, or who orders from the fast-food joint. Thankfully, the cameras are positioned to capture clear images of everyone's face as they come and go. At least if we do spot a person of interest, we'll have a clear view of their face.

But honestly, I'm not sure we're going to find anything of value. Even if Annabelle's killer came into the station, we have no way of identifying him. It's not like he's going to be wearing a t-shirt that says *New Mexico Strangler* written across the front.

"Hey Em," Zara says as I'm downing half a bag of chips. The benefit of working in a convenience store all day is we have plenty to eat. "Look at this."

I round the desk and peer over her shoulder. A young woman appears on the camera that faces the front doors, breezing through with a smile on her face. She's immediately recognizable as Annabelle Witter. "What time was this?"

"Nine-thirty-six last night," Zara replies. We both watch as Annabelle comes in, pokes around for a few minutes, then leaves without buying anything. I have Zara wind it back so I can watch Frank Crest on the other monitor, but he doesn't even seem to notice her. He's looking down at his phone the entire time.

"Shit," I say. "She was in here last night."

"Yep," Zara replies. "And Crest never even noticed."

"Wind it back again," I say, getting closer to the screen. On it, Annabelle comes in, heads to the shop area of the store, hesitates a moment, then leaves without so much as a word to Crest or anyone else. "Did she… just shoplift something?"

"I can't tell, the angle isn't great," Zara replies. "Maybe. We should check back with Hendricks to see if there's something from the store with her personal effects."

The thought of talking to that man again turns my stomach. But she's right. We need to double check to make sure. "Let's keep going, see if she comes back in." We take another twenty minutes to go through the rest of the footage between when she left the station and when her body was reported found, but she never appears again.

"A two hour and twelve minute window," Zara says. "At least we've narrowed down the time of death."

"For as much good as it does us." We head back to the front of the convenience store to find Crest and his employee both behind the counter doing paperwork.

Crest looks up. "Get everything you needed?"

"Annabelle was in here last night," I say. "She came in for about two minutes."

"What?" he asks.

I head to the shelf where she hesitated, noticing it's where the condoms are kept. "You have inventory numbers on these?"

"Yeah," Daryl, the other man says, coming over. "Should be a dozen packs there."

I count. "There's only four. Looks like you don't have strict control over your inventory."

Daryl shrugs. "It happens. We usually account ten to twenty percent to theft anyway. Better to let 'em take it than get into a shootout." He looks over his shoulder at Crest.

"Confirms Hendricks' suspicions," Zara says.

I hate to admit it, but she's right. More than likely Annabelle came in and stole the condoms for a John she'd met. "Yeah." I look out the windows at the lot where the trucks park. Because they take up so much space, they're further away from the station, though they're all parked in the same direction. "Wait a second." I head outside again toward the trucks, with Zara close behind.

"What are you thinking?"

I nod to the trucks as we trot over to where there are three parked at the moment. Standing in front of them, I can just barely see around the building to the back, where the dumpsters are visible. "The trucks have a perfect view of the back of the station," I say. "Which means someone's dash cam may have picked something up."

"Holy shit, Em," she says. "You're right!" She turns and looks at the row of five trucks that are currently parked in the spots. "Oh… but…"

"Yeah," I say. It means we're going to need to track down each of the trucks that were here last night around nine-thirty and after. We don't know for sure Annabelle's killer was a trucker, but it's a good possibility. Still, if any of them caught something on their dash cams, that might be the break we need. "I don't guess the cameras caught the license plates of the trucks that come through here, did they?"

Zara gives me a slow shake of her head.

I sigh. As if this day couldn't get any longer.

It takes us almost an hour to get back to the office by which point it is past dark out and I'm feeling the effects of a long day. On the drive Zara tried to compile a list of trucking companies that use Highway 17 as a major artery, but it's going to be a long process. We have to find every company that has trucks on that road, contact them and begin to collate a list of suspects and/or witnesses to the crime. Then we need to narrow it down to individual trucks that may have stopped at *The Speedy Stop* during the timeframe Annabelle was spotted there.

In short, it's going to be a ton of work for two people. It's times like this when I really miss Eliott and Nadia. The four of us could cut through this in half the time, but I highly doubt Strong is about to assign me a couple of additional agents, especially considering both Zara and I are "supposed" to be relatively fresh to the job. If she'd put in our backgrounds that we had a combined ten years of experience, that probably would have raised some eyebrows out here. It would have at least made a few people check closer into our backgrounds. So she opted for a less dramatic approach, whittling our combined experience down to three years instead.

By the time we get back to the office, the parking lot is almost empty and the lights are mostly off. We're not doing anyone any good if we're exhausted, so I call it, not even bothering to go back inside. Though, as we're about to pull away, I see the door to the office open and Agent Dent comes out, a stack of files in her arms. She heads over to a black Mercedes and gets in, not paying us any attention.

"Huh," I say, watching her.

"What?" Zara asks, her face lit up by the laptop on her lap.

"Dent," I say. "Drives a Mercedes."

She looks up, watching as Dent pulls out and heads off in the other direction. "So?"

I close my eyes and rub my temples. "Nothing, doesn't matter."

"You're exhausted," she says.

"That makes two of us," I say, noting the dark circles under her eyes. Normally I could go home and shower, relax with the dogs, have a nice dinner with Liam. I didn't realize how much I missed that simple unwinding until I didn't have it any longer. It was a pressure valve for me, a way for me to recoup from the day and prepare for the next. But here it's like I've been running on full blast all the time, never really taking a minute to unclench my jaw. "You said yesterday you're working on a new game?"

"Yeah," she says, closing the laptop. "Cthulhu's challenge. It's a puzzle game. Well, action puzzle. There's a lot of shooting. But also puzzle solving." She holds up one finger as if to emphasize the point.

"Would you mind if I… came over and watched?"

She looks at me under hooded eyes. "You. Emily Slate. Want to come over and watch me… play a video game?"

I shrug. "Yeah, why not?"

"Because I've been trying to get you into video games for what, three years? And you've never expressed one bit of interest. Why the change?"

I roll my shoulders and crack my back without meaning to. "I need to find a way to relax out here. Or if not that, maybe just recharge. And at this point I'm desperate enough to try anything."

She cackles, rubbing her hands together. "Oh, this is going to be fun. I'm gonna get you into it. You're gonna want to play."

"Let's not get ahead of ourselves here," I say. But it's like she's been taken over by a fever. "First, we gotta get you to create your own character. That shouldn't take more than a few hours. Then—"

"A few hours? Z, I just want to relax."

"It is relaxing, trust me. Oh man, this is going to be the most relaxing night you've had in a while. Head to the store, we gotta stock up on snacks."

"This is not a sleepover," I say. "I just want to unwind for a few minutes without needing to think."

"It is most *definitely* a sleepover," she says. "C'mon. Get it in gear. We need chips and alcohol. Stat."

I smile as I put the car back into gear. "You're the boss."

Chapter Seven

I YAWN as I flip through the stack of papers that we've spent the morning collating. Apparently even just the act of watching one of Zara's hobbies was a lot more involved than I expected. We didn't end up getting to bed until somewhere around three A.M. and I've got a crick in my neck from sleeping on her couch. Sure, it would have been literally twenty steps back to my apartment but by then I was so tired and woozy from all the wine, I felt it was better to sleep it off at her place. Plus, it was nice sleeping in a house with someone else there, even if we weren't in the same room. It felt more… normal.

But we had to be up at seven to be here on time, which means I'm running on four hours of sleep after a long day yesterday. I've already had three cups of coffee and it's barely keeping me upright.

"Okay, thank you very much," Zara says, hanging up her phone. She crosses a name off the list in front of her. "That's number sixteen."

I glance at my half of the list of companies we've identified that have trucks using that route. There are nine crossed off on mine, while four others are circled. "How many more?"

She scans her list quickly. "I've got another half dozen and that should be it. So far out of the forty-seven companies that use that route, we've got sixteen that had trucks in the state that day, and of those, seven that used Highway 17 as part of their route." She turns to her computer. "Thankfully, most of these guys have GPS tracking each of their trucks and so far we only have three that had trucks stop at that location during our time frame."

"Four," I say. "I just got off the phone with Mesa Inc. Add them to the list."

She writes the name down before picking up the phone again. For some reason, she doesn't seem nearly as wiped as I do. Maybe she's right, and I'm letting this thing drain me. She got the same amount of sleep as I did and yet she has been energetic and productive all morning, despite stifling the occasional yawn. Meanwhile I feel like I'm pulling a ten pound sled just to get up out of my seat.

As I pick up my phone and go through the script I've already been through with a dozen trucking companies this morning, I can't quit thinking about Ridout yesterday. He seemed so sure there was nothing to this case and so willing to dismiss it, he completely missed potential evidence on the scene. The lab hasn't gotten back to us yet with anything on the keychain and I don't know that they will, but I'm hopeful they can at least pull *something*.

And then there is the Reservation cop Andersen. I'm wondering if it might be worth reaching out to him to see if he's done any preliminary work himself. Strong said there was a jurisdiction issue; it's possible they're still running their own investigation. We got the file from Bernalillo County this morning, but there was nothing from the Reservation itself. I'm not sure what's going on between him and Ridout, but if there's bad blood there, Andersen might have information he wasn't willing to share. Information he might give us.

It's a reach, but at this point I'm feeling a little desperate.

No prints at the scene, no witnesses. No cameras. It's too clean—which usually means we're either trying to find someone who is *very* lucky, or who is a professional. At least someone who has done this a few times before. Which means things could get very messy if we're not careful. I put in a request to the morgue for any other related cases, but nothing came back, which makes me think we're not dealing with a local.

"Little Green Men Trucking, how may I help you?" a sweet, southern voice says on the other end of the line. I have to double check that I've called the right number on my list. Sure enough, *LGM Trucking*, out of Roswell, New Mexico. Of course. Why not?

"Good morning, my name is Agent Claire Dunn with the FBI," I tell the woman, then go into my spiel about what information we're looking for.

"Oh my," she says. "That sounds serious. Let me put you in touch with Greyson, he handles all our truck routes. He should be able to get you the information you need."

"Thank you," I say as she puts me on hold, elevator music filling the receiver. I glance over at Zara, put my forefinger to my head and pull the "trigger", miming falling on to the desk. She gives me a knowing grin.

"This is Greyson Bauers, what can I do for you?" a man says on the end of the line.

"My name is Agent Claire Dunn, with the FBI. I'm looking for information regarding your trucking routes. We're currently investigating a murder and—"

"I'm sorry, did you say a murder?" the man asks, interrupting me.

"Yes, sir," I reply. "Can you confirm for me your company uses Highway 17, west of Albuquerque, as one of its major trucking routes?"

He's silent a beat too long on the other end. "Well, yes, we do. Why?"

"Do you keep GPS on all your trucks?" I ask, going down my list of questions.

"No, we outsource our drivers. They come with their own cabs. They don't take kindly to companies keeping a close eye on them. We don't keep a tight leash here at LGM. As long as they get to their destinations on time, that's good enough for us."

I make a note. "So you don't know when and where your drivers stop?" I ask. I notice Zara poke her head up.

"No ma'am," he replies. "Though we require them to submit their expenses they want reimbursed to us. Usually that means fast-food receipts and the like."

"How many trucks did you have running that route on Monday the seventh?" I ask.

"This past Monday? Hang on, I'll have to check." The line goes silent. I put it on mute on my side just to be safe.

"Hey, check into these guys," I tell Zara. "Something feels off. LGM, out of Roswell."

"Got it," she says and turns back to her computer, even with the phone to her ear.

"Miss Dunn, are you there?" Bauers says on the other end.

"That's Agent Dunn," I correct him.

"Sorry 'bout that. I don't have any record of our drivers on that road on Monday."

"You're sure?" I ask. "Maybe early Monday from a late Sunday departure?"

"Nope. Nothing," he replies, his voice full of confidence. "Is there anything else I can help you with?"

I mark through the company's name on my list. "No, thank you anyway," I say.

"Yes, ma'am," he says. "You have a good day." I hang up and look over the rest of my list. There are only two names left.

"What did he say?" Zara asks.

"Said that none of their trucks were on the road that day."

I'm checking the rest of my list, wondering if all of this is going to end up being for nothing. Even if we find a trucking company that was there that night, what are the odds their cameras were recording?

"Looks like LGM doesn't use its own drivers, they subcontract," Zara says, screwing up her features. "Looks like a great bargain for LGM, not so much for the trucker. They get paid a flat rate per mile, no benefits."

I perk up. "None?"

"No, why?"

"Their shipping manager just told me drivers could submit their expenses for reimbursement."

She scans the screen, looking back and forth. "I don't see anything about that here. Maybe it's an unlisted perk?"

"Maybe," I say, though when I return to my list I circle LGM, despite having crossed it off already. "Let's add them to the list just for shits and giggles."

Zara levels her gaze at me. "All the way down in Roswell? You know that's like a three and a half hour drive, right?"

"Yeah," I say, yawning again. "I know. Which is why if we end up going down there, you're driving."

Chapter Eight

We ended up with four companies total who had trucks that ran that route on Monday night. Two were out of state, so Zara spoke with Strong, who coordinated with other FBI offices to assist us in the investigation. I hope these companies won't put up a fight just to look at a few hours of dashcam footage—should it exist. I'm also hoping they might have caught images of any other vehicles that might have been at the rest stop so we can cross-reference with what fuzzy images we pulled from the security cameras. We'll get lucky if we can even get makes on the non-commercial vehicles there that night because right now all we have are blurry colors.

First on our list is Triton Trucking, which is fortunately based in Albuquerque. But after about fifteen minutes with a rotund man with a thick beard, we leave empty-handed. Their truck was there until around five P.M., meaning it left far too early to catch anything of value.

Our second stop, Western Foods, Inc. seems more promising. Zara spoke with them earlier in the day and they confirmed they had two different trucks stop at that station on Monday.

"Crap," Zara says as we're about to head into the building.

"The Denver office just reported in. Nothing from Black Mountain Moving, LLC. Their truck left before four P.M. on Monday."

"Damn," I say, opening the door for her. "We're running out of options, quick. Let's hope we have better luck with one of these." I head straight for the front desk, where a young woman with a headset sits. I flash my badge, getting her attention. "We're here to see Mrs. Peterson. My colleague spoke with her on the phone earlier today."

"Oh, of course," the woman says and dials a number before speaking into a headset. She smiles and looks up. "She'll be right with you."

"Thanks," I say, taking in the lobby. All around us are images of powerful looking trucks, trains and ships, all in the process of moving goods from one place to another.

"Good morning," a voice says behind us. I turn to see a woman in her early sixties coming out to greet us. She's dressed smart, in no-nonsense slacks and a dark blouse. "I'm Myra Peterson."

"Agents Dunn and Laidlaw," I say, shaking her hand. "You spoke with my partner earlier?"

"Yes, I recall," she says. "I already checked into our trucks that pulled into The Speedy Shop on Monday. Unfortunately, I don't think we'll be able to help you."

"Why not?" I ask.

"Our first truck was only there from nine A.M. until around nine-thirty. And our second pulled in around eight and didn't leave until ten."

"That's perfect," I say. "Can we see the footage from that vehicle?"

"I'm afraid that's the problem," Peterson says. "That cab has a faulty tank on the right side, which meant the driver had to back the trailer in to refuel instead of pulling through. His camera was facing the highway—your partner said you were interested in footage showing the back of the building."

Damn. While that's not helpful, it may not be a complete loss. "Did your driver capture footage from any of the other vehicles in the lot? We're looking to build a comprehensive list of anyone who was there at that time." I also can't ignore the fact her driver was there during the period in which Annabelle was most likely killed.

She hands over a thumb drive. "I took the liberty of copying the footage for you, just in case. I hope there's something here you can use."

"Thank you," I say, taking the thumb drive. I take a second to appraise Peterson. "You strike me as someone who likes to be prepared."

"I'm paid to pay attention to details," she says. "I figured if someone was killed, it's in my best interest to clear my company of any wrongdoing as quickly as possible. Trust me, you have my full cooperation, should you need it."

"We'd like to speak with your driver," Zara says. "Obviously with him there during the time frame—"

She holds up a hand. "Say no more. I added his contact information on the drive as well, but here." She hands over her business card. On the back is a separate set of contact details. "He's currently on his way back from Carlsbad on a run and should be in this evening."

"Jack Carlin," I say, reading the card.

"I haven't informed him of the situation," she says. "I didn't want to appear as though we were trying to warn him of anything."

"What can you tell us about him?" Zara asks.

"Been driving with us for about fifteen years," she says. "Always been a reliable employee. No issues that we've ever seen."

"What about his background?" I ask. "What did he do before he drove for you?"

"Same thing, mostly," she replies. "Jack has been a trucker most of his life. I believe he had a few run-ins with the law when he was younger, but it wasn't anything serious. At least not serious enough to disqualify him from employment."

I flip the card back and forth in my hand. It's not much, but it might be significant. We'll need to look deeper into Jack Carlin. "He gets in tonight?"

She nods. "He's due back at his destination around seven. I just checked; he's still on time."

If he's our culprit, then he's obviously not on the run, otherwise he would have left Albuquerque and never looked back. The fact he's already on his way back says he either had no involvement, or is confident that he can't be caught. "Thanks for your help," I say, pocketing the card.

"For what it's worth," she says as we turn to leave, "I've known Jack a long time. He's a good man. I know you have to investigate him anyway. But he's not your guy."

I give her a nod. "Thanks again." Zara shoots me a smirk as we head back to the car. "What?"

"Too helpful?"

"Maybe," I say. As much as I appreciate Mrs. Peterson's help, I'm always a little wary of people who come off as overly accommodating.

"Think she wasn't being honest back there?" Zara asks.

"We'll find out," I say. "I plan on being at his destination when he arrives. I don't want to even give him the chance of sneaking away."

"And until then?"

I grunt, getting back in the SUV. "Until then we keep looking at everyone else."

Zara's phone buzzes and her face falls as she reads the message. "Seriously?"

We've been working almost nonstop trying to narrow down any other vehicles that could have been at The Speedy

Stop on Monday night. After going through Western Foods' footage, we managed to ID seven different vehicle makes and models, though tracking them down has been near impossible. Unfortunately the dash cam never glimpsed the license plates, so we're left with looking for a needle in a haystack. Searching just one state for a particular car type and color is hard enough, but try the entire country.

"What?" I ask, glancing up.

"Hang on," she says and puts the phone to her ear. "Yes, this is Laidlaw. How—" She screws up her features again. "And you're sure—no, okay, I appreciate the help. Okay, thank you. You too." She hangs up. "Sacramento office. Nothing on their end for DBS Transit Inc. The truck's camera was malfunctioning. Didn't record a thing for three days."

"Are they sure?" I ask. "That's awfully convenient."

She nods. "The company didn't even know the camera wasn't working until *we* inquired about it."

"But if that's the case, the driver could still—"

She gives her head a slow shake. "The driver is in a wheelchair. He uses a special winch to get in and out of the cab."

Shit. It's unlikely he would be our unsub. Not that someone in a wheelchair couldn't have killed Annabelle, but it's highly unlikely. "That doesn't mean he didn't see or hear something," I say.

"Well, add him to the list if you want. But Sacramento has done all they're going to do for us. If you want to interview him, you'll have to convince Strong it's worth the time to head up there."

There's no way he'd approve a trip for either of us to go interview a trucker out of Sacramento, especially given our "short" records. Hell, I'd have a difficult time getting Caruthers to sign off on that.

"Just… ugh. Keep them on the list." I check my watch. It's closing in on six. "Let's head out. I want to see what Mr. Carlin has to say."

"Yep." As she and I head for the doors, I glance up to notice Agent Dent, speaking with her partner walking towards us. Both of them shoot us appraising looks but they don't slow down. Though they do lower their voices as they pass.

"Ever get that feeling like someone's talking about you behind your back?" Zara says once we're out at the car.

"Why would Dent be interested in us?" I ask. "Doesn't she have enough on her plate?"

"Would *you* call that normal behavior?" Zara asks.

I shrug. It's not my job to analyze what *Special Agent Kelly Dent* does all day long. She can whisper until her lips fall off for all I care. Right now, I just want to get to Jack Carlin and look the man in the eye. He's the first actual suspect we've had, and I'm not about to let him get away.

It only takes us about twenty minutes to get to Ralston Distribution, a warehouse that sits in an industrial area of town. There are nothing but large warehouses around, trucking coming and going in all directions. We end up parking and keep a lookout for the Western Foods truck, far enough away we don't look too suspicious but close enough that we can catch up to Carlin if he gets spooked.

"You're going to wear down your nails doing that," Zara says. I look down at my thumb and forefinger and realize I've been chewing on the nail itself. That's not something I normally do. It's this place—I really think it's beginning to get to me.

"Heads up," I say, spotting the signature green truck as it makes the turn, headed for the loading dock. "Right on time."

"What's the play?" she asks.

"Wait until he's dropped off the trailer," I say. "Then we make our move." We continue to watch as Carlin pulls the trailer into the lot, then carefully and expertly backs it up to the distribution building. He handles the truck like someone with a lifetime of experience. Once the trailer is down, he gets out and speaks with the shipping manager, signing off the drop as another man comes over and unhooks his cab from the trailer. Carlin shakes the hand of the manager before climbing back into his truck.

"Em?" Zara asks.

Carlin isn't moving with any sense of urgency. Just a man going about his business. Which could fit the profile of our killer perfectly. He's someone who doesn't think he can be caught—or doesn't care. Either way, I want to be cautious about Jack Carlin. If he is our unsub, he may turn unpredictable if he figures out we're watching him. "Okay. Let's hit it."

We both get out of the SUV, also moving with no sense of urgency. Running for the truck would only make things worse. Instead, we approach slowly, directly in the light of the beams. A few of the men on the shipping dock stop to look, but my attention is focused on Carlin. He's in his cab, rooting around for something before he finally sees us. A crease forms on his brow and he rolls down his window.

"Jack Carlin?" I ask, but I already recognize his face from searching through the hours of footage with Zara. He showed up on the interior cameras, grabbing a bite to eat before heading back out.

"That's right."

I hold up my badge. "FBI. We'd like a word with you, sir." He doesn't react like someone who committed a murder two days ago, instead the crease on his brow deepens as confusion clouds his features. He opens the door, grabbing the handholds and lets himself down with the measure and grace of someone who has been doing it their whole lives.

"Am I in some sort of trouble?" he asks.

"Depends," Zara says, showing him her badge as well. "Did you visit The Speedy Shop on Highway 17 on Monday between the hours of eight and ten P.M.?"

"Yeah, I think I did," he replies. "It's one of the few stops out that way. It's usually easier to stop there than to refuel in town. Plus, with this tank issue I've been dealin' with—"

"One of your fuel tanks is leaking," I say.

He nods, his face still full of confusion. "We spoke with your manager at Western. Myra Peterson."

"Oh," he says. "Yeah, it started leakin' about four days ago, just haven't got it fixed. I was actually gettin' ready to drop it off for service."

"Can you tell me about Monday night?" I ask. "What did you do after you pulled into the station?"

"Well," he says, crossing his arms and putting his weight on his back foot. "I had to back in, cause of the tank and the rest of the spots were full. Only open one was on the wrong side, o'course. But I backed in, fueled up, went inside and grabbed a burger and took a leak. Then I headed back out. Why, what's this all about?"

He's certainly not acting like someone with something to hide. But I've dealt with liars before, and some of them can be very talented. "While you were there, did you see a young woman, early twenties with dark brown hair cut to the shoulders? She would have been wearing jeans and a red leather jacket."

"Not that I recall," he says.

"You said you just went inside for a few minutes?" Zara asks. He nods. "So why were you there two hours?"

"Part of that wasn't my fault," he says, beginning to get defensive. "I took a quick snooze in the cab, just thirty minutes to recharge. But when I got ready to leave, some other jackass had blocked me in. Took me a solid half hour to track him down and then I spent another twenty minutes arguing with him to move."

"Why didn't he want to move?" I ask.

"Who knows? He came across as an entitled little prick," Carlin says, working himself up. "Didn't seem to understand that I couldn't just turn my truck around in its place."

"Did you get his name?" I ask.

"Naw. Saw his ride though. He's with that outfit down in Roswell. MGL or something."

"LGM?" I ask.

"That's the one," he replies. "Got that stupid gray alien on the sides of all their trucks."

My heart picks up a beat. "Was he still there when you left?" I ask.

"Sure was, he made a big deal about pulling into the spot I'd vacated," Carlin replies. "Why, is that important?"

"Did you see him interacting with anyone else? Perhaps the woman I mentioned before?"

He shakes his head. "No, I never saw her. But I wasn't really paying attention. I didn't even really notice him until I had to track him down to move him. Found him out behind the station, having a smoke, but it wasn't a cigarette if you know what I mean."

I exchange a look with Zara. It's not concrete, but if what Carlin says is true, then LGM lied directly to us. Still, it doesn't clear him of any wrongdoing. "Did anyone see you and this other man arguing?"

"I couldn't really say," he replies. "All I cared about was getting back on the road. Wasn't payin' much attention to anyone else."

"Ok," I say, nodding. "Thank you, Mr. Carlin. Do you have any more shipments over the next few days?"

"Not while my truck is in the shop," he says. "I've got some leave time. Plan on stayin' home and catching up on basketball."

I hand him my card. "If you think of anything else that might be important, please give me a call."

He takes it. "Not sure what else I can tell you, but sure."

As we head back to the car, I turn to Zara. "Well?"

"No tells that I could see," she says. "He believes what he's saying. Or at least he thinks he does."

"Doesn't clear him."

"No, but the window is pretty thin. He would have had to kill Annabelle and dump her body in twenty-four minutes. As well as argue with the LGM driver and get his truck out of the way."

"Speaking of which," I say, climbing back into the SUV. "I think we know where we're headed next."

"Yeah, yeah," she says. "I know. My turn to drive."

Chapter Nine

"I SHOULD HAVE KNOWN that bastard was lying," I say for probably the fifth time since we got on the road. My knuckles are white and my nails are digging into my palms. It was too late to make the drive last night, so we headed out first thing this morning with Zara at the wheel. But the more I turn over my conversation with *Greyson Bauers* from LGM, the angrier I get. He lied directly to me about any of their trucks being on that route that night. Not only that, but if Mr. Carlin was correct, then the LGM truck would have been facing the correct way *and* was at the site right when we needed them to be. So even if the driver isn't forthcoming, we can still pull the dashcam footage. That is, if I can figure out *why* Bauers covered up their involvement. All of it points to someone who is acting very guilty.

"It's not a slam dunk," Zara reminds me. "We're working off the testimony of a man who might be implicated himself."

She's right. I can't get ahead of myself. Carlin could have told us that to throw us off his trail. But even if that's the case, why did LGM lie to me over the phone? I decided we couldn't leave it to chance. We need to confront them in person, so they can't do another run-around.

"Hey, did you talk to Strong about clearing this brief excursion?" Zara asks after a few minutes of silence.

I glance over before returning my eyes to the road. "No, why?"

"Don't you think it's going to be a little suspicious that we left of our own accord without informing anyone?"

"We're not junior agents," I say. "We do still have *some* autonomy."

"Yeah, but look at it from his perspective. This is our first 'real' case. And already we've used resources to interview a suspect. Running around town is one thing. Heading down close to the Mexico border is another."

She's right. We probably should have cleared it with Strong first. I'm just getting so sick of feeling like I have someone's thumb on my back all the time. I've gotten too used to a certain amount of autonomy and giving that up is just *another* thing to add to the pile of pains in my ass.

"We'll have to hope LGM reveals something useful. At least then maybe I can call him and explain."

"I'd have a good excuse if they don't," she replies, adjusting her sunglasses. With the giant frames she looks like a bug.

"Temporary insanity?" I suggest and she busts out laughing. "Plus, why are you complaining? Haven't you always wanted to go to *the source*?" It's a well-known fact to anyone who knows Zara that she *loves* aliens.

"I just never thought about risking my job to do it," she replies as a grin forms across her face. "It will be pretty cool though, won't it?"

"Yeah, it will," I say. But I have to stay focused. My plan is to confront Greyson or whoever at LGM that's making decisions and force them to give me information under the threat of lying to a federal officer. I can only think of one reason they would do that and that's covering up the truth. And given how none of our other leads have panned out, I'm hopeful this will at least give us *something.*

"Oh my God. I gotta pull over," Zara says, leaning forward in her seat. I take a second to realize what she's talking about, but then I see it. A big metal sign with a UFO perched on top of it that says WELCOME TO ROSWELL. Thankfully, there is an area to pull off where another car already sits. A young family stands in front of the sign, taking a picture.

"Ohmygod, ohmygod," Zara keeps saying as she pulls the SUV to a stop. "I can't believe we're here." She's out of the car without even turning off the engine, leaving me to kill it and grab the keys. The other family looks to have finished anyway and is heading back to their car just as Zara runs up to the sign before turning around and taking a selfie with it. I'm not sure I get the big deal. It's just a sign, but she's *enamored.*

"Em, c'mon, we gotta get a picture," she yells. I head over to meet her, noticing just how clear it is out here. It's clear in Albuquerque too, but there's something different about being this far out in the desert. There's a certain stillness that is hard to describe. That is, until a massive tractor trailer goes barreling by, blowing my hair all over the place.

Zara pulls me in, crushing us together as she holds her arm out and snaps a picture of us in front of the sign. But because of the height of it, she has to shoot us from below. "Isn't this cool?" she yells. The sign itself is practically covered in stickers of all kinds, presumably souvenirs from well-wishers all over the globe. I forget this place is a tourist mecca.

"C'mon," I say. "I want to get over to LGM as soon as possible." It's already close to eleven and once we speak with LGM, we're going to have a long drive back.

"Okay, yeah, lemme just get a few more pictures," she says as she snaps off half a dozen. "Man, I wish I could send these to Theo. He would *freak.*" As she says it, her gaze drops. She hasn't spoken much about the two of them since we arrived. Ever since the FBI cut his contract and Zara and I were sequestered here he's been out of contact. Even more than Liam has. I've tried bringing it up a few times, but she always waves me off and says it's no big deal. I know better than to push her. She'll open up when she's ready, but I know being this out of contact has to be gnawing at her as much as it is me.

"How about we head through the center of town?" I suggest as we head back to the car. Her face lights up a little. "Make sure you have your camera ready."

Driving through the middle of Roswell, New Mexico is nothing less than an *experience*. There are little green men on everything. They're on the signs, on the buildings, on cars. Full-fledged statues stand outside the buildings: alien life insurance, alien lawyers, alien home contractors. It's like if you don't embrace the alien motif in your business, you'll be ostracized and kicked out of town. And don't even get me started on the UFO museum—complete with the largest repository of UFO-related documents in the world.

Trying to keep Zara from quitting the FBI and starting life over as a UFO researcher was a challenge, to say the least. She practically jumped out of the SUV as we drove past the museum.

Finally, however, we reach LGM trucking, which is nothing more than a one-story warehouse building that sits next to a large parking lot. The parking lot contains six tractor trailer trucks, all emblazoned with the LGM logo while the building features two docks where the trucks can back into and load and unload their materials. Attached to the warehouse is a small office building with a glass door and large floor to ceiling windows on each side. A chain-link fence surrounds the property, which sits by itself right off Route 93, the closest neighboring business about five hundred yards in each direction. Fortunately for us, the gate is rolled open when we arrive and we park right in front of the office.

"Huh," Zara says. "I kinda expected a giant blow up alien on top of the building."

Knowing this place, it wouldn't be the strangest thing I've seen. "Maybe they like to be more subtle about their branding," I say. As we get out the wind picks up, drawing dust and dirt from the nearby fields across the bare parking lot. I have to shield my eyes from the sudden dust-up which is over in only a few seconds. "Let's get inside before I become a redhead."

"Aww," she says. "I think you'd look good in red. Could you imagine what Liam would say?"

I actually couldn't. Unlike Zara I've never had an inclination to color my hair and I don't plan on starting anytime soon. I make a motion for the door and we head in.

Inside there isn't a reception desk; instead a series of regular-sized desks sit to our left about ten feet from the door and extending all the way back to the wall. A man is behind the first one, scribbling something on what looks like a time sheet. I clear my throat to get his attention, as apparently the door opening and closing didn't do it.

He looks up. "Oh, sorry, didn't see you. What can I do for you?" He's tan enough that I can tell he spends a good deal of the day in the sun. What's more is even though he's wearing a button-down shirt, I can see it straining under the muscles of his arms, visible beneath the fabric. He certainly doesn't look like someone who works behind a desk all day.

"We're looking for Greyson Bauers," I say.

He flashes us a million-dollar smile, showing rows of perfectly straight, white teeth. "Then you're in luck. That's me." He stands and holds out his hand to shake mine, which I take. He's got a good grip, but not enough that I feel like he's going to crush my hand.

"Great. We spoke on the phone earlier. I'm Special Agent Dunn, with the FBI. This is my partner, Special Agent Laidlaw."

His smile drops and he lets go of my hand immediately. "Oh," he says. "I... uh... I don't understand. Was there something else you needed? I thought—" His body posture has changed completely, the confidence evaporating which is exactly what I was hoping for.

"I just wanted to confirm you were sticking with your story about not having any trucks on Highway 17 outside Albuquerque on Monday night," I say, leveling my gaze at him, practically begging him to lie to me again.

He fumbles at his collar and returns to his desk, keeping his back to us. "Oh... right... on Monday, um..."

"Remember?" I ask. "You said you had no trucks out there that night, right?"

"Well, you know what?" he says, rounding the desk again and fumbling with some of his papers. "I actually... I did some more research after we got off the phone and I think I may have been mistaken."

I share a quick glance with Zara, who takes up a position closer to Bauers' desk but further to the side. She leans up against the wall, her arms crossed. Bauers glances at her, then back at me and then back to the pile of papers on his desk. "Yes, here it is. We had one run that took our driver out that way Monday. Left Clovis headed for Shiprock. And... um, yep. He reached Shiprock around one A.M. on Tuesday." He gives us an apologetic grin. "That must have been why I didn't see it. It was marked as a Tuesday delivery."

"Uh-huh," I say, knowing full well that's a line of bullshit if I've ever heard one. "And did the truck stop at the The Speedy Stop on its journey?"

"Hang on, let me check the driver logs," he says and takes

a seat at his desk, typing at his computer. I motion to Zara and she moves closer so she can see what he's doing on his screen. She gives me a quick nod. But from the way Bauers is sweating, I doubt he even noticed her move. He is nervous about something, and it's more than just a couple of FBI agents standing in his office.

"I… uh… yeah. It's right here. Stopped to refuel. Twenty-one-oh-seven. Was back on the road by twenty-two-fifteen."

That's not a lot of overlap, but it's longer that the truck was there than Jack Carlin. And it's forty-five minutes where we might glimpse Annabelle on the truck's dashcam. "Great. We'll need the footage from the truck," I say.

He turns to me, a confused look on his face. "I'm sorry?"

"From the truck's dashcam," I reiterate, not sure what the problem is. "As I said on the phone, we're investigating an incident and need the footage from your driver."

"Oh… our trucks don't use dash cams," he says, his gaze shooting back and forth between us. Sweat is visible on his brow and if this goes on much longer he might start shaking like a leaf.

"Why not?" Zara asks. "What happens if one of your drivers gets into an accident? What about liability?"

He gives us a quick shrug. "I don't know what to tell you. It's not company policy to have them, so the trucks aren't outfitted with them."

You've got to be kidding me. "You mean you don't have any cameras on your trucks *anywhere*?"

"No, we don't," he says. "I'm sorry."

"Unbelievable," I mutter. "Is the truck that was out there that night in your yard?"

He nods. "Sure, it's the second one from the left, why?"

"I want to inspect it," I say. "And I want to talk to the driver."

He doesn't move as I head towards the door. "Don't you… I mean, isn't there like a warrant or something required for that? Our boss has some strict rules about who can access company property."

I pause. Something is going on here, and I don't like it. Why is he being so cagey? Is there something in that truck he doesn't want us to find? "Where's your boss?" I ask.

"Mr. Lambert?" he asks. "He's not in today."

Convenient. "Are you refusing us access to your truck?"

He stands, unsure at first but then straightens his back. "I'm… sorry. I can't let anyone access company property without Mr. Lambert's authorization."

If he's trying to hide something, he's doing a terrible job of it. Because this just became my newest obsession. "Will Mr. Lambert be in at any point today?"

"I… uh, I don't think so," he replies.

"How about tomorrow?" Zara asks.

"Yes, he should be," Bauers replies. "He usually comes in around nine."

"Inform him we'll be back with a warrant," I say, keeping my stare on the man, trying to gauge his reaction. He's exhibiting all the classic signs of someone who is trying very hard not to look nervous.

"Sure," he says, his eyes flashing between me and Zara. I hold for a few moments to see if there's any further reaction, but he seems determined. Finally we head back to the car, leaving Mr. Bauers to his work.

"Think he's in there calling Lambert right now?" Zara asks as we get back in the car.

"No doubt about it," I say. "This is going to be an uphill battle." I just hope whatever is going on here is actually related to Annabelle's death. I'm not sure I even have the evidence I need for a warrant.

"Well, look on the bright side," Zara says. "Now we don't have to drive back."

Chapter Ten

WITH LITTLE ELSE TO DO, we spend the rest of the day doing some light sightseeing. A trip to the UFO museum and heading out to some of the famous spots from the famous 1947 crash take up most of the day. I have to admit, it's nice to slow down and enjoy the town for a minute. Usually we're running ourselves ragged when we're working on a case. But since our victim is already dead, I don't see the harm in waiting an extra day to speak with this Lambert person. Plus, while Zara is fawning over something in the many gift shops around town, I work on pulling together a case to obtain a warrant.

After a full day we stop by the drugstore for some essentials before checking into the Roswell Motel, complete with alien signs and standees outside. It looks like any other motel I've stayed at, with the exception that there are about a dozen green beings with large black eyes pointing us to the check-in desk. *I* wanted to stay at the Holiday Inn, but Zara insisted. She said we couldn't come all the way to Roswell and not do it. Plus, I can't argue with the price. At least it shouldn't throw up any flags when it comes across Strong's desk.

That's another thing. If things were normal, I wouldn't be

concerned. But we're supposed to be keeping a low profile. And I'm not sure driving out to Roswell and asking a bunch of questions relating to a murder in Albuquerque qualifies. If someone out there really is targeting me and has access to the FBI database, then an action like this might be like sending up a flare.

"This is nice," Zara says, opening the door to our room. I have to admit, it's better than I expected. The room is clean, with two queen-size beds and a small table near the window. A tiny microwave sits on top of a small fridge itself on the only dresser in the corner of the room. A TV hangs on the wall over the table.

"Huh. I was expecting more aliens," I say, tossing my stuff on one of the beds. Zara heads into the bathroom.

"No creatures from outer space in here."

"You sound disappointed," I say.

She flops down on the other bed. "I guess I was just hoping this place would be decked out, you know? Like the entire room would be painted black with white specs for stars and instead of a ceiling fan there'd be a big metal ship on the ceiling with a little guy waving or something."

I chuckle. "I'm not sure they'd get much business that way."

"Are you kidding? People would love it. You saw the McDonalds, right?"

I did. The entire building was in the shape of a flying saucer. "I'm going to make a call," I say, holding up the burner phone I grabbed from the drug store. "Back in a minute."

"Tell him hi for me," she says as she flips on the TV. The first channel is automatically on some UFO documentary. If I didn't know better, I would say she somehow engineered Lambert not to be there, so we'd be *forced* to stay here overnight.

We're in one of the back units and as I exit the room, I'm

looking at yet another dirt patch that leads out to the horizon. There are a few trees and buildings out there, but they're off in the distance. The sun hasn't set yet, but it's close and the sky is a beautiful mix of blues and purples. As the phone rings, I catch the first glimpse of stars.

"Hey," Liam says on the other end. "I was hoping I'd hear from you soon."

"Hey," I say. The sound of his voice is like a salve for my emotions. "Sorry I didn't call sooner. We've been on a case."

"An actual case?" he asks. "That's good, right?"

I nod, even though he can't see me. But I don't want to talk about the case. "How are you? How are the pups?"

"They miss you," he says. "They keep looking at the door, waiting for you to come home." He pauses. "I miss you too. A lot."

I sigh. "I need to tell you something." He doesn't say anything, just waits for me to continue. "I almost quit on Tuesday."

"What?"

"I thought that by removing myself from the equation maybe I could at least come back home," I say. "But then we got this assignment. If it had come in an hour later, or even thirty minutes—"

"We're going to figure this thing out," he says. "I promise. In fact, I have news—I just needed to wait for you to call."

"News?" I ask, feeling something like hope deep in my chest for the first time in a solid month.

"Everyone here is being tight-lipped," he says. "They've compartmentalized everything. But I overheard Caruthers and Janice the other day. They were discussing the breach—and you. I couldn't catch much more than your name, but you and… your partner… haven't been forgotten there."

"What were they saying?" I ask.

"Something about timing, and something else about *the*

underground? I think they realized I was close and they quit talking, though they never actually said anything to me."

"The underground?" I ask. "What's that?"

"No idea," he says. "But rest assured, they're working on it. They haven't quit. And neither can you."

"I dunno," I say. "Aren't you tired of all this cloak-and-dagger shit? The constantly looking over your shoulder?"

"I know it's hard," he replies. "But for as long as I've known you, you've never been afraid to do the hard thing. Who knows, maybe this will all be over sooner than we think."

"That's what… *my partner* keeps telling me." I have to remind myself not to use my or Zara's name over the line, not that I think it will make all that much difference. But as far as the outside world is concerned, Emily Slate has disappeared off the face of the earth. "I think part of it is this place. It's so desolate out here. I feel like we're all alone. And I miss you." I know I already said it once, but I feel like it needs to be said again. We only get to speak once a week, which is a lot different from seeing each other almost every day at work and at home.

"Soon," he says. "Just hang in there. I'm going to keep working too. All of us here on the team are doing everything we can."

"All of you?" I ask.

"Yep. We're all pulling for you. Not just me."

Does that mean Nadia and Elliott are working on this too? I wonder if I should tell him about Zara's investigations, but it probably wouldn't be the best thing to broach over an open line like this. "It would be pretty rude to give up then, wouldn't it?" I say instead, kicking at a stray rock.

"Terrible manners," he replies. "My mother would not approve."

I snort back a laugh. "How is your family?"

"Everyone is fine here, don't worry about us," he says. "Also I show the dogs your picture every day to make sure they don't forget you." I know he's joking, but it tugs at my heart-strings, regardless.

"Give them a kiss for me," I say. "And one for yourself, though I'm not sure how you can manage that."

"I'll find a way, trust me," he replies which causes me to laugh again. "Talk again soon?"

"In a few days," I say. I instinctively know we're already reaching our five-minute limit. "Maybe I'll have this thing wrapped up by then."

"Whatever it is, I'm sure you're killing it," he says before pausing. "I love you."

"I love you back," I say, then whisper a quick "Bye" before hanging up. Turning off the phone, I remove the battery and the sim card, and smash the latter under my heel as my eyes well up with tears. This shouldn't be necessary, and yet it is.

I take a few moments to gather myself before heading back inside to find Zara on the bed, working on her computer.

"I thought you were watching UFO stuff."

"Got boring," she says. "I've seen that one before. Here, look at this." She turns the laptop to me, showing me the screen. "This is the list of commercial auto insurance requirements for the state of New Mexico. It says here that any commercially driven vehicle is *required* to keep visual recordings during operation in order to qualify for auto insurance in the state."

"So you're saying that LGM is lying about the dash cams, or they don't have insurance."

"Oh, they have it," she replies, pulling up another site—this one belonging to LGM. "See here? *Fully licensed, bonded and insured.* I even checked with the state corporation commission. If they don't have dash cams, they're lying to the state as well."

"Which gives us probable cause," I say. "And more ammunition for a warrant." I step back. "You did all this in five minutes?"

She shrugs. "It isn't like I've had a *real* challenge for a while now. I mean, other than… you know."

I take a seat on the other bed and roll out my shoulders. "Yeah. I know."

"How is he, by the way?"

"He says he's good, but I know Liam well enough that I can tell he's struggling too. Turns out Nadia and Elliott are helping him try to figure out what's going on."

"Aww," she says. "That's sweet. I don't suppose they've made any progress."

"Not much. He said he overheard Janice and Caruthers discussing something called *The Underground*. He said they mentioned it in the same sentence with my name."

A *V* forms across her brow. "The Underground? Never heard of it. Unless we're talking about London transit systems."

"Doubt it," I say. "Anyway, he said they quit talking as soon as he got close."

"You know what you should do—call Janice," she says. "Confront her about whatever this is. Make her tell you what they know."

I shake my head. "That would only poke the bear. I trust Janice. If there's a way to get us out of this, she'll let us know."

She closes her laptop. "Did he say anything else?"

"Not really. We can't discuss many details, you know?" I reach down and pull off my shoes, stretching out my toes. They feel like they've been smashed together all day. My gaze lingers on them a split second longer than it should. Zara is right, I *do* have pretty feet.

"You're thinking about it, aren't you?" she asks and I throw my foot down, covering up with the scratchy duvet cover.

"No," I protest.

She hops on the bed. "You absolutely were. Admit it." She tries yanking at the cover.

"Quit it!" I yell but can't help but laugh at the same time.

"Not until you agree to use my referral code!"

We end up in a tug of war with the duvet, each of us employing every trick in the book to get one up on the other. For a second I think my height will be an advantage, but she's quicker than I am, which evens it out. And unlike me, Zara hasn't been slacking in her training. I'm not sure if two grown women vying for control of a blanket is a scene anyone would believe, I'm just glad the sheers are drawn.

Finally we end it in a draw and end up lying on our backs, staring up at the ceiling and panting.

"Liam will get a kick out of this place when we get back," she says between breaths. "Imagine how jealous he'll be."

"Speaking of which," I say, trying to catch my breath. "I feel like this is the kind of place that would be right up Theo's alley." I expect an immediate retort, but when I don't get one I turn to look at my friend. She's staring at the ceiling like she's looking off into space. "Z?"

"Can I tell you something?" she finally says, somber.

"You can tell me anything," I say, sitting back up. "What's going on?"

"I… I'm not sure I trust Theo anymore," she says. "This whole thing started with his contract… when we went after that information Fletch was carrying. If not for Theo, we never would have even had Fletch on our radar."

"You don't think the Bureau missed something with him, do you?"

"I don't think they knew what to look for," she says. "*I* didn't even look, remember? I was so enamored to date someone whose entire backstory I *didn't* know. And the truth is, I don't know that much about him, outside of what little he's told us. Who knows? When he was working for Simon, maybe it wasn't a cover."

I think back to that harrowing case. The one that ended up with Zara and I with a bomb set to go off between us. Had it not been for Theo, the both of us would be dead right now. And since then, he's become a valuable partner with the Bureau. But I know what she means. Sometimes the Bureau takes shortcuts to get to their goals faster. Sometimes they make deals with unscrupulous people to get the more dangerous ones off the street. And sometimes they work with criminals if it serves their interests. And as much as I hate it, I have to accept it's part of the job. But it's not something I'll ever directly be a part of. Maybe that's why I don't want to get promoted. Because eventually I would end up facing that situation.

"You haven't spoken to him since all this happened, have you?" I ask. She gives me a small shake of her head. "Would doing a background on him now be helpful?"

"I don't know," she replies. "What if nothing comes up? Or worse, what if I find exactly what I'm looking for?" I get up and take a seat beside her, wrapping my arm around her shoulder. "You don't think he could be behind all this, do you?" she asks.

"It doesn't seem like him," I say, thinking back to all my interactions with Theo. Most have been professional, except when he and Zara would show up at a party or something together. But those occasions were rare because he is always traveling. I don't know how long he spends in the states, but it can't be more than a few weeks at a time. And he is sarcastic, always making a joke out of things. But I find him competent and trustworthy in the field, otherwise I wouldn't have agreed to keep working with him. Honestly, most of my trust in him comes from Zara's confidence in his character. "I hope not."

"I just have a bad feeling about it," she admits.

"Let's try not to jump to any conclusions," I say. "We don't know *what* is going on. And until we do, all we can do is work the case in front of us, right?"

She nods a few times, like she's trying to convince herself of that. "Right."

"Ok, let's get some sleep then. I want to get to the local courthouse early tomorrow. Get a jump on things."

"Yeah," she says. "You're right. One request though." I raise my eyebrows as she flips the channel back over to the documentary. "We go to sleep with the aliens on."

I give her a wink. "Whatever floats your boat."

Chapter Eleven

"What do you mean *denied*?" I nearly scream at the clerk as he hands my written request back to me.

We're standing in the Chaves County courthouse, which is a beautiful old building that sits right in the middle of town. The floors and columns are all marble and there's even a rotunda high above us, with frescos on the walls.

And yet the timid-looking clerk behind the glass wall is anything but as he sets his gaze to mine. "I'm sorry, but Judge Sloane has made her decision. Your request for a warrant is denied."

"On what grounds?" I ask, pushing the application back towards him.

"Insufficient evidence," he says, pushing it back.

I hold up my badge. "Does the judge not understand that Bauers lied to a federal officer?" I ask. "My partner witnessed it." I motion to Zara who is standing right next to me.

"I don't know what to tell you," the clerk replies. "This is the judge's decision."

"This is insane." I take the paper back and head for the doors, Zara alongside me. "We need to find a way to talk to that judge."

"Em, that won't help," she says as we descend the stairs back to the parking lot. "Berating a local judge isn't going to get you the warrant. It'll only piss her off."

She's right; I'm just so irked. I thought this was a slam dunk. And if we were in DC, it would be.

I say that, but then I think back to how many times I've tussled with the judicial system and I'm not so sure. Still, lying to a federal officer is an offense, and should at least provide enough incentive to investigate whatever the hell they're doing over at LGM.

"Great," I say, slamming the door of the SUV. "Now what? Go back to Albuquerque empty-handed? That's going to look great to Strong."

"I don't see that we have much choice," she says. "Unless you want to go confront Lambert personally. But I'd bet by now he's already covered up whatever they're trying to hide."

I sigh, the air leaving my lungs. "You're right," I say. Our talk with Bauers yesterday no doubt sent up the alarm for Lambert or anyone else in the company. "I just wish we could talk to the driver. If he was there that night, he's a potential suspect." I turn to her. "I don't guess there's any way you could find out who he is?"

She glares at me under hooded eyes. "Why, Emily Rachel Slate. Are you asking me to *break into* a private computer system and examine their employee records?"

"No, I guess not," I say.

"Good," she replies. "Because that would be illegal. And I think I have a better way."

It's closing in on eleven o'clock as we enter the bar. It's only been open half an hour, but the bar is already half full of patrons and the bartender is working overtime on drinks.

Zara scans the place, which has a western theme to it, but not overdone like some of those gaudy places. We just left a restaurant which had honest-to-God spaceships hanging from the ceiling. And not just one or two, but dozens, most of them bigger than me. The whole restaurant looked like an alien airport hangar.

"There he is," Zara says, pointing to a booth near the side of the restaurant. You would think a place like this would be gloomy, but there's so much light coming in from the big windows it's almost like we're still outdoors.

The man we're headed to speak with is hunched over a glass, half full of an amber liquid. He's wearing a plaid button- down and a tan cowboy hat sits on the seat next to him. He glances up when we approach, his eyes lighting up. "Howdy, ladies."

"Brandon Ruiz?" Zara asks. Confusion falls over his face. Obviously, he wasn't expecting to run into two FBI agents today.

"Yes?" he says, like he doesn't know his own identity.

Zara slides into the booth across from him and I follow. Considering this is her idea, I'm letting her take the reins on this one. She shows the man her badge. "I'm Special Agent Laidlaw, this is Special Agent Dunn. We'd like to ask you a few questions."

He looks down at his beer like maybe he's had enough to drink and he's hallucinating all this, but Zara snaps her fingers right in his face, bringing his attention back to us.

"What is this all about?" he asks.

"You currently own and operate a 2020 Peterbilt 389 flattop Sleeper, is that correct?"

His eyes grow wide. "Yes," he says. "Why?"

"Were you once employed by LGM Trucking, LLC?" she asks.

He snorts. "I think *employed* is a strong word. They hired

me occasionally for jobs, solely on an independent contractor basis. I never formally worked for the company."

"But you're familiar with their operations," I say.

"Familiar enough, why?" he asks.

"We're looking for some information about their drivers," Zara says. "And we think you can help us."

Ruiz looks at her, then me, then back to his beer again, keeping his eyes on the table. "Sorry, 'fraid not."

This is the third independent owner-operator we've approached about information regarding LGM Trucking. And so far each of them has been tight-lipped. I can understand wanting a bit of privacy regarding your company, but whoever this Lambert is, he has a tight noose on people who aren't even his employees anymore.

"I thought you might say that," Zara replies. "Would you like to know how we found you?" He glances up then back at his glass again, saying nothing. "It was your friendly former parole officer, Officer Danko. He was kind enough to let us know this is where you like to lurk on your days off."

Ruiz sighs. "Can't you just leave me alone? I haven't done anything wrong."

"Not according to Officer Danko," she says. "He informed us about a little trafficking ring you used to run. Out of the back of your own truck, no less."

"Look, I just got my license back," he says, pushing the beer away. "I've been without a job for six months and I'm behind. I don't need anything screwing up the contracts I have lined up."

"Which is why it's a good idea to tell us everything you can about LGM," Zara says. "Just so we can make sure nothing gums up the works."

Ruiz grits his teeth. "No, you don't get it. I'm not worried about you. I'm worried about *him.*"

"Who, Danko?" I ask.

"*Lambert,*" Ruiz whispers.

"Why is everyone so afraid of this guy?" Zara asks.

Ruiz drains his beer in one go and grabs his hat. "Look, I'm sorry. I can't help you. Please don't contact me again." He moves to get out of the booth, but my arm stops him.

"Sit down, Mr. Ruiz." He grimaces but resumes his place in the booth.

"What are you going to do, threaten me?" he says. "You can't do any worse than what that man has already done to me. He's the reason—" The man looks around, making sure we're out of earshot of anyone else. "He's the reason I got caught in the first place."

"He ratted you out," Zara says.

"When I refused to make a run for him, yeah," Ruiz says.

"What kind of run?" I ask. But Ruiz only shakes his head.

"Let me spell this out for you," Zara tells him. "We have a dead girl. Young, about the age of your daughter. Maria, right? Graduates from ENMU this year?" He nods. "And we think LGM is involved. No one else will talk to us. I'm asking for your help here. Not threatening. Not coercing. Asking."

Ruiz swallows. "You don't understand. You don't go up against Lambert. Not in this town. He's rich, and he protects himself." He leans closer. "And he has ears everywhere."

"You're sounding a little paranoid, Mr. Ruiz," I say.

"You would be too if you lived here," he replies. "Now please, I can't say anything else. I wish I could help you; I really do. But I have a family to think about. And they need me." I drop my arm as he gets out of the booth and heads for the door, not looking back.

"Damn," Zara says. "I was sure that would work."

"Seems Lambert has a real stranglehold on this town," I say. "All I wanted was the name of the truck driver."

"And to find out about the cameras," Zara reminds me. I glance around and notice a few looks from other people in the bar, but they turn back to their business as soon as they see me looking.

"Let's get out of here," I say. "I don't have a good feeling about this place."

"With pleasure," Zara says, following me to the door. We're parked around back and as we turn the corner to the car, I catch the sound of glass crunching from under the heel of a boot. My senses fire, telling me something is off, and adrenaline floods my system.

But I'm a split second too late as I look down the barrel of a gun.

Chapter Twelve

I RAISE MY HANDS SLOWLY, looking at the disheveled man, his dirty blonde hair and facial hair covered in dirt. His skin is tanned dark, just like Bauers, but unlike the other man he's skinny, looking strung out.

"Just calm down," I say, my hands up. Zara is still around the side of the building—at least I think she is—she's out of my periphery. She wouldn't be able to see him from her position, but from the look in this guy's eyes, he's strung out, which makes him *very* unpredictable. Somehow, despite everything, they found me. Whoever was responsible for the breach at the FBI has me dead to rights. One wrong move and it's all over.

"You're the FBI lady," he says, shoving the gun closer to me.

"Yes," I reply, trying to telegraph to Zara not to do anything.

"You've been asking about Lambert," he says.

I take a breath. *Jesus.* Ruiz wasn't kidding about the man having ears everywhere. Until a second ago I thought whoever caused me to leave DC had finally tracked me here; that maybe my call to Liam last night had been what had done it. But it turns out we're making Lambert nervous, and he decided to send us a message. Suddenly, I'm not so anxious anymore. "I'm performing an investigation."

"Where's the other one?" he demands.

"She's off following leads," I say. "It's just you and me."

"You shouldn't be asking questions about things you don't know about," he says, attempting to be intimidating, though it comes off more like pathetic. Even though all my focus is on him, I catch movement behind his head which causes my gaze to shift ever so slightly. It's enough to distract him to turn and as he does, I grab his hand, pushing it to the sky as he squeezes the trigger. The gun produces a deafening boom but I twist his wrist causing him to cry out in pain as he drops the weapon. Zara is immediately at my side and helps me wrestle him to the ground as we get him into cuffs.

"Where did you come from?" I was sure the movement behind the man was Zara, circling around the building. "I thought you were over there." I motion to behind the man, but it's only then that I see what caught my attention. It wasn't Zara, but it *is* a face I recognize. "What the hell?"

"What?" Zara asks, looking up.

At the other end of the parking lot stands the reservation cop we saw at the station who had been in an argument with Ridout. He's watching us with feigned disinterest as we get the other man back up, his arms locked behind his back.

"You got nothing on me," the gunman spits. "I won't talk! I'm loyal. Ain't the first time I've seen the inside of a jail cell!"

"Sit down and shut up," I say, pushing the man on his ass so he's sitting up against the wheel of our car. Already there's the sound of a siren in the distance. Someone must have heard the gunshot. I pull out my badge as a precaution.

"What is *he* doing here?" Zara asks, indicating the man from the reservation. Andersen, the clerk said his name was.

"Who knows?" I mutter, turning away from him. I don't have time to worry about Andersen or anyone else, at least not until this perpetrator is in a jail cell. "And right now, I don't care. If Lambert sent this guy, maybe now I can finally get Judge Sloane to sign off on a warrant."

"E—*Claire*," Zara says. "He's gone."

I turn to look and sure enough; the man has disappeared, like he was never there. I don't know what's going on here, but I don't like it. And I really don't like being stalked.

A squad car comes screaming down one of the side streets, its lights flashing. Zara and I already have both our hands up, our badges out so the officers can see them clearly.

"Get down on the ground!" one of them calls out as he gets out of the car, pointing the second gun at me today.

"We're federal officers," I yell back. "FBI. This suspect is in custody." The man lowers his weapon as his partner says something over the radio. He approaches slowly and inspects my ID from a distance before stowing his weapon. He motions to his partner who continues talking on the radio.

"We got a report of a gunshot," he says.

I nod to the man on the ground. "The weapon is over there. He decided to try to hold up an FBI agent."

The officer *tsks* and shakes his head. "Just can't stay out of trouble, can you, Jerry? This one is gonna cost you. Won't be no parole this time."

"I got friends," 'Jerry' replies. "I don't sweat you."

I motion to the cop. "He mentioned someone named Lambert. Does that mean anything to you?"

The cop blanches for a split second and then it's gone. "I wouldn't worry about that. Jerry's a transient, on drugs half the time and drunk with booze the other half. But don't you worry, we'll get him booked. Would you like to follow us down to the station so we can take your statement?"

"You can take it here, thanks," I say, though I feel something in the air has shifted. As I speak and the officer writes the series of events down, I have a bad feeling in the pit of my stomach.

Finally he flips the notebook closed. His partner already

has Jerry in the backseat of their cruiser, despite the man not for one second shutting up about the level of treatment he's receiving.

As they pull away, Zara looks at me. "Did you just feel something change there?"

I nod. As soon as I said the name *Lambert,* it was like all the air was sucked out of the space.

"How are you feeling about that warrant now?"

"Not good," I say. Whatever we've stumbled upon here, whatever is going on, it doesn't look like anyone in this town is willing to even go near Lambert.

"You will not find what you're looking for here," a voice says from behind us. I spin, my hand back on my weapon. But when I see it's the same man from before—Andersen—I drop my grip. He's walking slowly towards us, his truck parked in the next lot over. "This town is buttoned up tight. No one will break their silence for the FBI."

"I'm sorry," I say, sarcasm tinging my words. "We haven't formally met."

"Wendell Andersen," he says, though he doesn't hold out his hand. He just stops a few feet in front of us.

"Special Agent Dunn. And this is Special Agent Laidlaw," I say. "You're with the Navajo Police. From the service station." The man nods. "What are you doing here?"

"Investigating," he replies.

"More like stalking," Zara says.

Andersen doesn't react, his face is as hard as stone. Now that I see him properly, I can tell he has a strong build, though his belly sticks out over his belt. Even though he's wearing a hat, his dark hair has grayed, but his eyes remain piercing. "What do you know about Lambert?" I ask.

"You first," he says, not even blinking.

"No way," Zara replies. "This is a federal investigation now. We're not required to share anything with you."

"I'm conducting my own investigation," he says.

"How long have you been in Roswell?" I ask.

He hooks his thumbs into his belt. "Since yesterday."

"You followed us down," I say and the man nods. "Why?"

"I wanted to see if you could be trusted," he says. Finally, after he sees that neither Zara nor I are going to break, he sighs and glances out towards the horizon. "I've been after Lambert for years. The cops here... they don't go up against him."

"Who even is he? Why is everyone so afraid of him?" I ask.

"He's a known criminal. My office has seven different investigations open on him at the moment."

"Let me guess," Zara says. "No witnesses will come forward to testify."

"That," Andersen says. "And the evidence is circumstantial at best. We know Lambert is behind these crimes, but we lack sufficient proof."

"What crimes?" I ask.

"Drug trafficking," he says. "*Human* trafficking. Fraud. Assault and battery. And, of course, murder."

I share a quick glance with Zara. "How long have you been investigating him?"

"Almost three years," Andersen says.

"And in all that time you haven't had enough evidence to convict?" I ask. "Maybe this guy didn't actually do what you're accusing him of."

Andersen regards me for a moment. "There are more bodies."

I'm momentarily taken aback. "No there aren't. Bernalillo County would have told us if there had been any that matched the M.O.—"

"They didn't happen in Bernalillo County," he says. "They all occurred on reservation property."

I take a moment to process what he's told me. "How many more?"

"Five," he says. "Annabelle Witter makes number six."

"And Ridout doesn't know about them?" Zara asks.

Andersen takes a deep breath, like he's centering himself. "Officer Ridout doesn't believe they are connected. Which was what he and I were arguing about the other day at the station."

"Are you telling me Officer Ridout is intentionally obscuring the facts of this case?"

"I am," he replies. "And so are most of the police officers you will find out here. Lambert owns this place. No one will go against him."

"You could have told us all this that day at the station," I say. "It would have saved us a lot of time and trouble."

"I wasn't sure I could trust you," he replies. "But by coming here and asking around, you've already done more than any other department. You also see how dangerous it can be."

I roll my eyes. "It wasn't the first time I've had a gun in my face and I doubt it's the last," I say. "The odds of that man actually hitting what he was shooting at were fifty-fifty at best."

"Still, it's rare that you see that kind of response after only a few hours," he says. "This is why my investigations have stalled."

I put my hands on my hips, looking around. "Would you be willing to share your information with us?" I want to get a look at the other deaths, see if they really look like they're all by the same perp as he claims. He may be assigning correlation where there is none.

"If you agree to share what you've learned and what you continue to learn in the course of your investigation," he says.

I shoot Zara a look. Thankfully we know each other well enough we don't need to have a discussion about this. Her body language tells me everything I need to know. She's cautious, but intrigued, much like I am. "Okay," I say. "But I want everything you have on Lambert, top to bottom. If he's really behind these deaths, I want to make sure we nail him." I pull out my card.

"Easier said than done," Andersen says, taking it. "I will have the files to you tomorrow. Are you planning on staying in Roswell?"

Honestly, I'm not sure. I feel like there is something big here. But if Lambert really owns this town, how long until someone else comes after us? It might be the smarter move to head back to Albuquerque and work the case from there. At least that way we'd be out of the bullseye.

"We'll head back to Albuquerque today," I say. "I'm not sure how far we can get here if the whole town is zipped up."

"Very well," Andersen replies before heading back to his car without so much as a *see ya later*.

"Charismatic guy," Zara says once he's out of earshot. "Think he's telling the truth?"

"I'm not sure," I say, cautious. I don't like the fact he's been following us around the past two days. More than that, I didn't even notice.

She takes a deep breath, then lets the air out as we watch Andersen drive away. "Well, are you driving back, or am I?"

Chapter Thirteen

I STARE across the desk at my boss as he reads the preliminary report I filed last night, though I have to admit, I'm not feeling great about it.

Even though it was close to quitting time when Zara and I got back to Albuquerque late yesterday afternoon, she convinced me we should probably at least file *some* paperwork explaining where we'd been for the past two days before we got called into Strong's office. Unfortunately, I was called in this morning anyway, probably *because* of the reports. But she's right; we need to keep him in the loop. I can't be out here pretending like everything is like it is back in DC. I need to be more cautious. Working on a case again has made me fall back into old habits—some of which may not be tolerated here.

Strong looks over the top of the report at me briefly before returning his gaze to the file. All I can do is sit and wait for his judgement. I don't think he's going to kick me off the case, but he may want to tighten the leash, which will only make things harder.

Finally, he sets the file down and appraises me a moment longer. I recognize the tactic; he's trying to get me to squirm.

And maybe as a "younger" agent with less experience, I should be. But I'm not going to sit here and let Strong or anyone else intimidate me, cover be damned.

"There's not much here," he finally says. I conveniently left out the part where I was almost shot in the face, mostly because I don't want him to ask how an agent with zero real-world combat experience could disarm and detain a perpetrator so easily. That, and I don't want the incident to send up any flares surrounding our position here.

"No, sir. But I believe we have a solid foundation. We've found a genuine lead. Whether Lambert was involved with Annabelle's death or not is immaterial. But he's hiding something, and he may have the evidence we need to solve her murder."

Strong takes a deep breath, sitting back in his chair. "Agent Dunn, how long have you been with the FBI?"

"Seventeen months," I say, which is congruent with my backstory.

"Agent, I know you're itching to prove yourself. I've seen how much drive you have and how you think it's being wasted on menial tasks. Part of the reason I've kept a close eye on you and Laidlaw is because I wanted to see how you responded to different challenges."

I'm not sure where he's going with this. "Sir?"

"I was told to keep a close eye on you both. That you needed additional training before you were ready for the field." He glances down at the report again. "This is not the report of an agent who has only been with the Bureau seventeen months."

I freeze in my seat, not even daring to breathe. The man is staring at me, watching for any errant movement, anything that he can use to his advantage. And it's my job not to give it to him. "Is that a compliment, sir?"

He narrows his gaze. "I have never seen anyone with seventeen months on the job deliver this kind of report in two days." He leans forward. "You either have to be very arrogant, or very lucky."

"I'm sorry?"

"Taking an unsanctioned excursion based on a *hunch*? Perhaps you don't know this, but for someone in your position, that kind of thing needs approval."

"But not for someone like Agent Dent," I say, unable to stop myself.

"Agent Dent has been with this office for four years," he says. "She's *earned* my trust. You haven't." He closes the file and pushes it back towards me. "From here on you are not to make one move on this case without my say-so. Don't make me sorry I gave you this opportunity, Dunn."

I nod. "Sorry, sir," I say, and I am. The last thing I want to do is to be put back on desk duty.

"Good. Get Laidlaw in here. She's next."

I stand. "Sir, it was my idea to go to Roswell. Agent Laidlaw actually tried to talk me out of it. She said we should wait for approval. I… I didn't think it was necessary."

"Is that so?" He glares at me, tapping one finger on his desk.

"Yes, sir. She's blameless in this. It was my fault… and my responsibility."

The man huffs, then finally waves me away, turning back to his computer. "Get back to work."

"Sir…" I say, knowing I'm right up against the line here.

"Don't you know when to leave, Dunn?" the man asks, his brow heavy as he glares at me.

"You said you wanted me to keep you informed of our progress. On our drive back, Agent Laidlaw located Annabelle Witter's former roommate. We'd like to interview her to find out if anyone was stalking Annabelle. I thought it might be an additional lead we could follow."

He's silent for a moment before finally giving me a nod. "Very well."

"Thank you," I say and head out, not wanting to poke the bear any further. As I get back to my desk, Zara is typing away on her computer.

"So?" she asks, not looking up. "Did you tell him about Andersen?"

"No," I say, taking a seat at my desk. "I didn't want to bring it up until I know there's something real there. Andersen could just be jerking us around. I don't guess those files have showed up yet?"

"Nothing in my inbox," Zara replies.

I check my computer again. "Me either. But the good news is you don't have to go in there and get reamed out. And bonus, we're clear to speak to the roommate. But we're not to make a move without informing him first."

She scoffs. "Kind of reminds me of when you took that little airplane excursion. You know, the one with the *champagne*?" There's a huge grin on her face though she hasn't looked away from her computer.

"That was an honest mistake," I say, recalling the time I accidentally booked a private airplane while investigating a case.

"Uh, huh. You may look straight-laced, but secretly you're a rebel in your core. More than I ever was." She finally stops typing and eyes me. "The difference is you pretend not to be. It's like a secret identity you keep deep inside."

"Can we not psychoanalyze me today?" I say. "We can't wait on files that may or may not show up. Let's go talk to the roommate."

"Let's just hope she has something substantial."

If Lambert is behind Annabelle's death, I'm not sure her roommate would have known about it. But we need to continue exploring all other avenues. Zara tracked Annabelle's location to an apartment complex here in town, though she wasn't formally renting the property. The name on the contract is Suzanne Fray. And we still don't have concrete evidence anyone with LGM or any trucking company was involved. I want to make sure we're not overlooking something obvious. But at the same time, we need to be careful.

There's no telling what we could be walking into.

~

"Ta-da, the apartment of Suzanne Fray," Zara says as we pull the SUV up to the apartments. There are two identical buildings with an alley running between them. The unit is part of a two-story block that sits on pillars above the parking spaces. Zara pulls into the alley and parks the SUV at the end near the dumpsters. We get out, noting that each building has a unique address.

"It's this one," Zara says, pointing to the one on the right. I glance up, noticing that each apartment has its own balcony that overlooks the alleyway. We make our way around to the front. There's no code to get in the front doors, and they lead to a narrow open-air courtyard which comprises two staircases, one right in front of us and the other at the far end of the block, along with a few planters with lush ferns. The place looks like it was built in the seventies, but seems to be well-maintained. It's not the Shangri-La, but it's not a hovel either.

We take the steps up to the second floor and file past each of the units until we reach apartment 6C. "Would you like to do the honors?" I ask.

"Hmm." Zara rubs her chin thoughtfully. "Would Fiona Laidlaw be the kind of person who bangs hard on the door? Or would she be more subtle?"

"I don't really care as long as *she* does something," I say.

She purses her lips and then knocks politely. There's some shuffling from inside, but no one opens the door. I see the peephole darken. "Fiona" knocks again, this time a little harder. "Ms. Fray?"

"Who is it?" a timid voice on the other side finally asks.

"We're with the FBI," Zara says. "We'd like to talk to you about Annabelle."

There's no answer from the other side.

"Ms. Fray?" Zara asks again.

"No thank you," she says and I hear more shuffling behind the door.

She knows, right? I mouth to Zara.

"She must. Witter hasn't been back in three days." Annabelle's death was on the news yesterday, but given not everyone watches TV these days, it's possible she could have missed it.

This time I knock, a little harder than Zara. "Ms. Fray, please. We'd just like a moment of your time," I say. "You and Annabelle were roommates for the past six months, correct?"

Finally the chain on the other side slides and the door opens to reveal a small woman—girl, really—dressed in sweatpants, a tank top and an oversized robe that's stained on one side. She has mousy brown hair that's in a mess around her head and her eyes are red-rimmed. "Can't you just leave me alone?"

Yep. She knows. "I'm sorry about Annabelle," I say. "But my partner and I are trying to figure out what happened to her. I promise we won't take up much of your time and we'll make this as quick as possible."

The girl huffs and turns away from the door, but leaves it open for us. She heads back inside and flops down on the only couch in the living space. There's a bag of chips on the floor, spilled open, along with a package of cigarettes on the table, accompanying a few empty beer bottles. The slight tinge of smoke hangs in the air, but not enough for me to believe she's been smoking in here. She probably goes out to the balcony.

I close the door behind us as I take in the apartment. It's small, but clean enough. Other than the area around the couch, there's not much here. A few other pieces of furniture and the errant box or two. There's also nowhere else to sit, so Zara and I end up standing beside the wall-mounted TV.

Suzanne's attention isn't on us at all, but is on the TV where she's watching some reality show. She picks up the remote and starts the program again, right in the middle of an argument between some of the "stars."

"Would you mind turning that down?" I ask.

Without looking at me, she reduces the volume a few bars. It's not much, but it helps. She picks up the bag of chips and shoves a few in her mouth, completely ignoring us.

I shoot a tentative glance at Zara who only raises her eyebrows. "Ms. Fray, when was the last time you saw Annabelle?" I ask.

"Saturday," she says.

"What time?"

"I dunno. Afternoon, I think." She crunches down on another chip.

"Did you see her here at the apartment or were you out somewhere?" I ask.

She huffs, pausing the show again. "Here, okay? She said she was going out, and then I didn't see her at all on Sunday."

"Was that normal?" I ask. "For her not to be here when you return after working all night?"

"No," she says. "But she was... working extra. She was trying to save up some money."

"For what?" Zara asks.

"Her mother, I think," Suzanne says. "She helped her out sometimes."

"Where is the money she saved now?" I ask. Suzanne just barely flinches then looks at me. It's the first time she's made eye contact with me since we arrived.

"I'm keeping it safe."

"Then it's in this apartment," Zara says.

"I didn't steal her money, okay?" Suzanne says. "She asked me to hang on to it for her." She sighs. "It's in the back of my dresser if you *have* to know. She told me in case I needed a few extra bucks. But I've never touched it."

"How much?" I ask.

"I didn't count it. Last she told me was about three grand," she replies. Not an insubstantial sum.

I take a few steps towards the couch, crouching down in front of Suzanne so I'm blocking her view of the TV. "We know what kind of work Annabelle was in. We also know you two didn't have a formal rental contract, that you were basically letting her stay here for free. And I don't care. What I do care about is if someone might have been after her. Did anyone else know about that money? Did she have a boyfriend, or a pimp who might come looking for it?"

Suzanne pulls herself in tighter. "There used to be this guy she dated. Todd. But he's been out of the picture for a few months now. She didn't have a pimp. We…we worked alone."

"Dangerous job," Zara says.

"Yeah, you try surviving on minimum wage and see how far it gets you," she shoots back. She turns back to me. "At least this way I'm not working sixty hours a week."

"Did Annabelle have problems with any of her Johns?" I ask. "Anyone who might have followed her around, or made her feel nervous?"

Suzanne shakes her head. "No. Most of the guys we deal with are in and out; they don't stick around," she says. "They don't want to."

"Ever heard of the name LGM Trucking?" I ask.

She shrugs. "Doesn't ring a bell."

"Do you know if Annabelle owned a little yellow keychain? One with the Disney Castle on it?"

"She wasn't into that fluffy stuff," she replies.

I glance back at Zara. "Mind if we look at her room?" She waves absently like she doesn't care. I shoot a glance at Zara as we head back down the hallway.

"The one on the left," Suzanne calls out.

When we get into the room it's fairly sparse. Just a bed, a nightstand and a small desk. Not many personal items. That is, until I open the closet. "Whoa."

Zara comes up behind me. "Now *that's* a wardrobe." It's full of lingerie and other attire, including boots, short jackets and even a few wigs up on the top shelf. It appears Annabelle had her choice of looks. With this much stuff she could have worn a different outfit every day for a month and never taken the same thing off the rack twice.

A cursory search of the closet doesn't reveal anything other than clothes and accessories. Unfortunately it doesn't seem like there's much here. We head back into the living room where Suzanne hasn't moved.

"You said you didn't see Annabelle on Sunday. Did you talk or text with her?"

She doesn't move for a second, then I see her flinch and her eyes well up before she wipes them away. "Yeah… I… uh, I texted her not to forget to get some milk when she came back." She takes a shuddering breath. "Stupid last thing to say to someone."

"You guys were friends for a while, huh?"

She shrugs again, like it's no big deal. "Seven or eight months is all." I take a deep breath and one more look around the room. I don't think we're going to get what we need here.

"Will…will there be a funeral?" Suzanne asks as we get to the door.

I turn back to her. "Did Annabelle have a will?" She shakes her head. "Then it will be up to her family." As I put my hand on the door handle, I think about the keychain again. "Oh, you may want to get your locks changed. Annabelle didn't have any keys on her, just her ID and phone."

"What does that mean?" she asks, sitting up further.

"It means someone out there could have a key to your

apartment," Zara replies. "Tell your landlord. He can re-key the locks for you."

"Okay," she says, tentative. "Thanks."

I take out my card and leave it on the side table. "If you think of anything else that might be helpful, give me a call anytime."

Suzanne glances at the card a moment, then turns her attention back to her TV, taking it off pause. "Yeah, sure," she says with an air of sarcasm. I feel like there's something else here, but I don't want to push her too hard. She's already defensive enough. I can only hope given time to think about it, she'll come around with anything else she may have.

As Zara and I head back out to the car, I can't help but be a little deflated.

"Disappointed?" Zara asks as she heads back around to the driver's side.

"Yeah. But not surprised," I say. This was a longshot. I just don't like the idea of relying on Andersen to further this investigation along.

As we head back to the station, I get the feeling this case isn't going to be as open and shut as I'd hoped.

Chapter Fourteen

When we return to the office I'm forced to report to Strong that the roommate was a bust. While I don't like admitting defeat, I get the sense that keeping him in the loop is better than not. There's still no email from Andersen, which is beginning to make me nervous. It's already closing in on quitting time and I don't think we have time to drive all the way out to the Reservation P.D. before it empties for the weekend.

"I'm going to check with Receiving," I tell Zara as the clock ticks closer to the big hand on the five. "Maybe he overnighted a file or something."

"Or maybe he was yanking our chain just to get some free intel," she says. She seems a little more on edge lately, which I'm betting has to do with this whole Theo business. Of course I can't blame her. It's not like I've been a barrel of laughs myself.

I head over to the other side of the office to speak with the clerk, only to find Agent Dent sifting through the mail when I arrive. She nods as I approach. "Dunn."

"Hello," I say. "You don't see anything for Agent Laidlaw or myself in that pile, do you?"

"Nope," she replies, pulling out a manilla envelope with

her name on it from the stack. "Who was the sender? Maybe they didn't put your name on it."

"Nevermind," I say. "I can look."

"Dunn," she says, her tone flat. "I just went through this entire pile. Tell me the name. Why do the same work twice?"

I hesitate. Agent Kelly Dent is like the star pupil around here. Stellar reputation in the field, working on all the biggest cases, and Strong's personal favorite, of which he's made no secret.

"It would have come from the Navajo Reservation Department," I finally say. That is, assuming Andersen didn't send it from his home.

She furrows her brow. "The girl found out by the dumpster? That's your case?" I nod. "Reservation claiming jurisdiction?"

"Not exactly," I say.

"Listen, don't let them push you around," she says, placing a supportive hand on my shoulder. "I work with guys like that all the time. They think just because they've been on the job longer they're *owed* something. Well, they're not. This is your case. You run things how you see fit."

"Thanks," I say, appreciative of how supportive she's being. She sees me as the new kid who still doesn't know how the job operates. And she's just trying to be helpful. "I'll keep that in mind."

"Didn't see anything from there in the stack, though," she says as she heads past me. "Call them and tell 'em to get their butts in gear. We don't take time off here until the job's done."

"I'll do that," I call after her. Funny. Agent Dent has been more or less ambivalent towards Zara and me since we arrived. This is the first "real" conversation we've had. Maybe that's because we finally have a case. Or maybe it's just the first time we haven't just passed each other in the halls. Either way, she seems like a solid agent.

I double check the stack anyway before heading back to

my desk. "No dice," I tell Zara. "But I had a very nice talk with Agent Dent."

"Oh yeah?" she asks. "Did she ask you to get her a coffee? Extra cream?"

I chuckle. "She's actually really nice. No envelope from Andersen, though." I check the time again. "Should I call his office?"

She shrugs. "Can't hurt. But do we really think he's going to have anything useful? Maybe we should just forget it and move on. I'm still not convinced about that guy."

She's right. I'm putting too much stock into an interaction that was dubious at best. We need to focus on our own investigation and if he sends the files, great. "Ok, then. Do we keep going after Lambert, considering he might be the only one who has footage of what happened that night? Or do we try a different angle?"

Zara pulls out the file, flipping through it. "What about her parents? Suzanne said Annabelle was stowing money for her mother. Maybe we should check out that direction. You always say 'Follow the money.'"

I do say that a lot. "I'm just not sure this is about money," I say. "If someone killed her for a few thousand dollars, why haven't they come to collect?"

"Maybe Suzanne was lying and there was a lot more there," Zara suggests. "She could have been skimming off the top."

I lean back in my chair and rub my eyes. The problem with all of this is we don't have any actual *evidence*. How are we supposed to track down a killer when they didn't leave anything other than a dubious keychain behind? There could be a million different reasons behind what happened. It could have been random for all we know, which means the odds of finding the guy are about one in a billion.

"Let's just call it," I say. "I need to stop thinking about the case for a minute. Maybe then something will come to me."

"Hey, I don't mind a little extra downtime," Zara says, grabbing her stuff. "Think you can handle another round of Cthulhu tonight?"

"I'll pass, but give Cthulhu my best. I'm going to take a hot bath and try not to think about anything."

Strong wishes us a pleasant weekend on his way out the door. It's strange. Back home I never would have not planned on coming in on a weekend when I was working a case. But people here don't dedicate their entire lives to the job—at least not like they do in DC. Things move a little slower here. Not that the agents in this office aren't up to snuff; they're as hard-working and dedicated agents as I've ever seen. But they don't kill themselves for this job. Except maybe Dent. Then again, to be fair, I was notorious for putting in longer hours than I should have on my cases.

As we pull up to our apartments and get out, I notice a small brown parcel sitting on my front porch.

"Em," Zara says, her voice cautious.

"I see it," I say. Ever since arriving here we've had to be very careful of anything that comes directly to us, considering no one is supposed to know us out here. I haven't received a package in a month. And the fact one is sitting at my door is just a little alarming.

We approach cautiously. Given someone is out there potentially hunting me, I have to treat anything that comes along like a potential threat. But as soon as I see the name on the top, my shoulders relax. "It's the files," I say.

"From Andersen?" Zara asks.

I approach the box and see *Agent Claire Dunn* written across the top. Then below that *From Andersen.*

Zara comes up beside me, inspecting the box. "How does he know where you live? It's not on the business card and it's not like you're listed in the white pages."

I glance around, looking for Andersen's truck sitting somewhere in the parking lot, but there's no sign of it. "I guess if he can follow us to Roswell he's good enough to follow me home one day." Not that it gives me the greatest feeling. I would have much rather him dropped this at the office.

"I'm telling you, Em. There is something off about that guy. I don't like it."

"Let's deal with that later," I say. "I want to see if he actually has anything we could use."

After inspecting the box again just to make sure, I cart it inside where Zara and I remove all the files, examining each of them one by one. Thankfully, she has the presence of mind to order some takeout, as there is a lot here and it will take some time to parse.

"Well, he wasn't lying," Zara says once we have everything laid out on the floor. There are nine different investigations Andersen has opened into Lambert, ranging from Racketeering, Money Laundering, Bribery, Smuggling and a host of others. Unfortunately, most of the files are small, without much to go on other than a few allegations from witnesses that have disappeared or bits of evidence that have come back inconclusive.

I reach down and pick up the first of the murder cases Andersen has given us. Sure enough, it was an eighteen-year-old girl from the reservation who went missing over two years ago. Her body was found six months later in a ditch off some no-name highway. There are five other similar cases, however two of the victims are still reported missing and have yet to be found.

"M.O. matches," Zara says. "Autopsies conclude each of the victims died from strangulation."

"Yep, and look who signed off on all of them," I say, turning around one of the files so she can see.

"Hendricks," she says with distaste in her mouth. "Of course the worst coroner in the state didn't mention any connection. Why would he?"

"He probably didn't think they were worth mentioning," I

growl. "No fluids or trace evidence left on any of the bodies. Whoever is doing this is thorough and careful. Which means Annabelle wasn't just a lucky break."

Zara shakes her head as she looks over the files. "So why would he suddenly change his tactics?"

"What do you mean? The M.O.s match."

"The details do," she says. "But if it's the same killer, Annabelle was the first victim that wasn't a member of the tribe *and* that was killed in a public place. Or at least left in a public place. The rest of these were much more sporadic."

"Could be escalation," I say, pulling out a sheet of paper as I jot down the dates when the victims were taken along with when they were found.

"Or they might not be related at all," she suggests. "This Andersen guy might be trying to piggyback on our investigation when there's no real meat here."

I shake my head. "I don't think that's the case. What are the odds New Mexico has *two* killers who both use gloves, strangle their victims and leave them with their IDs and effects? Most killers aren't going to leave their victims to be ID'd. That's what makes this one different."

"I guess," she replies. The doorbell rings and Zara heads to get it, paying the delivery guy for the food. As she comes back in, the smell of Kung Pao chicken and Chow Mein fills the room.

"Thank God, I'm starving," I say, heading for the bag. We pull everything out and go to work, not bothering with plates. Chinese food just doesn't taste as good off a plate—I can't explain why.

"The bigger question is if we actually believe that this is the same killer, how do you explain it to Strong? Do you really think he'll accept evidence like this, with no solid connection?"

"That's a good question," I say. Again, this shouldn't be an issue. But at the same time, I need to remember I'm being closely watched here. "But we don't have a choice. We have to inform him."

"And if he asks how we came upon it?"

"I'll tell him the truth. We ran into Andersen and decided to cooperate." I stuff a saucy chicken into my mouth, relishing the taste.

"I dunno, Em. If we're to believe this, we just went from one body to possibly seven. How do you know he won't pull us from the case and give it to someone like Dent?"

I look over all the files Andersen has given us. Zara raises a good point. This is growing into something for a more seasoned investigator, not someone who has only been with the Bureau for seventeen months. But I can't obscure this case for my own personal benefit. "I guess that's a chance we'll have to take," I finally say. "I don't see any other way around it."

Zara shovels a bunch of noodles in her mouth. "Neither do I."

Chapter Fifteen

Zara sits on the edge of her bed, examining her computer. She's been staring at the blank screen for probably thirty minutes, trying to figure out how to proceed.

"It's not a big deal. It's just a background check," she whispers to herself. But she knows better. This could be what breaks her relationship with Theo, which proves once and for all he isn't who he says he is. Then again it could exonerate him. In which case she'll be forced to come clean with him and admit she had her suspicions. And that might end things too. Either way, her relationship is on the line.

"This is stupid. Just do it," she says a little more forcefully, but she can't. Unlike Emily, she hasn't had the best of luck in the romance department. And that was fine for a while. But she gets lonely for companionship. And a lot of the time Emily is with Liam. She hates to admit it, but she envies their relationship. They are a good fit, and they support each other without undermining the other's accomplishments.

Back when she was in Intelligence, Zara used to have her pulse on the number of office relationships that were going on at any given time. And nine times out of ten they didn't survive, because putting two highly driven, competitive and type-A personalities together was a recipe for disaster. But it's not like that with Emily and Liam. And she had hoped she could get that lucky too.

Unfortunately every guy she's dated has either come with a load of baggage or has been pretending to be one thing while secretly being another when things become comfortable. She had hoped that maybe with Theo things would be different. Mostly because their relationship would be more transient, given the nature of his job. But considering how they met and how their relationship developed, she's not so sure she didn't just step on a land mine.

"Stop stalling," she says to herself. "You know you're going to do it, so you might as well get it over with."

She stares at the screen a beat longer. "Screw it."

Her fingers fly over the keyboard as she runs through her normal background checks. She opens up databases she hasn't used in *months*, looking as deeply as she can into the name *Theo Arsenault*.

The first thing that comes up is his MI6 record, which causes her to breathe a sigh of relief. At least he wasn't lying about that. The record isn't public and she shouldn't be able to access it, but this is a personal matter and she's decided she needs to suspend some of her ethics in order to get to the bottom of this.

From what is in the official record, Theo was part of MI6 for almost eight years, having been recruited from his job as an investigator with the Met Police in London. He resigned two years ago to work as an *independent consultant* for various agencies around the world—all of which lines up with what little he's told her.

"Ok," she mutters. "So that's what's on the surface. Now it's time for the deep dive." She begins doing several various searches in places that most people who access the web don't know about—nor would they care to. And she doesn't use his name, only his face. She wants to see if anything comes up at all before she works on the various aliases she's heard him use over the past year. She hates to admit she's been keeping a mental list.

But as far as she can tell, his record is more or less what she expected. He grew up in Leeds, went to primary then secondary school before moving to London, where he began working as a constable investigator. He was recruited from there and then moved into independent contracting work.

It's all very above-board.

However, something still seems wrong. She can't put her finger on it, but Theo is… unique. And she can't find even an instance of being tardy from school, much less making trouble elsewhere. It reminds her of a cover someone would write for someone else. And the problem with most covers is they are *too* clean. Which is why when she created the covers for herself and Emily when they came to New Mexico, she threw in a little teenage rebellion and a few other incidents to make their pasts seem a little more realistic.

It's the polish that reveals the defects.

She sits back, reading over the information she's discovered. It's believable, but something in the back of her mind tells her it isn't the complete story. She needs to go deeper, but as she does, she comes up empty. It's like the further she digs, she just keeps hitting bedrock. That's all there is, there's nowhere else to go.

As a seasoned investigator and someone who crafts personas for a *living*, she doesn't believe it. No matter how ironclad it looks. Whoever crafted this background knew what they were doing, but they left just enough to make her suspicious. And that doesn't leave her with a good feeling.

What's worse is now that she's opened the box, she can't put everything back inside. And it isn't like she has any evidence that she can show anyone to prove she's right. But she just knows it in her gut. Something about all of this is wrong.

Zara flops back on her bed, staring up at the glow in the dark stars she's put up all over the ceiling. She's not upset, just disappointed. Disappointed in herself that she waited this long to do what she's been thinking about doing for a solid month now. Ever since the breach at the FBI she's been suspicious. She can't help it; it's in her nature. And maybe that means she'll never be able to have a relationship like Emily and Liam. Maybe she just needs to know everything there is to know about a person before she really gets to know them. But when she does that, it takes all the fun out of growing with someone.

She wants to smack herself upside the head for being such a basket case. But she doesn't. Instead, she goes into her small bathroom and gets under the shower, letting the hot water flow over her. It's the closest thing she can get to white noise for her whole body; the only way she can turn her brain off. She just stands there, letting the world melt away.

Tomorrow she will figure out what to do. But tonight she just needs to soak it all in.

Chapter Sixteen

"ISN'T today supposed to be our day off?" Zara asks as the wind whips at her hair. This time *I've* rolled down the windows as I'm feeling more invigorated this morning. We spent most of the evening going through Andersen's "evidence" and finding very little that's actually useful. It's mostly a bunch of supposition and accusations without anything solid. Zara was right, we couldn't rely on him to give us a slam dunk. I think somewhere in the back of my mind I knew that, because if he had everything he needed to convict Lambert, he would have already done so. What I was really hoping was that we could use something from one of the other murders to help us track down Annabelle's killer, but the information in those files more or less matched what we had from her scene. Little to no evidence left behind and nothing that would point to a particular culprit.

Despite all of that, I awoke this morning focused and determined to figure this thing out. And what I can't get out of my head is that money Annabelle had socked away. For someone in her position that was a lot of cash to be keeping, so it's worth looking into. At this point, I'll take anything.

Not only that, but because this is my day off and I'm not

on the clock, I don't have to inform Strong we're taking this little jaunt to Arizona. Nor do we have to inform him just how large this case is growing. That can wait until Monday.

The only problem is it's another long, desolate drive.

"No days off for the wicked," I say, grinning at Zara. She just rolls her eyes at me. Last night she ducked out a little early while I was still going over the information in the files. I think she's feeling the pressure of this place as much as I am. But she puts on one of her playlists and for some reason, it doesn't annoy me as much as it normally would.

I think having this case has really changed my attitude; it's given me something to direct all my energies on. And maybe that's just a temporary Band-Aid, but at this point I'll take whatever I can get. Sitting on my butt in the office trying not to go crazy was not a winning solution. At least this gets me out of the chair and moving around a little.

Which reminds me, my workout regimen has been very sporadic lately. I need to get back into a regular groove. I think when this case is over I'm going to start getting up earlier—see if I can't get in some early morning training. There's certainly no shortage of gyms around where we live.

My mind wanders as the vast landscape opens up before us. It can be really beautiful out here, but also so barren. But I see why some people refer to it as big sky country. The clouds seem to go on forever and the sky looks about ten times as big as it does anywhere else. I guess that's because you can see so far out into the distance. Almost like looking out into the future. I just wish I could see that far ahead in my own life.

As we cross the border into Arizona, I look for the sign for the town. Having pulled Annabelle's family records, it was easy enough to get an address for both her parents. It appears they've been divorced for almost fifteen years. And given Suzanne said Annabelle was trying to support her mother, I figure we should speak to her first.

"That's it, isn't it?" Zara points to a small sign that says *Sanders*. It was so small I almost missed it.

I turn off onto an old highway that leads into what used to be a mobile home park that now sits abandoned. Weeds and shrubs grow up through the concrete where the homes used to sit, the partitions between them having become distorted and ragged. Driving past the lots, we reach a T-intersection which stretches as far as the eye can see in both directions, without a single structure anywhere in sight.

"*This* is where her mother lives?" I ask.

"Maybe the community is bigger than it looks," Zara suggests.

The GPS indicates we should turn right; there's the promise of *something* out there. I make the turn and head down the road, pushing the needle of the SUV up to seventy before finally letting off. That's the thing about driving out here; speeds feel different because everything is so far apart. Seventy feels like fifty back home.

I lean forward to get a better look as a few more buildings come into view. There's another mobile home park, presumably that replaced the abandoned one back at the turnoff as this one is filled with homes, most with some semblance of landscaping and vehicles sitting out front. As we pass people sitting out in front of the homes glance up, watching us drive by.

Further on are a few community buildings and a church, along with the occasional person walking on the side of the street, bag in hand. However, there are no other cars on the road. And every person we pass observes us carefully.

"Guess they're not used to visitors," I say, as we drive by an older style home where a man stands outside shirtless, a cigarette hanging from his mouth.

"It's like Children of the Corn out here," Zara mutters. "Except, you know, with adults."

Finally the GPS tells us we've arrived and I pull up to a

small two-story duplex. It can't be much larger than a thousand square feet in total but there are two entrance doors. The information from Annabelle's file indicates that we want the left door: 102B.

Sitting outside the other door is an older woman with a darker appearance. She looks like she might be a member of one of the tribes given her complexion and her shiny gray hair. In her hands she holds a pair of knitting needles as she works on crafting what looks like a shawl.

We head up to the other door and I knock, making sure it's loud and clear. But there's no movement on the other side and no one comes to the door. I try again but to no avail.

"Excuse me," I say, approaching the woman working on the shawl. "Do you know if Mrs. Witter is home?"

"No, she's not," the woman replies.

"Do you know when she'll be back?" Zara asks.

"I don't." She continues knitting, not even bothering to look at us.

"Do you know where we can find her?" I ask.

"No."

Wow, most helpful person of the year here. "You're her neighbor I assume?" The woman doesn't respond. "Did you know her daughter?"

The woman's needles stop clacking and she lays them in her lap. "I did. Sweet girl. Shame what happened."

I guess I shouldn't be surprised. It isn't like these people are living in the dark ages. No matter how desolate the community, everyone has access to the world these days. And no doubt with both Annabelle's parents living in this small town, word has gotten around.

"We're trying to find out what happened," I tell the woman.

"It's obvious what happened," she replies, picking up her needles and working again. "A man she was charging for sex killed her."

I'm taken aback by her bluntness. "Well, yes. But we're trying to find out who."

The woman only scoffs.

"If Mrs. Witter comes back, could you have her contact us? I'll leave my card under the door." I return to the door and slide my card underneath.

"You'd do better to leave that poor woman alone," she says. "She has enough demons to manage without dealing with the police too."

"We're not police," Zara says. "We're with the FBI."

"Same difference," she replies. "You come around here only wanting what *you* need, never considering what other people might want."

"What does she want?" I ask.

"To be left alone."

I narrow my eyes. This woman is awfully cagey to be nothing more than the next-door neighbor. "Jolene?"

She turns to me, her eyes sharp now. "Leave me be," she says. "Can't you see I'm in mourning?"

"I'm very sorry for your loss," I say. "All we want is to find out who did this so they can't do it again. And to give your family some peace."

Her mouth turns into a grimace. "I won't know peace until I'm dead," she replies. "And no amount of talking will ever make it better."

I sigh. Mrs. Witter seems like someone who could be reasoned with, but she has all these barriers up. And I'm not sure I can get through them. "Did you know your daughter was saving money for you?"

She huffs, putting down her needles again as she closes her eyes and breathes out slowly through her nose. "I sent it back," she finally says. "I never wanted her foul money."

"Why was she sending it to you in the first place?" Zara asks.

She lifts her skirt just enough to reveal she's missing a foot.

It ends in a nub, but I don't see any crutches or a wheelchair around. "Gout two years ago. Haven't been able to work since. And these don't bring in much." She indicates the shawl.

"So she was supporting you," I say.

"Don't you listen? I never took her money," she says. "After I found out what she was doing—she used to have so much potential. She was a smart girl. And then she went and wasted it all, giving her body away for what? A few measly dollars?" She crosses herself and bows her head before returning to her knitting.

"Do you know if she was having problems with anyone?" I ask.

"I haven't spoken to my daughter in over a year," the woman replies. "Except when I sent her a letter telling her to stop her foolishness and come home. If she'd listened, she'd be here right now."

Empathy doesn't seem to be one of Mrs. Witter's strong suits—at least not where her daughter is concerned. I can understand not agreeing with your child's profession, especially if it's something as controversial as what Annabelle was doing. But at the same time, I'm beginning to see why she left Sanders.

"Sorry for bothering you," I say, taking a step back. "And again, sorry for your loss."

The woman doesn't respond, doesn't look up or even acknowledge us as Zara and I head back to the car. I'm left with a profound sense of sadness from this place—like it is empty and devoid of anything meaningful. It's a feeling that strikes me so hard I have to physically restrain myself from tearing up, and I'm not even sure why.

"Jeez," Zara says once we're back in the car. "That was a downer."

"Yeah," I say, turning the engine back over. I can't even count how many times I've had to speak to parents who have lost children, but never in my entire career have I encountered someone so emotionless and cut off that it barely even registers for them.

"Em, you okay?" Zara asks, and I realize I'm just staring into space.

"Yeah, fine," I say and blink a few times, coming back into myself. "What's the father's address? Maybe we'll have more luck."

"810 Rim Road," she says. "About fifteen miles east."

I nod and back the SUV up, taking one last look at Mrs. Witter as we pull away. The woman never stops her knitting.

Chapter Seventeen

Rim Road is nothing more than a dirt path off the highway. And at first I'm not sure it's the right way, but Zara insists that I keep going. Every few hundred yards there's another house that sits off the road, their own dirt path leading off from Rim Road. As we pass, I notice these are a nicer crop of homes, each of them a little different but most in the same southwestern style. I catch one with a pool and a sun deck, but as I look in the rearview mirror I see we're kicking up a ton of dirt. Easing off the accelerator, the SUV stops bouncing as much and the dirt settles a little behind us.

"Thought you were headed to a fire there for a second," Zara says, relaxing her grip on the armrest.

"Sorry, I guess I was just distracted," I say.

"By Annabelle's mother?" she asks.

I nod. Even though it's been almost a year since my mother's sister nearly killed us, my mom still weighs heavily on my mind. I spent a lot of time with Dr. Frost trying to come to terms with her past and how her actions ended up shaping me in ways I didn't even realize. Ever since we arrived here in New Mexico, she's been on the edge of my mind, and I think that's because I haven't had an outlet for everything that's still bottled up in there. I don't know what it was, but something about Annabelle's mother triggered something for me. Odds are I won't even know what until I get a chance to speak with Frost again. And who knows when that will be.

"Should be this one right up here," Zara says, pointing ahead to a stucco house that is out almost on an outcropping. The surrounding land drops away about five or ten feet, giving it the illusion it's sitting on top of a crest. The dirt drive leads to a paved driveway about halfway up, where a large tractor-trailer cab sits beside a Dodge pickup.

I pull in behind the Dodge as we get out. It's quiet out here, barely even a sound other than the occasional bird or gust of wind.

We head around to the front of the house, following the walk alongside some nicely maintained rock gardens, complete with cacti that line the house. Given what we just witnessed with Annabelle's mother, I'm not sure how this is going to go, but I knock anyway.

"Second time's a charm," Zara says.

After a few moments the door opens to reveal a woman in her early fifties, her blonde hair pulled back in a ponytail and an apron around her waist. "Hello," she says. "Can I help you?"

"I'm sorry," I say. "We're looking for Daniel Witter. Does he live here?"

"Dan?" the woman calls out. "Company."

A man appears behind her, tall, with a full beard and moustache. He's got on a light plaid button down shirt over jeans and greets us with a quizzical look. "Help you folks?"

I show him my badge as Zara does the same. "I'm Special Agent Dunn; this is Special Agent Laidlaw. We're investigating your daughter's murder."

The woman steps back a little further, allowing Daniel Witter to come forward. He regards us for a moment, then holds out a hand, shaking both of ours. "If you don't mind me asking, what are the FBI doing investigating my daughter?"

"May we come in?" I ask.

"I'm sorry," he says. "It's been a stressful few days. This is my wife, Margaret. Please." He stands aside, opening his home to us. Both Zara and I shake his wife's hand as we enter; I hadn't realized Annabelle's father was remarried.

"Let's go into the kitchen," he says and we follow him through the house. It's not huge, but it is tasteful and clean. Above us wooden logs cut through the adobe ceiling and large windows all over the house allow the maximum amount of light inside. The kitchen sits at the back of the home, built into a round alcove with a breakfast nook attached on one side. Beyond the kitchen is a deck that leads to an above-ground pool.

As soon as we enter the kitchen, I catch a blur of movement out by the deck and a second later, a small opening in the kitchen door flaps as a medium-sized Australian Shepherd comes bounding towards us, panting.

"Oh, no, Chuck, down!" Margaret says but I'm already bent down to greet the dog as he drives towards us. A second later he's sniffing me profusely, his tail wagging all over the place.

"I… uh… sorry, we should have had him contained," Daniel says. "We weren't expecting company."

"It's okay," Zara says. "We love dogs. Especially her." I presume she's pointing at me but because I'm being assaulted by a dog snout I can barely look up.

Chuck is a big lovebug, very sweet. But what's worse is he's making me miss Timber and Rocky even more now and I have to stand back up before I start bawling. But I make sure to get in a few good head rubs before I do.

"He's friendly," I say.

"He's friendly to people," Daniel says, pulling out one of

the chairs around the breakfast nook table. "Deadly to groundhogs, though."

Zara and I join him around the table as Margaret brings everyone water before taking a seat herself.

"You said you wanted to talk about… Annabelle?" Mr. Witter asks after taking a long drink of water.

"Yes," I say. "I'm sorry, I know everything is still raw. But we hoped you might help us in our investigation."

"You're looking for the man who… well, who did that to her," Margaret says.

I nod. "When was the last time you saw or talked to your daughter?"

Mr. Witter lets out a slow breath. "Friday… Saturday maybe? We talk every few days." He swallows. "We *talked* every few days."

I nod, softening my expression. "I'm sorry, I know this is hard. When you spoke to her did she say anything that might indicate she was having a problem with someone? Or that she was fearful in any way?"

"No, nothing like that," he replies. "Seemed normal as far as I could tell."

I shoot a quick glance to Zara. "I assume you know what she did for a living."

He nods. "I do."

"Did she ever mention any problems she had with her clients? Anyone in particular?"

"We didn't talk about her… work," he says. "She knew I didn't approve. But at least I didn't cut her out of my life because of it." Margaret reaches over and takes the man's hand in her own and I see him squeeze hers back.

"Did you know she was saving up money to give to her mother?" I ask. "She had a couple thousand for her."

"Doesn't surprise me," he says. "Annabelle had a big heart. And she was desperate for her mother's approval. Well, her acceptance anyway. But Jolene is…she's had a hard life, some of which is her own fault and some of which isn't. But she took a lot of that out on Annabelle." He turns to Margaret. "I think that was one of the reasons she left in the first place."

"How long ago did Annabelle leave Sanders?" I ask.

"A few years," he says. "Not long after she got out of high school. She had a scholarship, you know, to Northern Arizona. Could have had her pick of majors."

"Why didn't she go?" Zara asks.

"Money," he says. "The scholarship only covered two semesters, and we didn't have enough to pay for any more. She said she didn't want to start something she couldn't finish, so she was going to make enough money to get her through before she accepted." He sighs. "But she just… never came back. And the deadline to accept the scholarship came and went. She missed her chance."

Margaret pats her husband's hand. It's obvious from the way he's deflating that this is a tough subject for him. He's having almost the opposite reaction as his ex-wife. We continue to ask him a few more questions but the more we do the more I can see we're losing him. Finally, he excuses himself and heads outside, Chuck following along.

"I'm sorry," I say. "We've taken up enough of your time," I say to Margaret who remains at the table with us.

"That's alright," she says. "Dan is a soft soul and when it comes to his daughter… well, he puts on a brave face, but it's killing him inside."

"Did Annabelle ever stay here with you when she was living in Sanders?" I ask.

She shakes her head. "No, her mother got custody in court so she only ended up visiting." She leans closer to us. "Her mother wasn't much of a disciplinarian. Let Annabelle do whatever she wanted. If you ask me, that's where she got into turning tricks or whatever it is you call it."

She says *turning tricks* with a particular distaste and also without the practice of someone who has said it often. It's obvious the subject isn't discussed in this household.

"Dan won't tell you this, but he found Annabelle… *working*… one night. Just about ended in a massacre," she continues.

My ears perk up. "How's that?"

She motions outside. "He was driving for some company, I forget which, and he pulled into a rest stop. He saw her getting into another truck driver's cab and couldn't control himself. Just about beat the man senseless."

"Was there ever a police report filed?" I ask.

"I don't think so, the other man was so afraid I think he didn't want to deal with it. But that was the straw that broke the camel's back. Their relationship was never the same afterwards."

I turn and look out the window at Dan who is staring up at the sky, taking deep breaths. "But he said they used to speak on the phone all the time."

"For a minute or two, and Dan was always the one calling." She shakes her head again. "That girl had one good parent, and she decided to pander to the bad one. I just don't get it."

She leans back to her side of the table as Mr. Witter comes back in. His complexion looks a little better, but I can tell we've about tapped the well here.

I stand up, giving them both an appreciative nod. "Thanks for taking the time to speak to us. I know this isn't easy."

"I just hope you find the bastard," Daniel says. "You talk to the girl she was staying with?"

"Suzanne?" I ask.

He nods. "Those two were thick as thieves. Knew everything about each other. If something was going on in Annie's life, Suzanne would know about it."

I think back to our conversation with Suzanne. She acted

like she and Annabelle were mere acquaintances. "How long did they know each other?"

"Since high school," he replies. "They were classmates here in Sanders."

I give Zara a pointed look. That isn't what she told us. It may be time to go back and put some pressure on Ms. Fray.

They walk us out and as we're getting ready to head back to the car I stop. "Oh, one other thing. You're an independent owner-operator of your own vehicle, is that right?"

Dan nods. "For almost twenty years."

"Have you ever done business with LGM trucking?"

"No, I don't think so," he says.

"What about the name Lambert? Does that mean anything to you?"

His gaze darkens and I know I've hit a nerve. "Let me know if you find anything out about my daughter." And before I can say anything else, he closes the door in our faces.

"I'd say that was a pretty clear answer," Zara says.

"You think there could be a connection?" I ask.

"I dunno. But we're not going to find out from him."

Chapter Eighteen

"Oh, you've got to be *shitting* me," I say as we pull back into the parking lot surrounding our apartments. Given the amount of time it took to drive out to Sanders and back, the sun has already set and I'm tired from being in the car all day.

But right there, in front of my apartment, sits Wendell Andersen in his truck, just staring out the windshield. As soon as he sees us, he gets out of his vehicle and waits for us to park.

"Great," I say. "Now we get to deal with this."

I expect some smart retort from Zara, but when I look over she's practically glowering at the man. It's enough to put me on edge.

As we get out of the car, Andersen watches us carefully. His hands are locked behind his back and he's almost standing at attention, like he's in the military.

"Is there something we can do for you, Officer?" I ask as we approach.

"Your investigation into Lambert, how is it proceeding?" he asks.

"It has literally been one day," I say, stopping about five feet from him. "We haven't even begun. Not to mention there is nothing in those files that connects any of the victims to Annabelle Witter."

"The method of death would seem to be the common denominator," he says.

Zara appears in my periphery. "I don't know what your deal is, but showing up here like this is not cool," she says. "It's an invasion of privacy. Not to mention creepy."

"I wasn't aware standing on public property was considered creepy," he says, though I know he's just being obtuse. Andersen doesn't strike me as the kind of man who likes to wait. But he's about to find out I'm not the kind of woman who likes to be pushed.

"You should have sent the files directly to our office," I say. "I don't like coming home and finding strange boxes on my doorstep." Even though there's no way Andersen can know about why we're really here, I wouldn't tolerate this kind of behavior from anyone.

"I did not come here to be reprimanded," he says, lowering his voice. "I came to find out what you've managed to discover about Lambert. You've been away all day; I assume you've made *some* progress."

"What progress we do or do not make is none of your concern," I say. "We will inform you when we've made progress. When *we're* ready."

He glances to the side. "I see. It seems you're not so different from law enforcement here after all."

"*Excuse me*," Zara says, stepping forward again. "What was that?"

"None of your people consider our problems relevant," he says. "Not that I would expect you to understand. But the two of you struck me as detectives who wouldn't let racial boundaries limit your investigations. For everyone else out here, the examination stops at the border to our land and never goes any further. You were supposed to be better than that."

"Are you calling us racist?" Zara demands. She's practically heaving and for the first time since I've known her, I consider if I'll have to hold her back. Normally, Andersen's words would be enough to put me in a similar state, but I'm so preoccupied with her that they pass right by me.

He shrugs. "You can't help it. It's in your nature. I will take my files back now, please."

"Those files aren't going anywhere," I say, holding out an arm to keep Zara from progressing any further. "As soon as you turned them over to us, they became Federal property. File a complaint with our office, but until I have Annabelle Witter's killer in handcuffs, those files stay with us."

"If that's the way you want to do things," he says. "Your office will hear from mine first thing on Monday."

"You've got a big pair on you, you know that?" Zara calls after him as he walks away. "Coming here demanding results on an investigation you can't even manage yourself!"

He stops, but doesn't turn around.

"Maybe if you had actual evidence in those files, we'd have something to work with. But it's the biggest nothing burger I've ever seen in my life. If Lambert is guilty of anything, it's of having a stalker. And to be honest, I'm starting to see where he's coming from!" My eyes are like saucers watching Zara's outburst. It's not something I see often from her. If ever.

When he reaches his car, he finally turns back around. "You will never find out what happened to Annabelle Witter if you're not willing to look beyond the limitations of your case. This is bigger than you want to admit." He closes the door and drives off.

As soon as he's gone, I turn to Zara. "Are you ok?"

She stares after him. "I don't like it," she says. "Something is wrong with that guy. I've been saying it from the beginning."

I furrow my brow. "You think he's connected to what's going on in DC?"

"I don't know. But what kind of man just randomly follows

us back to your apartment and sits and waits while we're out all day? He's keeping tabs on us and it's enough to make my hair stand on end." She turns to me. "I was told to keep an eye out for anything suspicious." She points in the direction of his taillights. "And that's suspicious."

"Ok, I see your point," I say. "I don't like it either. So what do we do? Begin investigating Andersen?"

"Maybe," she says, but I can see the interaction with him has really rattled her. She's breathing faster than normal, and I'd bet her heart is about to burst out of her chest.

"C'mon, let's go inside," I say. "I'll make some tea."

She nods and allows me to lead her to my door. As I grapple for the key I smile. "It's kind of nice having a body-guard. But you don't have to… what would you call it? Hulk out?"

She smiles despite herself and I see some of the old Zara returning. "Yeah, sorry about that. It's just guys like that, you know? People who assume they know everything about us when really they don't know jack." We head into the apartment where all the files from last night are still lined up on the floor in front of the fake fireplace. I sit her down on one of the stools in front of the counter as I head into the small pantry drawer in the kitchen.

"There's something else," she finally says as I locate a bag of English Breakfast.

I head over to the coffee maker and turn it on just to get some water hot. "What?"

"I did the background search on Theo."

My hand stops in mid-air, the tea packet half open. I turn to her, slowly, trying to gauge her emotions. She's pulled herself in tighter, though she's looking straight at me, her brown eyes wide, waiting for judgement that I'm not about to deliver. "What happened?"

"I didn't find anything," she says.

I allow myself a breath. "That's good, right?"

She shakes her head. "No, Em, you don't get it. I didn't find *anything.* He's got a background, and it all matches up with what little he's told me. But it's too clean. It's… it's manufactured."

I know Zara well enough not to question her expertise. If she says it's manufactured, then I have to believe her. I drop the tea bag into the empty mug, waiting for the water to warm. "What does that mean?"

"Someone made it up for him, or he made it himself," she says. "I don't know which. And it doesn't really matter."

I return to the other side of the counter while the hot water pours over the tea bag. "That's what has you so on edge, isn't it?"

"Well, that and the possibility that someone is out there hunting you. Hunting *us.* But yeah, mostly the Theo thing."

I laugh. "Thanks a lot. What if Theo's background cover is for a good reason? Like the ones you made for us here? Maybe it's what's keeping him safe?"

One edge of her mouth quirks up. "*Safe* and *Theo* don't exactly go well together," she says. "I dunno, Em. I don't have a good feeling about it."

"What are you going to do?" I ask.

"I have to confront him, don't I?" she says. "What else can I do? I can't keep pretending I don't have any suspicions. Not that I'm likely to talk to him anytime soon. But I have to believe our paths will cross eventually."

Heading back over to grab the mug now that the water is finished, I can't imagine being in a relationship with someone and not knowing where they were or if they were safe. Not that I have a tracker on Liam, but I at least know he's in the general DC area and isn't going anywhere for the foreseeable future. But Theo could be anywhere in the world right now. He could be in Albuquerque and we might not even know it.

"I'm sorry," I say. "I know how much you wanted this one to work out."

She waves me off. "It's okay. I should have figured since both of us met undercover trying to infiltrate a terrorist, it wouldn't be the most stable relationship."

"But you were so happy when you were together," I say.

"Remember when I told you I needed to be with someone whose past I didn't know every little detail about? Yeah, apparently I can't handle that. It was nice at first, not knowing anything about him; but I can't keep going that way."

"Have you ever *asked* him about his past? Beyond the basics, I mean?"

"Sure," she says. "He'll tell me bits about his time with MI6 or his hometown. But anytime I mention his family he changes the subject. And anytime I ask about what he used to do before MI6 I get a standard answer that could apply to any situation." She takes the mug from me and lets the steam waft up to her nose, taking in a deep breath. "I think that's what started getting me suspicious in the first place. It sounded like he was manufacturing memories to tell me instead of telling me what *really* happened." She takes a sip of the tea. "This is good."

"Z, I'm really sorry," I say.

"Me too," she replies. "I'm not quitting, though. You know those contacts I have that were looking into our little problem at the FBI and not finding anything?" I nod. "I gave them a new task. And I've got just enough feet money to cover their expenses for a few weeks."

I chuckle and decide to make my own cup of tea. As I'm grabbing a second mug, Zara pipes up again.

"That's not the worst part," she says.

"How can there be a worse part than that?"

"I think… no, I suspect, I don't know. But I *think* he might have something to do with all of this." She waves around the room.

"This… you mean, us being here?" She nods and I furrow my brow. "You think he's connected to the breach?"

"All I know is he was with us on that Op to get the information from Fletch and that's when everything went to shit. One of the reasons I blew up at Andersen was because I feel like he's trying to use us to run his own game. And I'm really afraid Theo is doing the same thing."

"But he's been triple vetted," I say. "How would he even pull something like that off?"

"I don't know," she replies. "All I know is he's been an integral part of our operations for almost seven months straight. Even if he's not wholly responsible, I feel like he's connected to what's going on."

"You don't have any proof of that… do you?"

She glances down at her mug, watching the liquid steam some more. "No. And if he's as good as I know he is, we probably never will."

"Should we inform Caruthers?" I ask.

"And tell him what? The agent who brought Theo to them now suspects him of being a traitor based on a feeling?"

She's right. That's not going to fly. "What if I just give Liam a heads up? So he can be on the watch for anything that might help."

"No, I don't want to get him involved. Theo isn't sloppy enough to leave behind anything concrete." She frowns, looking at me.

"What?"

"I don't know," she says. "But something feels very familiar about this."

I think back to the case at hand. "You thinking about Lambert? And how Andersen hasn't been able to get anything to stick?"

She taps her chin with her forefinger. "I wonder… do you think Lambert has connections in the intelligence community?"

I motion to the pile of papers by the fireplace. "If we go by what Andersen believes, he's got connections in *every* community. I wouldn't put it past him to buy off a few officers or government officials. But actual *agents*? I think that's a stretch."

"Maybe not current agents," she says. "But what about *former* agents? People who know how to make records disappear?"

"Holy shit," I say. "You might be onto something. We need to go back through what Andersen left us. Maybe there's something we overlooked."

Her face lights up in a way I haven't seen for a few days. She gets up, heading for the door. "I'll get the drinks."

"Perfect," I say. "I think this occasion calls for a pizza."

"Why Ms. Slate," she says as she reaches the door. "You know me too well."

Chapter Nineteen

It turns out finding the names of retired FBI Agents from the Albuquerque office was the easy part. Even though their records and cases are sealed and not available to what the system considers "new agents," there is a very convenient dedicatory on the wall just inside our office. It lists the names of every FBI agent from our office who was either killed in the line of duty or who retired along with their years of service. There are only sixteen agents that are listed as KIA going back to 1949, which is an impressive record. All we had to do was pop in for a minute, snap some pictures, and we were on our way.

However, the list of retired agents is much longer. There are over a hundred names in that section and Zara and I spend a considerable amount of time parsing through them, trying to determine how many may have already died and how many could still be alive. We spend most of the day doing background research on our own office, trying to determine if any of the retired agents might have a connection to Lambert in any way. At the same time the results finally come back on the keychain we found under the dumpster. It seems we're not the only ones who like to work weekends. There were no fingerprints on the keychain itself, and nothing else that could identify it as connected to the case. I'm forced to admit it was probably just trash that some tourist had thrown out.

But my bigger concern is Suzanne Fray. I want to know why she lied to us about how long she'd known Annabelle and try to figure out what else she's hiding. I don't know what impetus she had to lie, but we need to confront her about it regardless. After we finish narrowing down the list of potential agents, that is next on my agenda.

"Do you really think this rogue agent theory is going to help us find Annabelle's killer?" Zara asks, bent over her computer as she continues her search.

"It's a shot in the dark, I admit," I say. "But we need some way to pressure Lambert. From what we've seen, the man is nearly untouchable. If we can figure out how to apply a little bit of stress on him or his operation, maybe we can get that footage from his truck. I don't think it's a coincidence that the only person who might have footage of that night is also the same person who sent someone to scare us into shutting up." I shoot her a grin. "That's how we know we're on the right track."

"If you say so," she says. "We still don't even know who was driving that truck."

"Ask yourself this. If you weren't involved in a murder, but you had evidence that showed what happened, why wouldn't you hand that over to authorities?"

"Because you *are* involved. Somehow," she says.

I nod and point to her. "Yep. Whoever he's protecting, whether it's himself or one of his employees, he's doing it for a reason. And I'm betting that reason is crucial to his operation."

"But we haven't even met this man yet," Zara says. "Just one of his lackeys."

"We're going to change that soon enough." I stretch out my legs, having been sitting on them for a solid hour. "But not until we have something solid. We're only going to get one shot at Lambert. I don't want him to see it coming. He's already on edge. As evidenced by our friend in Roswell."

"I hope you're right," Zara says. "Because tracking down every single one of these agents is going to take some time. So far I've managed to eliminate twenty-two. Nine that are dead and thirteen that no longer live in the United States."

I frown and glance over to her.

"Yeah. Over half of those have retired to another country. But some are still active, working in consulting jobs in Europe and overseas. Sound familiar?"

"Yeah, yeah," I say. "Let's not worry about my future career prospects. Let's just see how many we can eliminate before doing a deep dive on the rest."

"Speaking of which," she says, grabbing her nearby mug of coffee. "How many have *you* eliminated?"

"None," I say. "I'm looking at Suzanne Fray's subscription service."

Zara scrambles up and over to the same couch as me, pushing me to the side. "Don't tell me she has a *Footsie* account."

"No," I say. "It's a little more than that."

Her eyes go wide as she sees the variety of videos Suzanne offers up on her personal page. "Ohhh. Got it."

"Looks like both girls weren't in the same line of work after all. Fray's was exclusively online," I say.

"I wonder why Annabelle didn't have one of these," Zara says, sitting back. "Seems a lot safer. You can do everything from the privacy of your own home—there's very little risk. Assuming the site's security is up to snuff."

I point to Suzanne's subscribers. She only has two hundred and sixty. "I don't know if that's enough to make a living on. Maybe Annabelle figured she could do better with more… *traditional* work. Especially if she was trying to save up money."

"I still don't get that," Zara says. "Why save up money for someone who doesn't want it? Especially if it means getting into strangers' trucks and potentially getting murdered? We know Annabelle wasn't stupid."

I shrug. "Who knows? Maybe that was just a cover story, and the money was for drugs. Don't forget what was in her system from the autopsy."

"Yeah, I guess," Zara says. "But how many druggies do you know that can save anything, much less three thousand dollars?"

I tap my finger on my knee. She's right. Something doesn't add up here. "Did Annabelle have any other contacts or acqu—" My phone buzzes beside me, causing me to pause.

"What is it?" Zara asks.

I furrow my brow. I don't often get a call from a number I don't know. But given how much I've given out my card over the past few days, I shouldn't be surprised. "Hello?"

"Agent Dunn, this is Suzanne Fray. From yesterday?"

I mouth *Suzanne* to Zara. "Ms. Fray, what can I do for you?" This is serendipitous. There's no way she could know we want to speak with her again, not unless Mr. Witter somehow informed her. But I didn't get the impression they were close enough for something like that.

"Can we meet?" she asks, her voice tight and ragged. It sounds like she's been running.

"Are you okay?" I ask.

"I—I don't know. I think I'm being followed."

"Where are you right now?" I ask, motioning to Zara to get ready. She hops off the couch and goes to grab her jacket.

"It's a restaurant—um, Loyola's. Do you know it? It's over on Central. You know, the old 66?"

"I know it," I say. "Stay there, we'll be there as soon as we can. Don't leave the restaurant and stay in public. Don't even go to the bathroom."

"Okay," she says, her voice sounding small.

I'm trying to pull on my shoes as I calm her. "You'll be safe there. Do you know who's following you?"

"No," she says. "I just saw a van outside my place when I got home last night. And then I saw it again this morning, but it was parked in a different place. And I just saw it drive by again."

"Is there anything else?" Zara grabs the keys as both of us head out of the apartment.

"I got a weird call last night. Someone just called then hung up. I—I didn't get much sleep."

"Okay, just stay right there," I say. "We're fifteen minutes away."

"Yeah," she says. "Okay."

I hang up as we get into the SUV. "She's being followed?" Zara asks.

"I don't know. It could be an overreaction. She says she keeps seeing the same van, and she got a strange call last night."

"That's not much," Zara says.

"No, but if she wants to talk, I don't want to lose the opportunity." I back the SUV out of the space and hit the accelerator, pulling onto the main road. "She'll be much more likely to tell us anything we want now. Maybe we can actually get something out of her this time." She lied to our faces once. But she's not going to get away with that again.

"And if she really is being followed?"

"Then maybe let's just hope traffic is light."

As we pull into the parking lot of Loyola's, the place is packed. I guess Sunday is the busy day. I'm forced to park across the street in an empty lot. After trotting back across to the restaurant, Zara and I head inside. Modeled in the style of a fifties diner, stepping inside is like stepping back in time. But it's not done up like one of those kitschy places with checkerboard floors and a jukebox in the back blasting Elvis Presley. This place really *feels* like it was built in the fifties and hasn't changed much since. Large pane-glass windows dominate the front and sides of the building, and the back is full of tables and chairs while the front section is all booths, except for the line of stools that line the low counter. The kitchen is split up into two sections in the back and the place is an absolute buzz of energy. There's a line to get in, obviously, and every seat has been taken with servers quickly hurrying back and forth as they take orders and deliver food.

"Do you see her?" I ask, surveying all the seats. It's mostly families and older people. I don't see a single woman sitting by herself anywhere.

"No," Zara replies.

"Hi, there will be a thirty-minute wait, is that okay?" a young server says, coming up to us. Her hair is dark and pulled back into a low ponytail and she's wearing a red shirt with the restaurant's logo on the left pocket.

I show her my badge. "Did you see a young woman come in here, about your age?" I ask. "She's about five foot six, short brown hair with green eyes? She probably would have been wearing something baggy."

"Oh," the server says. "I think I saw her earlier, she was sitting over there." She points to the front of the restaurant where all the booths are full of people much older than Suzanne.

"Which one?" I ask.

"Hey Shannon?" the server calls out to another server, a larger man with a goatee and pink fingernails. "Was that short-haired girl in your section?"

Shannon, two plates in his hands as he heads to another table, nods as he passes by. "Yeah, she was there for a while. Only ordered a drink."

"Where is she now?" I ask.

"I didn't see her leave," Shannon says.

"She left without paying?" the original server asks.

Shannon sets the plates down on another table before returning to us. "I haven't had a chance to tell you." He pulls out a five along with a bunch of other bills—presumably tips, handing the five to the first server. "She left this on the table. But I didn't see her get up."

"Excuse me," an older woman says behind me. "You're in my way."

I barely register her as I turn back to the original server. "No one saw her leave? How long ago was she here?"

"Maybe ten minutes?" Shannon says. "Sorry, I need to get back to my tables."

"*Excuse me*," the woman behind me says again.

I spin around to face her, biting my tongue so I don't say something I'll regret. "Ma'am, calm down. You'll get to your table."

"You're blocking the way," she says. I motion to Zara to speak to the woman while I turn my attention back to the server.

"Are there any other ways out of the restaurant, other than this door here?"

"Through the kitchen," she says. "But she wouldn't have gone through there without anyone seeing. And there's another exit on the side, by the restrooms."

"Show me," I say. She heads past the counter to the far side of the building—the only side that doesn't have glass windows. There's a door there with a diamond-shaped piece of glass set into it which leads to a small hallway. At one end is the women's restroom and the men's is at the other end, right beside an exit door.

I whistle to get Zara's attention as she's still arguing with the older woman who is now no longer blocked. She trots over as I thank the server.

We head down the hallway and out to the alleyway that

runs beside the restaurant. It would have been the perfect way to get out of the restaurant without being seen. There wasn't even a fire alarm on the door.

Unfortunately, there's nothing out here, not even tire tracks. Whoever took Suzanne, they are long gone.

Chapter Twenty

"WHY WOULD anyone want to kidnap Suzanne?" Zara asks as we head back to her apartment. We did a thorough search of the restaurant, but because they didn't have any security cameras, we were limited to what little remained of Suzanne's short visit. We did manage to learn that she'd been in a few times before and because she doesn't own a car that we're aware of, we have to assume she took the bus. The bus route runs right beside her apartments *and* the restaurant, so it makes sense. I also have been trying her phone nonstop, but it just goes to voicemail, which means it's probably off. Which also means we can't even get a general location on her.

I have to agree with Zara. I don't know why anyone would want to kidnap her. We have a lot of moving pieces here and I'm not sure how they fit together. "I guess it could be a stalker—someone who watches her online that's become a little too obsessed?"

"And who do we know who exhibits stalker-ish behavior?" she asks.

"That seems like a stretch, doesn't it?" I ask. "Why would Andersen kidnap Suzanne?"

"I don't know," she replies. "But what are the odds that

two roommates both go missing and one of them ends up dead within a week of each other?"

"Low, I agree," I say. "But Andersen has no reason to kidnap Suzanne. He's trying to nail Lambert. As far as we know, Suzanne and Lambert have no relation to each other."

"As far as we know," she says.

"I know you're just being cautious because of our situation. And I don't like Andersen any more than you do. But do you really think an officer of the law is going around kidnapping women?"

"Then why did she leave the restaurant when you specifically told her not to?" Zara asks.

"It had to be under duress," I say. "Someone came in using the crowd as cover, forced her out without making a scene. I just wish places around here had freaking surveillance cameras. Why is that such a hard thing?"

"At least the apartments do," Zara replies. "Maybe we can get a look at this van she said was following her." I also want to use the opportunity to check her apartment again, just to make sure we're not missing something.

We pull into the apartment complex and park beside the office, heading inside. A young man sits behind the counter, playing on his phone. He puts it away as soon as he sees us though, straightening his collar. He looks like he's about two weeks out of high school.

"Good afternoon, are you looking for an apartment for rent? We have a variety—"

"I'm Special Agent Dunn with the FBI. This is Agent Laidlaw. We need to see your security footage from yesterday and this morning," I say, holding up my badge and ID.

"Oh," he says, completely thrown off his sales pitch. "I… uh, let me call my manager. He'll want to—"

"Listen," Zara says, leaning over the counter and getting into the kid's face. "We don't have time for you to run this up the chain. We have a missing woman—who happens to live in *your* apartment complex. Now show us the footage."

I have to admit, I'm starting to like Intense Zara. She has an edge I haven't seen before.

The boy pulls at his collar. "I… uh… well, I mean, I'm not allowed…"

She leans closer. "*I'm not going to ask again.*"

He nods. "Okay, yeah, sure. I can do that. One second, um, just follow me." He fumbles with his keys to a door that's to his right.

"Easy, killer," I whisper to Zara. "We need this one alive."

Finally, he gets the door open and allows us in. It's a standard office with cabinets and drawers on one side and two desks on the other, both straddling a window that looks out onto the courtyard with the ferns. He heads to one of the computers and wakes it up, logging in and bringing up the security program. "Um, when did you want to see?"

"Here," Zara says, sitting down. "It'll be faster if I do it." She scrubs the footage back to yesterday on the camera that looks over the parking area where we first parked when we arrived the other day to speak with Suzanne. As the footage advances to around eleven A.M. yesterday, a white van pulls in just below Suzanne's balcony. But no driver steps out.

"There it is," I say. "Did you see a driver?"

"No, the angle isn't great. I couldn't see anything when they pulled in. But I can get the tag." She jots down the tag from the back of the van before scrubbing the footage forward again. The van sits there for about two hours before backing back out and disappearing again. As far as I can tell, no one ever got out of the vehicle.

Zara keeps running the footage forward until around ten P.M. the same van shows up again and does the exact same thing. Pulls in, parks and sits there for about an hour and a half, and then backs out and disappears from view again.

"That's not one of your maintenance vehicles," I say to the clerk.

"No, we only have one and it's a pickup truck with writing on the side," he replies.

"Ever seen that vehicle before?"

"I mean, maybe," he says. "It's just a white van."

"The choice of kidnappers across America," Zara mutters. She finishes going through the footage but the van doesn't appear again.

I turn back to the clerk. "We need the key for 6C."

"I'm not sure I can—"

Zara stands, causing him to flinch. "Okay, yeah. I have the unit keys right over here. But… um, you'll need to sign a waiver." He heads to one of the drawers and uses a key from his set to unlock it, pulling out a large case. He also digs around inside for a piece of paper that he puts in front of me. I give it a quick signature and he unlocks the case, handing over the key for 6C.

We head back through the courtyard to the stairs. Zara's phone is to her ear, and she's already calling in the plate on the white van. She rattles off the number to whoever she has on the other side while I pull on a pair of gloves before inserting the key into the lock.

"Yeah, okay, thanks," Zara says as I open the door cautiously. I check the inside, but everything looks to be in order. Nothing is out of place from when we were here a few days ago and the door to the balcony is shut. The smell of smoke still lingers in the air, though.

"No luck on the plate, it's expired," she says. "And the last vehicle it was registered to was a Pontiac Sunbird. If that tells you anything."

"It really doesn't," I say, looking around the apartment.

"Plate was probably stolen from a scrapyard," she says. "At any rate, I don't think there's any point in putting out an ABP for a white cargo van, do you?"

"Probably not, but we should do it anyway. I'm going to need to inform Strong." Our time has run out. Now we have a missing woman who could become victim number seven. More than likely the kidnapper chose that vehicle because they knew it would be hard to pinpoint. We're going to need something else to track down Suzanne.

"And it started off as such a nice Sunday, too," Zara says, pulling on her own pair of gloves. I'm not sure what I expect to find here, but I think it's worth looking, just in case. I just don't understand why someone would take Suzanne. Zara's right, there's no way it's a coincidence that *both* women are involved in separate crimes. This is all related… somehow.

I head back through the hallway and take a right, which should be Suzanne's room. It's plain enough with one window and a small desk in the corner with a laptop. An exercise ball is rolled beside the bed and a couple of mats are in the corner, a fine layer of dust on them. A photo board hangs on one of the walls. Funny, I didn't think people used those anymore. But there are a lot of pictures of her and Annabelle seemingly confirming they've known each other a long time. I pull open the drawers of the chest in the room and root around in the back until I find what I'm looking for. As I pull out the heavy sock and unwrap it, my eyes go wide.

"Hey, uh, Agent *Laidlaw*?" I call out.

Zara appears in the doorway. "Yeah?"

"Does this look like three thousand dollars to you?" I wave the stack of bills at her.

"Not unless that's all ones," she says.

I hand half the stack to Zara and we unfold it all, counting it out. "Ten thousand," she says. I reach back into the drawer and pull out two more identical socks, both with the same amount of money in each. "Okay, *thirty* thousand. What the hell?"

"I don't know. Suzanne had to know this was more than three grand, right? Or was that just another lie?"

She shrugs. "She said she never counted it. Maybe she really didn't know."

"I wonder if someone else did," I say.

"Wouldn't they have come looking?" she asks.

"Maybe they still will," I suggest. "Maybe the plan was to get Suzanne and Annabelle out of the way before trying to find the stash." I check my phone for the time. "It hasn't even been an hour since Suzanne went missing."

"But if they were going to do that, why not just wait until Suzanne was out of the apartment? They obviously had someone watching her schedule. I'm not sure this is about the money, Em."

She's right, it doesn't make a lot of sense. "Still, I think we should put surveillance on the apartment. Just in case someone comes looking."

"You'll have to get Strong to approve that," she reminds me.

"*Fuck.*" I am so done with this babysitting crap. "Fine. We need to inform him about Suzanne anyway."

"What do we do about the money?" Zara asks.

"We'll need to take it for evidence," I say. "Once we've figured this out, then we can determine who it belongs to."

"Wanna flip a coin to see who calls Strong?"

"No, I'll do it," I say, wrapping the money back up and placing it back in the overstuffed socks. "This is my mess and I'm the one who has to clean it up."

Chapter Twenty-One

How do I keep finding myself in these situations? After spending roughly thirty minutes on the phone with my boss yesterday we had no choice but to head back home, since he more or less grounded us until this morning when all three of us could sit down face to face. I tried to impress upon him the urgency in which we needed to find Suzanne Fray, and he at least has an APB out on a white sprinter van with expired plates, though I'm willing to bet the plates we saw on the cameras are already long gone.

I take a deep breath and open the door to SSA Strong's office, Zara right behind me. We both made sure we were here bright and early, but considering our access to the case has been temporarily suspended pending his review, we have no idea if Suzanne has been found or not.

"Morning," he says, motioning us inside. "Close the door behind you." He sounds more cordial than I'd expected, though given my history with supervisors, I've experienced a bit of whiplash in the past and know how quickly this can go sour.

We both take a seat as he finishes typing something on his computer.

"Has there been any word on Suzanne?" I ask.

"Nothing yet," he replies. "Four vans were stopped overnight, but they all came up empty." He turns and folds his hands on his desk in front of him. "You two are more driven than I've given you credit for. Most of my agents prefer to take a day off."

I exchange a look with Zara. We discussed how to play this before coming in here. *Do everything you can not to stand out.* She reminded me we're supposed to be keeping a low profile and any light shining on us is not what we want.

"Just eager, I suppose," I say. "Considering this is our first case."

"Still, you have good instincts, even if your methods are less than… official." He says. "You should have procured a warrant for the footage and search of the apartment."

"But I thought—" One look from Zara shuts me up. "Yes, sir."

He turns back to the screen. "And this information that was provided from the Reservation Police. You've turned it all over to records?" I nod. We had no choice and didn't have time to make copies of everything. Thinking back, I should have copied it all as soon as Andersen gave it to me, but everything just happened so fast. I didn't expect it to spiral so quickly.

"I want to reiterate this, you're not in trouble here. You've done some fine detective work. But I'm taking both of you off this case."

My hands dig into the arms of the chair and it takes everything I have not to stand up and start yelling at the man that he can't take away the one thing that's keeping me sane around here. "May I ask why, sir?" I manage.

"Well, to be frank, this case has grown beyond your capabilities. You are both fine agents, but we're looking at possibly seven murders here, not to mention these allegations against a local business owner, which are, frankly, a lot. We need to give this our full attention. Which is why I'm assigning it to Agent Dent's team."

My teeth grind together.

"Don't get me wrong, even if you two were the most seasoned agents in the field, this would be too much for the two of you alone. I feel better with a full team working the case. But you have done some excellent work. I'm going to recommend to the section chief that you're awarded for your efforts. Obviously, I can't promise anything specific, but it's work like this that really puts you on the map. I'm sure you two will be promoted out of this in no time."

"Um," Zara says before I can blurt out what's on the tip of my tongue. "We really don't need any special recognition. We were just doing our jobs."

"Are you kidding?" he says. "You may have uncovered a massive crime ring here. This could be one of the biggest cases New Mexico has seen in years."

Any words of protest die in my throat. I forget that not every office is as busy as ours at home. That serial murderers and child trafficking rings aren't as common in the satellite offices as they are back on the east coast. There we're dealing with multiple metropolises, lined up from Boston all the way down to Richmond. Cases like this, while not common, are less of a spectacle there, because they happen a lot more often. But out here, this could be huge. And that would be bad for us.

"She's right, sir," I say. "Please, don't go out of your way. We just happened to stumble into something here. It was honestly unintentional."

"Unintentional?" he asks. "You've put more hours in on this in five days than most agents would in two weeks. Don't sell yourselves short." He gives us a warm smile. "I just wish I'd put the two of you in the field when you first arrived. At any rate, we can discuss it later. I want you to coordinate with

Agent Dent and make sure she and her team have everything they need to proceed with the case."

"We can do that," Zara says.

"Good. Once you're finished, you can both take the rest of the day and tomorrow as a well-deserved reward for all your hard work since you didn't get a weekend. But come back on Wednesday ready for more. I want to see how you two handle something more advanced."

I exchange another glance with Zara. Since Strong doesn't say anything else, I guess that's our cue to leave. We both thank him before heading back out, shooting looks at each other the whole way. A special recognition? The biggest case in New Mexico? Not only that, but I have to hand over everything I have to Dent, which means I don't get to see this through to the end. And that's a hard pill to swallow. Even on cases where I've failed, I've *always* been the one who took it from start to finish. I've never handed off a case in my life.

"Are you okay?" Zara asks as we head back to our desks.

"What are we going to do? He wasn't supposed to say *that*." Honestly, I thought we were going to get reamed out for breaking protocol again. But I guess in this case the ends justified the means.

"You gotta contact Caruthers. Let him know what's going on," she whispers. "We need to give him a heads up that—"

We both turn as someone appears in my periphery. I look up and see Special Agent Kelly Dent beaming at us. "So. Turns out you two are the real deal. You ready for the briefing?"

My eyes are practically bugging out of my skull. What the hell am I supposed to do now? "Can you…uh, give us a few minutes? We have some—"

"—last minute prep," Zara finishes.

"No time like the present," she says. "C'mon, I don't care if you have to read it off a notepad. Time's wasting and we have a missing woman out there." She turns and heads for the briefing room.

To say my heart is in my throat would be an understatement. We are *fucked.* As we follow Dent to the briefing room, I wonder how long it would take us both to pack and leave town. Most of my stuff is still in suitcases. But Zara—she'll have to leave it. There's no telling how long we have.

"Dunn, Laidlaw, you know the rest of the team," Dent says as she breezes through the glass door. Three other agents are already sitting around the conference table. "That's Morrow, Tocker and Stockham." The three agents give us a quick nod. Morrow is Dent's partner and a seasoned agent, having been with the Bureau almost twenty years. Tocker and Stockham, otherwise known as *the brothers* because they look so much alike—bald, muscular and both with glasses—transferred in from Sacramento a year or so ago. I see one of them in the halls all the time and I always think it's the other one. Seeing them sitting here together, it really is remarkable how much they look alike.

"As we all know, Agents Dunn and Laidlaw cracked a big one," Dent says, rounding the table and inviting us to take a seat. "What started out as a single murder has ballooned into a case with possibly six other related deaths, a potential conspiracy and the matter of thirty-thousand dollars stuffed into a sock drawer." She finally takes a seat right across from me, clasping her long fingers together and leaning forward, her attention completely on me. "We read over the case notes this morning. But I'd like to hear about what you *didn't* write down."

"We included everything in the reports," I say. "There's really nothing else to add." Why do I feel so warm in here? Maybe it's the fact that I'm being torn in three different directions and I don't see a clean escape.

"No, you didn't," Dent replies and my stomach bottoms out. I chance a look at Zara, who seems just as shocked as I am. "I want to know your theories. Your suppositions. I want to know what you think is going on here."

"But that's just conjecture," I say. "We don't know *what's* going on. That's why we were investigating."

"You must have some idea," she says. "After all, you did just open up what might be the *biggest case* in New Mexico history."

My heart is going about a million miles per hour. Those were Strong's words. And now that I think about it, Dent's tone has gone from friendly to something decidedly less than. Is she *threatening* me? She's leaning forward, almost like a predator, her gaze fixed on mine. And her smooth black hair is only contributing to the mental image my mind is making up all on its own of a bird of prey, glaring down at its next meal. All eyes at the table are on me.

And I've got nowhere else to go.

Chapter Twenty-Two

"Agent Dent," I say, taking a slow, calm breath. I can only see one way out of this. And while I really don't want to be in this room right now, I can't put my pride above the investigation. *Either* investigation. Which means I have to do something I've never done before.

"I'd rather not comment on my personal beliefs about the case as I wouldn't want to influence your line of thinking. Frankly, this has stumped us. I'm honestly glad Strong gave this to you because we're at a loss."

"Oh, come on," she says, sitting back. "You must have had some theories."

I glance around the table. "It's like you said. We fell into this and… it's outside of our league."

Dent works her jaw, staring at me. I feel like I'm in an interrogation room, like she's trying to break me. And I get the distinct feeling Agent Dent knows more than she's letting on.

Finally she blinks and turns to the brothers. "I want you two running down these other murders. Let's try to get as much information on them as possible. Find out if they really could be related or if the Reservation is just trying to get us to do their work for them."

"Got it, boss," one of them, Tocker, I think, says. He and Stockholm stand and head out.

Dent turns to her partner. "Want to start on Fray? Let's see if we can't figure out who might have wanted to take her. Check old boyfriends, acquaintances, anyone she might have owed money. She worked in a dangerous business. Maybe someone came looking for payback."

"Yep," Morrow says, closing the file in front of him. "I'll get right on it." He heads out, leaving us with Agent Dent.

Again, I find her glaring at us like she's looking for something. "It's too bad we don't have any additional information. Suzanne probably doesn't have long."

I shoot Zara a nervous look. The more I open my mouth, the greater the chance I accidentally say something that will only make this situation worse. Strong is already looking to shine a spotlight on us when we were meant to keep a low profile. But a young woman's life hangs in the balance here. Can I really sit here and do nothing knowing that I might have been able to change her fate? And if she ends up dead like Annabelle, can I live with that?

I clear my throat just as Dent is about to get up. "What about Lambert?"

She stops, staying in her seat. "What about him?"

"Aren't you going to investigate him?"

She pauses, looking from me to Zara and back. "Why? Do you have something that's not in the file? Because the only thing I see are a bunch of accusations from the Reservation."

"He owns the one truck that might have recorded what happened to Annabelle," I say.

"If he did, then that footage is long gone by now, trust me," she says, rising from her chair.

I should be figuring out how we're going to get out of this office without making a scene and yet all I can think about is Suzanne and how she might end up just like Annabelle. I glance at Zara again, looking for some kind of guidance only to find her features pinched, almost like she's in pain. This is killing her just as much as it's killing me. If it were just me, I wouldn't even hesitate to expose myself if it could help find Suzanne. But I can't put Zara in that kind of danger. I feel like I'm being ripped in two.

"Wait," I say as Dent reaches the door, the file tucked under her arm. She stops, watching me closely. Zara gives me a subtle nod. "There's something else."

"I'm listening," Dent replies.

"Lambert… sent someone after us in Roswell."

She takes her hand off the door and returns to her seat, her attention never leaving me. "He looked like a hired gun. Tried to intimidate us for asking too many questions after we visited his boss's plant."

"Was he armed?" she asks. I nod. "And how did you respond?"

"We managed to disarm and subdue him," I say, trying to be as careful as I can with my words.

Her eyes narrow. "How?"

"It was luck, mostly," I say. "He became distracted, and I was able to get the upper hand."

"That's… impressive," she says. "And it's not in the file."

"It didn't seem relevant," Zara says.

"And Strong doesn't know." It's not a question, just a statement as if she's confirming it for herself. I don't bother answering. "You two transferred here from Portland, isn't that right?"

I nod.

"I had a chance to visit up there once. The gorge was beautiful. What's that river that connects up with the Columbia up there? I always forget."

"The Willamette," I say, thinking back to the prep work Zara had us do when we arrived. We have complete dossiers on our "new" backgrounds and I have just about every fact memorized, including my new birthdate and social security number.

But I don't like the way she's looking at us. It's as if the air in the room has shifted ever so slightly. "Right," she says. "The Will-AM-ette." She emphasizes the last syllable, whereas I didn't. "How could I forget? After being stationed up there for six years."

It's as if I'm glued to my chair. Where before I felt the distinct need to run, now I can't even move. Did I just blow our entire cover?

"It's funny," she says. "I like to know who I'm working with. And after you two arrived, I contacted one of my old colleagues up there and asked him about you. Surprisingly, he didn't know what I was talking about." My heart is hammering in my chest and sweat has broken out across my brow. I don't normally crack under pressure, but given she's about to expose us, I'm starting to understand why Caruthers was hesitant to allow us to continue operating. He should have just locked us in a box and thrown away the key.

"That's… strange," I say. "Maybe he was under orders not to say anything."

"Maybe," she replies. "Still. I've known Boyle a long time. And I can usually tell when he's covering for someone. But he genuinely didn't seem to know who you were."

"Listen, Agent Dent," I say.

"No," she replies before I can get another word out. "Don't say another word. Whatever you're into, whatever is going on, I don't want to know about it. You're obviously here for a reason and that reason is clearly above my pay grade. But don't think that I'm stupid. Neither of you are 'new' agents."

"No," I admit. "But that information stays with you. Otherwise, it puts people at risk."

"Fair enough," she says. "So if you're as seasoned as I expect you are, I'm guessing you didn't report the assault because you didn't want anyone looking too closely at your response."

"We're trying to keep a low profile," Zara says, her voice flat. I can't tell if she's upset that I blew our covers or not. But it's something we'll have to discuss later.

"Understandable. But given the way Strong was going on about you two I'm not sure you accomplished that. He's determined to make sure you're rewarded for your work."

Ugh. What I wouldn't give to have Wallace back in this situation. At least he could be counted on to take the credit of others, leaving them to languish in the shadows. But no, we had to get the altruistic boss. "I know. And that's going to be a problem."

She knits her fingers together again, thinking hard. "I think I might be able to help there. Provide some time, if you will. Strong isn't the kind of boss who really digs into the details of a case. He likes to take a bird's-eye view. I might be able to convince him that everything you've found here, everything about this case was nothing more than pure dumb luck."

Zara sits up, her eyes wide. "Really?"

"It may take a little convincing," she says. "But I think I can do it. Maybe then he won't be so willing to show you off."

"That would be amazing," I say. "But...why would you do that?"

She regards me for a moment. "Because I believe in this organization. And what it stands for. And whatever you two are involved with that's required you to set up new identities and leave your lives behind, it must be important. So I want to help."

"Wow," I say, exchanging another glance with Zara. "That's... thank you."

She nods. "But in return, I need a favor. Can you at least give me your assessment of what's really going on here? This report reads like it was written by a robot."

Zara chuckles. "Sorry about that. We were trying not to be too obvious."

I lean forward. "The thirty thousand is the key. I think Annabelle was into something that got out of control. No one just has thirty grand stashed in their sock drawer. And I think it has to do with Lambert."

"Now that you told me he threatened you, I'm inclined to agree."

"The money had to come from him. Or maybe she stole it. I'm not sure. But he's the only one who knows what happened that night. And his truck was conveniently the only one that could have caught it on video."

"Video that has no doubt been destroyed by now," Zara says.

Dent shrugs. "Maybe. Maybe not. From what I know about him he can be one vengeful son of a bitch. If he could use that video as leverage, it still exists."

"Either way, I think we're looking at him or one of his men who's responsible for Annabelle."

"And what about Suzanne?" she asks.

"Maybe Lambert thinks she knows where the money is?" I say. "But if that's the case, I don't know why he hasn't raided the apartment. It's not like he doesn't know where she lives."

"So you think Lambert kidnapped Suzanne?" Dent says.

I nod to Zara. "That's the working theory, though we know it doesn't exactly fit. The problem is putting pressure on Lambert. So far we've been blocked at every turn. Including official ones."

She nods. "He's slippery, and he has his hands in every pot, which makes him hard to pin down. Fortunately, I know a way."

"You do?"

"The Bureau has had a file on Lambert going back as long as I've been here," she says. "There's not a ton there, amounting to little more than what the Reservation cop gave you, but it's enough that if anything big—anything like this were to come up, we have a way to force him out of his weasel hole."

I crack a smile as Zara chuckles. "Weasel hole?"

"What would you call it?" Dent asks.

"I guess that's as good a descriptor as any."

She nods, standing. "You know, I could use two more good agents on this. My team is solid, but I'm never one to turn down some additional help."

"Strong told us to take the next two days off," I say. "And if you're not able to convince him everything was just luck, we're going to need to make a quick exit."

"It's not that we don't appreciate the gesture," Zara adds.

"I get it," Dent says. "Say no more." She holds up the file. "Thanks for your help. Don't worry, I'll get Strong to come around. But it doesn't hurt to be prepared."

As she leaves, I can't help but feel deflated. Even though I believe she'll keep our cover intact, letting go of the case isn't easy.

"You okay?" Zara asks when it's just the two of us.

"Yeah," I say too quickly, turning to her. "Fine. Are *you* okay? I wasn't sure what to do back there. She had us pinned in a corner."

"No, you did the right thing," she says, placing her hand on my arm. "We're between the proverbial rock and hard place."

"Do you think she'll be able to get Strong to back off?" I ask.

"With the amount of pull she has in this office?" Zara asks. "I think so. I'm not sure anyone else could do it. But I bet she can."

"So what do we do?"

"*You* need to follow her and take her up on her offer," Zara replies. "While I go home and prepare, just in case we need to make a quick exit."

"What? No, I'm coming with you," I say. "We need to stick together."

"Em," she says, looking at me like a lost puppy. "You know if you don't see this case through it's going to drag on you. And that's just going to annoy me, so you need to not argue with your best friend and take her advice for once. Plus, you're already packed and ready to go. I've got an apartment to disassemble."

"But—"

"Don't argue when we both know this needs to happen. I can't take any more of your pouting. This is your case and you're not going to let someone else finish it for you. Got it?"

I smile despite myself. "You're a real pain in the ass." I pull her in for a hug.

"Right back 'atcha," she says. "Now hurry before she leaves."

I pull back, thinking how lucky I am to have someone like Zara. I honestly don't know what I would do without her.

Heading through the doors after Agent Dent, I am more determined than ever to get to the bottom of this.

Chapter Twenty-Three

"So," Dent says after we've been on the road for a solid hour. "Do I keep calling you Claire or is there another name you'd rather go by?"

"Claire is fine," I say, though I don't feel like the name fits me very well. Mostly when I'm undercover I keep my first name, just for simplicity's sake. But that wasn't an option here. And getting used to a new first name until it became second nature took a lot of training from Zara. She managed to pick up on it faster than I did, which is one of the reasons why she is so suited for undercover work. Unfortunately, it's not something she's eager to explore.

"Probably simpler that way," Dent says over the open windows. "This is usually the part of the drive where I try to get to know my co-workers but I don't really think that will work in this case."

"No, I guess not," I say.

"I bet you could probably rattle off a thousand facts about Portland though, couldn't you?"

"As long as I make sure my pronunciation is right," I say.

She grins. "Don't worry about that. It was a shot in the dark. Hell, unless you're born there half the time you get it wrong anyway." I catch her looking at me. "You look younger than you really are, don't you?"

"I get that a lot."

"You don't have to confirm this, but I'm going to guess you've been in the Bureau at least five years. Maybe longer."

Wow, she's good. "How about you?" I ask.

"Almost nine. They recruited me out of high school. Of course by then I was halfway through my college courses already anyway. I finished the rest of them off and got my degree in criminal studies before joining. Started in Dallas and then transferred to Portland before coming out here."

"Which office did you like the best?" I ask.

"Definitely ABQ," she replies. "Dallas is too fucking moist and funnily enough, so is Portland. Plus, out here you get all four seasons."

"Really?" I ask.

She nods. "High desert. We usually see snow in the valley at least once a year. Have you been up to the Sandias yet?"

I shake my head.

"They'll be skiing up there until May," she replies. "Tons of courses if you're into that kind of thing."

"I've never been much of a skier," I admit.

"That's the other thing about being out here," she says. "There's always something to do outside. And because the weather is so good most of the year, you really don't have an excuse not to." It's easy to tell Agent Dent really likes where she works. And she's beginning to give me a new perspective on this place. Where before all I could see was a hot desert wasteland, seeing it through her eyes is making me wonder how much I've been missing.

I have to admit, the view the entire drive so far has been amazing. I haven't been letting Zara do enough of the driving, which means I really haven't had the chance to just watch the landscape pass us by. I've been too focused on getting from one place to another.

She's back at the apartments and has been sending regular updates of her progress. I think she'll probably be good to go tonight if push comes to shove, but thankfully Dent has already begun sowing the seeds with Strong that we don't deserve nearly as much credit as he wants to give us. As far as I can tell, she's both a capable agent and someone who can be trusted. Given that she could have gone to her boss immediately about us but instead decided to help us keep our cover was enough to convince me she's not as bad as I thought.

"Are you sure about this plan?" I ask. "There seem to be a lot of variables."

"One thing is for certain," she replies. "Lambert may not be a creature of habit, but his cronies are. And we've been keeping this in our back pocket for just such an occasion."

"If you had the ability to go after Lambert all this time, why didn't you?" I ask.

She shrugs. "Most of what we had wasn't concrete enough to risk it. Strong decided it was better to go after targets we had a better chance of nailing rather than go out on a limb with Lambert. But your case changes everything. It's still a risk, but it's one I believe is worth taking, especially if he really is behind all these deaths."

"You seemed surprised to learn about them," I say. "Didn't the Reservation Police fill you in before we came along?"

She shakes her head. "Hadn't heard a word from them. But I can't really blame them. There's bad blood going back decades. The FBI hasn't always been the… *kindest* to them, so I can understand their distrust." She nods to the box in the back of her SUV—the same one Andersen left on my porch. "That cop probably thought since because you were new to the Bureau, maybe you wouldn't be as indoctrinated as the rest of us. He probably saw you as his one chance to solve those deaths."

"I just can't believe there could be that many," I say.

"That's one of the unfortunate things about our position here," she says. "Not only do you have Albuquerque police, but you have the Navajo. And those two *definitely* don't like each other. So it's like trying to play referee when one of the teams thinks you're working for the other side. It doesn't make for a very conducive working environment. So we're left doing a lot of work twice."

"Which is frustrating and a waste of time," I say.

"You must run into the same thing wherever you're from," she says. "Federal departments are always going to clash with the locals. Egos get in the way and as a result, nothing gets done."

"Yeah," I say knowingly. "I've run into that a time or two."

She chuckles. "Okay, we're here. You good covering the back?"

I nod. "Happy to do it." We agreed she should be the one going in the front as these people will know who she is and we're looking to get a reaction out of them. Though I kind of wish we had some more backup. This might be a lot for just the two of us to handle. I hop out of the SUV and spot our target ahead. It's a small, one-story restaurant with a large neon sign out front advertising *The Southwest's Best Tacos*. But the neon on the sign itself is broken and so the only legible part of the sign in the waning light just says *The Southwest*. There's no name of the business on the building or sign. Yeah, I can see how a place like this might be a front.

I position myself around the back where the door to the kitchen is propped open with a cinder block. A couple of dumpsters sit about fifty feet off the back of the building and a few vehicles are parked back here, all of them with spoilers and racing stripes. I draw my weapon with my back up against the wall, waiting. After a few minutes I hear Dent coming through the front door making an announcement.

"This is the FBI," she calls out. "I'm looking for Joseph Quezada." There's a shuffling inside as a bunch of men start yelling. All I can hear is chairs moving and tables being pushed aside and I have to hope Agent Dent knows what she's doing. A man in a white T-shirt and jeans with an apron on comes running out of the back of the building, sprinting for one of the cars. He can't be older than eighteen and he's not who I'm here for, so I let him go.

A moment later two more cooks come running out, headed in opposite directions as a slightly heavier-set man pours out with them. He's got on a tweed sports jacket and has thinning hair, and exactly matches the picture Dent gave me before we arrived.

"Joseph Quezada," I say leveling my gun at him. "Don't move another inch."

He turns and sees the gun, falling back on his butt and trying to scramble back. "You ain't got nothin'" he says, though there is genuine terror in his eyes.

I check my six to make sure no one is coming up behind me, but it seems like the kitchen staff isn't staying around to defend poor Joseph. "You're under arrest for solicitation," I tell him. "Stand up and put your hands behind your back."

I can see him debating it, scanning his periphery and looking for a way out, but he's got nowhere to go. Not unless he plans on scaling one of the eight-foot high chain link fences that happen to run around the businesses that neighbor this property.

"It ain't gonna stick," he says as he gets up, dusting himself off.

"Shut up and turn around," I say. "Anything you say can and will be used against you in a court of law."

"My brother will have me out before the eleven o'clock news."

Who still watches the news? I turn him around by one shoulder and lock his wrists in cuffs before stowing my weapon. As two of the vehicles that were parked behind the building throw up dirt peeling out, I walk Joseph around the other side of the building to find Dent outside the restaurant already, arguing with one of the other patrons.

"—care what the charge is, you can't just come in here and—"

"Let me stop you right there," Dent says to the older man who is probably in his seventies. "We have sufficient evidence to make an arrest and your nephew-in-law is going to be charged, booked and jailed. The judge will determine when he'll stand trial tomorrow."

"Stand trial? For what?" the old man spits.

"Don't listen to 'em," Joseph says as I march him to Dent's SUV, opening the back door. "Just get Karl!" I push him inside, lowering his head. He tried fighting me as we walked, pushing against me, but his balance isn't very good and nearly sent himself sprawling more than once.

"You can bet we'll be there first thing tomorrow," the old man tells Dent as she comes to join me at the SUV.

"That's your right," she says. "But I wouldn't get your hopes up. The evidence speaks for itself."

"This is bullshit," Joseph says from the backseat as soon as we're both inside. "You know who you're fucking with, right? He's going to steamroll right over top of you."

"Is he?" Dent asks without even looking in the rear view. She pulls out of the parking lot without looking back at the small crowd of patrons that has formed in front of the restaurant.

"You know he is. All you're doing is making yourselves a target."

I turn around, looking him dead in the eye. "You sure about that?"

"You don't scare me," he says.

"Then what would you call all that cowering you did back there on the ground?"

He just grimaces as I turn back, though as I do, I catch a smirk on Agent Dent's lips.

Chapter Twenty-Four

It takes an hour to get back to the office and another forty minutes to process Quezada. Rather than taking him back to the FBI office, we take him to the local precinct instead. Dent thought it might be better than trying to process him ourselves as this way he'd be thrown in with the "rest of the garbage," further incentivizing his brother-in-law.

Unfortunately, she chooses the one building where Officer Ridout works, and from his attitude I think he's still salty about the FBI taking over the case he'd been working. He makes no attempt to hide the fact he's watching over our shoulders the entire time we're booking Quezada. By the time we finally get him in an interview room, Ridout is practically staring down our throats.

"Is this another FBI operation we're not meant to know anything about?" he asks once Quezada is situated in one of their interview rooms.

"Something like that," I say, breezing past him on my way to the monitoring room. Dent stays behind, outside Quezada's door. She's planning on interrogating him. Despite wishing I could do it myself, apparently the two of them have some history, so I'll have to be content to watch from the other room.

"And I don't guess it matters you're going to rain hellfire down on everyone here," Ridout says, following me down the hallway.

"What's wrong, Ridout? Afraid of actually doing your job for once?"

"What's that supposed to mean?" he asks, vitriol in his words.

I spin on him, staring him straight in the face. "It means you missed a potential piece of evidence at the site where Annabelle was found. You were nothing but dismissive and rude, and to be frank, I don't enjoy working with incompetent detectives."

"What evidence?" he says.

"The keychain, remember?" I say. "Under the dumpster."

"Don't tell me you actually got something off that," he says.

"It doesn't matter," I reply. "You were so eager to get out of there and button this case up you didn't even look. And now we have another missing girl. That man in there is our best chance at finding her before she ends up just like Annabelle. If it's not already too late." I turn and head for the recording room again.

"Best of luck," he calls after me in an overly sarcastic tone. But I don't have time to babysit detective Ridout. I head into the room and take a seat beside the video tech who has two different cameras set up in the interview room. She turns to me, removing her over-the-ear headphones.

"Ready?"

I nod and she flips on the record button, which should turn on the little red lights on the cameras in the room, letting Dent know we're ready for her to proceed.

She approaches the desk where Quezada is sitting. And the closer she gets, the more he tries to push away from the table. But there's only so far he can go. Since his crime was technically a nonviolent offense, he isn't cuffed to the table or the floor, but the room is small and doesn't allow him to move away from her. Which is on purpose.

"Joseph," she says. "How've you been?"

"Better than you in a couple hours," he says, his attempt at bravado falling flat. "As soon as my brother gets here with our lawyer. Your boss is going to cut you back down to parking attendant."

"The FBI doesn't actually handle parking enforcement," she says without missing a beat. I like this lady. She's as unflappable as they come. "However we *do* handle multi-state sex crimes."

"*Sex crimes?*" he asks, incredulous.

"Let's see," Dent says, making a show out of opening the folder in front of her and pulling out a variety of photographs, spreading them out on the table before them. "We have you soliciting nine different prostitutes over a four-month period." She turns each of the photos around so he can see them. "That's about one every two weeks. Are we that hard up for companionship?"

"Fuck you," Joseph says.

"I'll take that as a yes."

"So what?" he says. "You're gonna arrest me because I got a little action? What is it, a petty misdemeanor?"

"That *would* be the case," Dent says, looking back down at the file. "If not for this one. I believe you knew her as Amanda. And unfortunately, Amanda was only seventeen at the time and underage. Which, as you know, is a felony."

"Now wait a second," he says, some of the fight going out of him.

"Not only that, but this isn't the first time you've been charged, is it? Which means the DA is probably going to want to bump this one up a few notches. Make an example out of you." She closes the file. "I wouldn't expect to see daylight again for, I dunno, fifteen years?"

"She told me she was eighteen!" he insists.

"Doesn't matter what she *told* you," Dent says. "I could tell you I'm twenty-two. Doesn't make it a fact." She stands up dramatically, her chair sliding back on the linoleum floor. I can't help but smile. She's doing a great job in there. I just wish I could see it in person. Watching Quezada sweat is probably the most fun I've had since getting to Albuquerque.

"Look, there has to be a way around this," he says. "I'm sure there's something I can help you with. I got all kinds of connections."

"I know all about your connections, *Joey*," Dent says. "Not interested." She turns and heads for the door.

"Wait, wait," he says, the panic really setting in. "Anything, okay? Anything. Just… let's make a deal, huh?"

Dent pauses and waits one, two, three seconds before turning back around. Just as I would have done it. "What kind of deal?"

"What do you want?" he asks. "Anything. Name it and it's yours."

Dent returns to the table and takes a seat. "Really? You mean that?" She's being slightly saccharine but Joseph doesn't seem to notice.

"Yeah, of course."

"Lambert," she says and his face immediately falls. "What's wrong, Joey? I thought you said *anything*."

"I… I can't do that," he says, swallowing hard.

"What about all those connections you just told me about?" Dent probes. "I thought you could *make a deal*."

"What…uh…what is it you want to know?"

"Everything," Dent says without a hint of emotion on her face. She's staring right into the man's eyes; in very much the way she was staring into mine. I know what kind of pressure he's under. I'm a trained agent and even *I* felt uncomfortable when she did that. It must be killing him.

"I… I don't know everything," he says, his voice growing smaller.

"You work for him, don't you? Tell me what you know and we'll see if it's enough worth making a deal over."

"I mean," he says. "What do you want me to say? We see each other a few times a week, he invites me over for dinner—"

"Tell me about his *business*," Dent reiterates. I'm getting the impression Joey isn't the sharpest knife in the drawer. "Specifically, about his trucks."

"His trucks?" he asks. "The trailers, you mean?"

"All of his trucks," Dent says. "Other than the tractor-trailers, what other kinds of vehicles does he use?"

Joey's eyebrows go up, producing significant lines on his forehead. "I don't get what you mean."

"White Sprinter vans, Joseph," Dent says, spelling it out for him. "Tell me about the white Sprinter vans."

"Lambert doesn't use Sprinter vans," he says. "Not big enough. The man works on scale; he only uses full trailers or sometimes double trailers. A van wouldn't be big enough to haul all the material he needs to move."

Dent sighs.

"Damn," I whisper. But that doesn't mean he couldn't have rented or stolen a van for the express purpose of kidnapping Suzanne. Obviously, he wouldn't do it in a vehicle that was one of his. It would have been pretty stupid to have pulled up to the apartment with the LGM logo on the side of the van.

"Okay, let's go back to his tractor trailer trucks then," Dent says. "Does he keep GPS on all his trucks?"

"Of course," Joey says. "We have to keep track of the trucks to make sure the drivers are taking the quickest routes to their destinations. A few miles difference can really screw up the entire schedule."

"And what about surveillance in the trucks?" she asks. "How is that handled?"

"Each truck has three different cameras," Joey replies. "One on the driver, one on the front that gets a good view of the road ahead and one on the back of the trailer, in case anything rear-ends the trucks."

I *knew* that bastard was lying to me the other day. Of course they have cameras on all their trucks.

"Covering all your bases, I see," she says.

"Yes. That way we can review anything that happens on a haul," he says. "Or if the driver is in an accident, we can see if he fell asleep at the wheel or if he had nothing to do with the accident. The insurance company requires us to provide all copies of the incident whenever we report an accident. They wouldn't cover us without those cameras."

"What happens to that footage after a haul?" she asks. "Is it overwritten?"

He shakes his head. "We have to keep it for a minimum of six months. So it's stored on a remote server."

"Do you have access to this server?"

"No, only Karl and his father have access."

After we'd arrived back at the station and Quezada was in processing, Dent explained that the old man who she'd been speaking with outside the restaurant had been Karl Lambert's eighty-eight-year-old father. Apparently he was the man who started the business fifty years ago before leaving it to his son. Though I have no idea if it was as… *intense* back then as it is today. One thing is for sure, we definitely have Lambert's attention now.

"Okay," Dent finally says. "Give me a moment." She gets up to head out. This helps, but it isn't the slam dunk either of us were hoping for. The fact that the footage may still exist that could tell us what happened to Annabelle gives me hope though. Still, I don't see Lambert just handing that over without a court order.

And Suzanne may not have that long.

"Hey, what about my deal?" Joey asks. "I gave you what you wanted, right?"

Dent turns back to him. "I'll pass word of your cooperation along to the DA. I'm sure she'll be happy to hear about your willingness to help." She closes the door behind her as I get up and head back towards the interrogation room, meeting her halfway.

"It's not much," she admits.

"But the evidence may still exist. It can show us exactly what happened."

"Not if Lambert was the one involved," she says. "There's no way he'll provide access to something that may implicate him."

"I don't think it was him directly," I say. "But probably one of his drivers. Maybe if we can get him to—"

Someone behind us clears their throat. Dent and I turn in unison, along with half of the rest of the office, to see Karl Lambert standing there, two large men flanking him on either side.

"Agents," he says in a deep, baritone voice. "We need to have a discussion."

Chapter Twenty-Five

Lambert is a tall man, probably six-one or six-two. So it really says something that the two men behind him are even taller. He's clean-shaven, wearing a nicely pressed suit which probably cost the equivalent of my entire year's salary. And while his words may have been cordial, the tone in which they were delivered were not. He's a man out for blood, and if we're not careful, he'll end up draining the both of us dry.

One of the men behind him steps to the front and I notice he's carrying a briefcase. "Where is Mr. Quezada?"

Dent hooks a thumb over her shoulder. "Interview Room 2."

The man lets out a breath so long it might as well be a growl. "We had to talk to six different departments before we tracked him here."

Lambert's frown deepens. "If I didn't know better, I would say you were trying to hide him from us."

"Does that sound like me?" Dent asks. Lambert only narrows his gaze. "Because it wasn't on purpose. Scout's honor." She holds up two fingers tight together.

The man with the briefcase moves past us and Dent nods for one of the officers to escort him to the interview room. I presume he's Lambert's lawyer, though I've never seen a lawyer that's so… hulking.

"You're treading on thin ice, Agent," Lambert says. "What is it you think you're doing here?"

I notice more than a few of the officers around us have taken an interest in the conversation. And I think Dent is picking up on it too. There are too many eyes on us and I get the distinct feeling they all may not be on our side. It's very possible someone in this office alerted Lambert to Quezada's location. We were hoping he wouldn't find us until the morning.

"Let's have a conversation," Dent replies. "In private." She still has the file folder under her arm.

I don't take my eyes off Lambert, although he's barely even glanced at me since he's arrived. This was the man who sent someone to shut me up, maybe kill me. And now he's standing right in front of us like he's done nothing wrong. He knows his power and influence protects him and I'm getting really sick of men who think they can just come and go as they please through life, who think the rules don't apply to them. Rarely do I meet someone with so much arrogance, but this guy is swimming in it.

"You know what?" he says to Dent. "A little talk sounds nice. We have some things we need to… work out." Every word is dripping with condescension and sarcasm. I notice he's wearing a large gold ring on his pinky, engraved with something I can't make out. But he holds that finger slightly tighter than the others, as if to protect it.

"Fine," she says. "We can use one of the meeting rooms."

"And subject myself to being recorded unlawfully? I don't think so. I'm sure you pulled a similar stunt with poor Joseph. Who will be exonerated soon enough, I assure you. If we're going to speak, we'll do it in a… friendlier venue."

This chance to speak to Lambert may not come again.

And despite what the man did to me, I'm not going to let this chance slip through my fingers.

"What do you suggest?" I ask. I can practically feel the tension crackling in the air like electricity.

Lambert addresses me for the first time, really giving me the once over and I have to suppress a shudder. "I own a restaurant down the street." He checks his watch. It's a Bvlgari Chronograph, and he makes no attempt to hide it. "They'll be open for another few hours. Allow me to show the FBI my hospitality."

"Thanks, but that's not really convenient," Dent says. "We meet here, or not at all."

Lambert gives us a smirk. "You've gone to all this trouble to get my attention. And now that you have it, you're willing to throw it away?"

We exchange a glance. He's not willing to have any kind of discussion if it's not on his terms, which shouldn't surprise me. But heading into hostile territory, surrounded by Lambert's people? That's asking for trouble. He's already come after me once, but going into a situation like that would be like walking straight into the lion's den. At the same time, he's the reason we have Quezada, the entire reason behind all of this. And an opportunity like this might not come along again. We need to press him while he's still willing and open, before he puts up *all* his defenses.

The only problem is if we walk into a place like that and things go wrong, we might not walk back out.

"Okay," Dent says. "Half an hour."

"The Panther, on Juan Tabo. Don't be late," Lambert replies. "I'm not a patient man." He turns and heads back out with his other goon following close behind. Dent motions for me to follow her to one of the empty offices that line the corridor.

"Thoughts?" she says as soon as we're inside.

"High risk," I admit. "He'll have guns on us the minute

we're in sight of that place. And he won't respond kindly when he learns what we've got on his brother-in-law."

"What's the alternative?" she asks. "Let him slip through our fingers?"

I pause, thinking. "Hang on. Let me make a call." I pull out my phone and dial Zara.

"Y'ello," she says.

"It's me."

"I know it's you. I have Caller ID. Your face pops up on my screen, *Grandma.*"

"*Any*way. We got some info from Quezada. He says Lambert keeps all the truck video stored on a server for six months. Do you think you could remote access that server?"

"Depends on if it's connected to a network or not," she replies. "If so… maybe. What are you thinking?"

"That I don't want to find another gun in my face. Lambert just issued us a personal invitation to his restaurant where we can 'work all this out'."

"Too risky," she says.

"I agree. He can't be trusted. But we need to see what's on that server. It may be our only clue to finding Suzanne before she ends up like her roommate."

"I have an idea," Zara says. "But the odds of it working are… well, let's just say it'll be a challenge."

I look at Dent, who is watching me with interest. "Why don't I like the sound of that?"

"Because in order for it to work, you'll be putting yourself in mortal danger?" she suggests.

I sigh, putting the phone on speaker so we both can hear. "Okay. Gimme what you got."

THIRTY MINUTES LATER WE'RE PULLING UP TO THE restaurant. There are no other cars in the parking lot except for one black Escalade. As we get out, there isn't a sound for what seems like miles. The restaurant is right off the busy Juan Tabo Blvd, but for some reason there's no traffic right now. It's like the world has stopped and we're the only pieces that are left moving.

"I'm trusting you, Dunn," Dent says as we head for the restaurant. "This better work."

"Fiona knows what she's doing." My heart is in my throat and I almost accidentally say Zara's real name before taking a deep breath and focusing my emotions to the back. I can't afford to lose my nerve in there.

"How are you feeling?" Zara says in my ear. She's outfitted me with a tiny earpiece that's completely invisible unless someone were to shine a light down my ear canal.

"Anxious," I admit. Before, when it was just one hired gun in a parking lot, I was barely fazed. But walking in here, where I'm sure I'll have a target on my back the second we enter? This is something different. And given Lambert has already come after me once, I wouldn't put it past him to kill two FBI agents in cold blood if he felt they were becoming too much of a problem.

Dent still carries the file folder she showed to Quezada.

"You got this," she says. "All I need is five minutes. Then you guys can get out of there."

"Unless he doesn't have access to it," I say.

"In that case I wouldn't stick around longer than five minutes anyway." I can hear her shuffling in the background. She set up her workstation in her apartment even though she's still in the middle of packing. We already informed Strong—who wasn't happy with the idea but agreed that this was the best shot we'd get at him. Though Dent made it sound as if it was just her team working the case; she made no mention of me or Zara, which is for the best. She also got on the horn with Morrow, Tocker and Stockholm and had them take up positions around the restaurant, which should make me feel better, but doesn't. We get one shot at this and that's it.

Dent pushes through the door and I follow, entering into a cafe-like space. There's a large oval-shaped counter in the middle of the restaurant and booths line the walls on all three sides. A man in a black suit stands by the front door and motions to Dent. She raises her arms, and he pats her down, removing her weapon and placing it on the counter just out of reach.

I follow suit as he does the same with my weapon. I hate coming into a situation weaponless, but we knew this would be the drill. No doubt Lambert's men are armed to the teeth and already have us in their sights. But that was a risk we knew we'd have to take. I just hope Morrow is as good of a shot as he's purported to be, in case we need it.

In one of the booths sits Lambert, eating what looks like a quesadilla. He's alone, though there are two men in the booth behind him, their eyes on the back of his head. We head around the counter and take a seat at the booth, only for another man to sit in the booth behind us. We're effectively surrounded on all sides.

"I must admit," Lambert says with quesadilla in his mouth. "yanking Joey to get my attention was a bold move. You could have just requested an appointment."

"Would you have accepted?" Dent asks.

"In a month or two, maybe," he says, wiping away an errant bit of cheese. "But I guess you're in a hurry."

"Okay," Zara says in my ear. "Go ahead."

Carefully I reach into my pocket and activate my phone, tapping out the sequence without looking, just like I practiced the whole way here.

"And we're good. I have a signal," she says. "Stand by."

"Your brother-in-law is looking at some serious charges," Dent says, setting the folder down.

"Please," Lambert replies, not even looking up. "Solicitation and prostitution? You arrest him, you'd have to arrest half the judiciary. Not to mention your boss, SSA Strong."

My eyes go wide as he finally looks up and meets our gaze. "Oh, you didn't know? Ol' Reggie used to have a penchant for the ladies of the night. He doesn't venture out much anymore, but that's the great thing about video. It lasts forever."

"The statute of limitations—"

"—won't matter to the court of public opinion," Lambert says. "And I'm betting Mrs. Strong won't really care about that either." He wipes his mouth again and throws the napkin down on the half-eaten quesadilla, pushing the plate aside. "So. Drop the charges against Joey, and this all goes away."

"Until you need something else from the FBI," Dent says.

"Look, I don't really care about your little organization," he says. "I have better things to do with my day. But you were the ones who came into my place of business, started harassing *my* employees." He shoots a pointed look at me. "You started this brawl. Don't get upset when you get a bloody lip."

"We want the footage," I say. "Then we can talk about Quezada."

"What footage?" he asks.

"Still looking," Zara says in my ear. "Keep him talking."

"The footage from the night of March seventh," I say. "From your driver who stopped at The Speedy Shop gas station off Highway 17 from approximately nine p.m. until eleven-thirty."

He stares at me, amused. "Wait. You can't be serious." He holds up a hand, chuckling to himself, and as he does I'm getting increasingly wary.

"This isn't a laughing matter," I say. "We have a missing woman and right now, you're looking like our prime suspect."

"Ah, shit," Zara says in my ear. I don't care that I've just shown our hand. There's only so much of Lambert's superiority complex I can take.

The man works his jaw for a second, the smile fading from his lips. "And here I thought this was about something *important.*" He snaps his fingers, nearly causing me to flinch as a man brings over a briefcase. Lambert presses his fingerprint to the case, and it opens, allowing him to remove a laptop.

Dent and I exchange a quick look as he opens the computer and types hurriedly on the keys before turning it around to face us. On the screen are the video feeds from three cameras, all of them with the date and timestamp in the lower corners matching when Annabelle should have been at the station.

"That's it," Zara says. "I'm copying the raw files now."

"This is what you've been looking for?" Lambert says. I don't like how free he's being with this information. Dent herself admitted he would never show us something that implicated him or anyone he employs. So why…?

"Here, let me speed it up for you," Lambert continues. He advances through the whole video and we're able to see the entire thing, his driver getting out of the vehicle, heading into the station, coming back a while later and getting in the truck before driving off. The truck has a perfect view of the dumpsters behind the station and Annabelle Witter never shows up during the entire feed.

I sit back, deflated. "Got it," Zara says, though now I don't know what the point is. She's not on there. Which means Lambert's driver didn't have anything to do with her death. He was gone before her body was dumped. He couldn't have been responsible.

"I assume that's satisfactory?" Lambert asks.

"It is," Dent says, shooting me another look.

"Then I expect Joey to be released within the hour." He closes the computer and places it back in the briefcase before handing it back off to his man.

"You want us to just… what? Make the charges disappear?" Dent asks.

He shrugs. "You can go through with the prosecution. But don't be surprised if a couple of photographs leak to the local papers. Might cause quite the stir in the FBI."

Talk about shining the light on the Albuquerque office. Not only would Strong be implicated, but something like this would for sure expose Zara and me. Plus, Quezada is worthless to us now. Prosecuting him won't get us any closer to Suzanne.

"You have a deal," I say as Dent turns to me, her eyes wide.

"Good. I think you know the way out." His gaze doesn't leave us as we get out of the booth and head to the door, retrieving our weapons on the counter.

"Have a good evening, Agents," he calls as we head back out into the night.

Chapter Twenty-Six

"I CAN'T BELIEVE you just capitulated to him like that," Dent says as we head back to the office. "What were you thinking?"

"That Strong being ousted as SSA wouldn't get us any closer to finding Suzanne. With the investigation that would follow, we'd never find her. She'd be lost in the shuffle somewhere. Not to mention tracking down Annabelle's killer."

"You said Lambert was behind all of it," Dent says. "You were certain."

"I..." My words die in my throat. I *was* certain. His people were just being so evasive and difficult about the whole thing I figured it had to be him. Lambert's video also exonerated Jack Carlin, if only by accident. And now we don't have any suspects. Which means Annabelle's killer had to be someone else. A random driver, perhaps. Just someone out on the road for a little fun. Which makes tracking them down impossible.

But that doesn't make sense. Because why would they come back and take Suzanne? Unless they're somehow, inexplicably, not related. I guess something like that is statistically possible, however improbable. But now I really don't know where to go.

"I need to talk to Strong about this," Dent says. "He needs to know Lambert has dirt on him."

"You can't do that," I say.

"The hell I can't," she replies. "Strong may not be perfect, but he deserves to know."

I stop her, holding my hand out. "I'm asking you not to. Anything that brings more attention to this office will be bad for everyone. Trust me."

"What are you really into?" she asks. "What are you hiding from?"

"I can't talk about it, but trust me, it's in our collective interest not to make waves. If it was just me, I wouldn't care. Hell, I'd tell you to go ahead—I deserve as much for screwing this up. But there are more people involved here, a *lot* more. And the more attention we draw to ourselves, the worse things will get."

Her eyes go wide again. "How deep does this thing go? Is my team in danger?" She takes a step back.

"Not if you don't talk to Strong," I say, holding my hands out. "Just let me and Agent Laidlaw handle this, okay?"

"I can't do that, *Dunn*," she replies. "I'm not really the kind of person who lets other people make my decisions for me."

I nod. "Completely understand. But if people start investigating, if Strong or anyone else begins making a fuss and my partner and I are thrust into the spotlight—and make no mistake we would be, IA would see to that—it could be disastrous. I need you to trust me right now, as someone who has been doing this job and has seen more than her fair share, believe me when I tell you it's imperative that we keep a low profile."

"We can't just hang Strong out to dry for Lambert to do with as he pleases," she argues.

"I don't think he will. It sounded like he'd been sitting on this information for a while, which tells me he was waiting for an opportunity like this. Lambert is the kind of person who deals in secrets and favors instead of money. I think if we let Quezada loose, he'll back off."

"Or he could have been bluffing and then ends up releasing the pictures anyway," she replies. "I don't know about you, but I don't exactly trust the word of a mob boss."

She has a point. "Fiona, are you picking all of this up?" I ask.

"Sure am," she replies, even though I'm the only one who can hear her.

"What's your take?"

"I cloned a good chunk of his database when he had his computer open," she replies. "Far more than I expected to get. Let me see what I can find. Maybe it will be enough to shut Lambert up for good. But I need time to do some digging."

I relay what she's told me to Dent. "Trust me, she's the best at this kind of thing. We can still protect Strong."

Dent looks me square in the eyes. "I don't like it. There are too many unknowns."

"We need to focus on Suzanne," I reiterate. "Not something that may or may not happen to our boss. Agreed?"

She furrows her brow. "Agreed. But if you've already cleared all the trucking companies, how can you ever hope to find the person who took her?"

"I don't know for sure, but I suspect because it's the same person who killed Annabelle. Maybe they're not as transient as we originally thought. We've been looking for someone who was passing through. Perhaps we should be looking for a local. Have Tocker and Stockholm found any more information about those other killings yet? Anything that might connect them to Annabelle's death?"

"I need to check in with them," she admits. "No doubt they saw that shitshow back there." Finally, she turns back towards the car and I follow. It feels like this is the best solution I'm going to get from her. A temporary stay, though I have no idea how long it will last.

"Do you really think we can trust her, Em?" Zara asks in my ear. "I mean, obviously don't answer. I'm just… how much do we really know about Dent? Because from what I've found out she's more of a by-the-book agent. If we don't come up with something soon, she'll go to Strong behind your back."

She's probably right. And to be honest, I wouldn't blame Dent one bit. How would I feel if a pair of new agents suddenly came into my office with a bunch of secrets and manufactured backstories, telling me what information I could and couldn't relay to my boss? She has already given me more leeway than I probably would in her situation.

"We need to go back to the beginning," I say to both Zara and Dent, climbing in the car and fishing the earpiece out of my ear. "Start over from scratch."

"No," Dent says. "We need to keep checking the sprinter vans. She has to turn up eventually."

"Whoever took her knew there were cameras," I say. "Otherwise why would they use fake plates? She's not in the back of someone's van anymore." My only hope is whoever took her isn't as quick as they were with Annabelle. "I think Witter is the key. Except it just doesn't make sense. Annabelle is seen on the station's security feeds around nine P.M. Then she doesn't show up again on anyone's cameras. But her body is found behind the station at ten minutes 'till twelve."

"Which means someone dumped her within a twenty-minute window," Dent says. "They obviously waited until there was no other traffic at the station to do it."

"I think we need to speak with Andersen again," I say.

"The reservation cop?" she asks. "Why?"

"He was the one who gave us all the info on the other women. He might know something else. If all these deaths *are* related, maybe he can help point us in the right direction. You said you wanted my feelings on the case, because I didn't put them in the file. Maybe we need the same thing from him."

Dent grumbles. "Yeah, and look how that turned out."

Because we're so late getting back, we have no choice but to wait until morning to drive out and speak with Andersen. I take the opportunity to head back to the apartment and do more preliminary packing. If we need to leave, we'll need to be quick, so I make sure I have everything I can't leave behind. When I go to check on Zara, she's made amazing progress with her place, but stopped in the middle to do research on the information she cloned from Lambert's computer via my phone.

"It worked like a charm," she says as I watch her parse through the information. "I thought I'd only get snippets, but the second he unlocked that computer, it came flooding in. Never really expected him to give that away, you know?"

"It's like Dent said. He wouldn't have given us anything that could implicate him. But to clear up some 'confusion', he was more than willing. He probably thinks we owe him a favor now because he did one for us."

"Deluded people tend to think that way," she says. "I'll get to the rest of my stuff later. But I thought this was more important."

"No, I think it's the right call. Anything yet?"

"Nothing but a bunch of schedules and data from the trucks themselves," she replies. "I have so much video now I don't know what to do with it all."

"Great. Now that we have it, we don't need it."

"You never know," she says. "There might be a golden nugget in here somewhere. I just need to find it."

"Anything we can use to pin down Lambert? Maybe something about hiring someone to threaten a couple of federal agents?"

"I'm betting he doesn't keep records of that kind of thing," she replies. "But I'm looking, regardless. There's *something* here, I'm sure of it."

I sigh and take a seat next to her. "I would offer to help but I know it's futile. You could do in five seconds what would take me an hour."

She gives me a quick smile. "It's the thought that counts, so thanks anyway." A moment passes before she speaks again. "Think Dent will keep her word?"

"I hope so," I say. "If she doesn't, well… I don't think she's going to tell him first thing tomorrow, but if we don't make fast progress, she'll probably feel like she has no choice."

"It's a hard place to be," Zara says. "Do you think you should tell Liam?"

I've been grappling with that. I don't want to alarm him, but if Zara and I are going to disappear—*really* disappear this time, he should know it's coming. I would hate for him to hear from Caruthers or Janice that we've just vanished off the face of the earth and no one can find us. But if this thing blows up here, I don't see that we'd have much choice. If whoever is targeting me finds out I'm here, there's no telling what would happen. And I'm not about to put these people in danger because of whatever is happening with the Bureau.

"I guess I should call him."

She stops typing for a moment and looks over. "It'll be okay, Em. And tell him to let Nadia and Elliott know I appreciate all they're doing."

I nod. "Will do."

I head back over to my apartment and dig around in one of the kitchen drawers for the last of my burner phones. I've had this one since we arrived and it was always my backup phone, in case I needed to call and didn't have a chance to go buy another one. Guess that day has finally arrived.

I unwrap it from the sleeve and activate it, dialing Liam's number. It rings three times before he picks up.

"Is that you?"

"Hey," I say. "You're getting pretty good at recognizing these restricted numbers."

"What's going on? You're off schedule," he says and I can tell I've woken him. It's closing on ten o'clock here and he's two hours ahead of me. "Is everything okay?"

"No," I say. "We may have a problem here. My *partner* and I are at risk of exposure."

"How high of a risk?" he asks.

"Right now, moderate. But something could happen in the next day or two that could… make us a lot more visible."

"Do you need us to retrieve you?" he asks. "I'm sure I could clear it, especially if it's dire."

"No," I say. "I can't leave. Not yet. But I wanted to let you know that if you see something that comes across about a specific office and a high-profile case and/or the department head, we'll have no choice but to run."

"You *do* have a choice," he says. "You could be like the others."

"And go into witness protection?" I ask. "Do you know me at all?"

"As opposed to disappearing and never seeing each other again?" he asks.

"It wouldn't be forever," I say. "Just until all this is over." There's silence on the other end for a moment. A silence I don't like. "Are you still there?"

"I was going to wait to tell you this, but if I don't get another chance, I might as well tell you now," he says. "We've been working round the clock on what's going on. They've called in *everybody*. But the problem is we still don't know who is behind it. And I don't mean like *I* don't know. The *Bureau* doesn't know."

My free hand forms a fist. "Is that confirmed?"

"By one of your old team members," he says. Shit. Probably Nadia. She must have been doing some serious digging if she's managed to find out that much. "There's more," he continues. "Three more have been targeted. They've been removed from active duty for their own safety."

"You're kidding," I say. "Which makes—"

"—nine so far."

Nine agents, targeted and removed from active service. Well, except me, of course. "Is the breach growing?"

"As far as we can tell, yes," he says. "Every department is locked down. Communication has ground to a halt."

"And no word from whoever is doing it? No demands?"

"Nothing," he replies.

"Which means I couldn't come home even if I wanted to," I say.

"You could, but you wouldn't be able to leave the house," he replies. "For who knows how long."

"It's almost worth it," I finally admit.

"If I want to be selfish, I'd agree," he says softly. "But it wouldn't be the best thing for you. I wouldn't feel comfortable with you back until we know why, and preferably *who*."

It's as if all the air has been sucked out of the room. The breach is getting worse, and the FBI seems powerless to stop it. Congress will only let this go on for so long before they step in, and then what will happen? A breach of this magnitude could compromise national security.

"What are we going to do?"

"I don't know," he says. I have never felt more alone here than I do right now. What am I even doing here? The case is falling apart, my life is in shambles and Zara and I are about to go on the run.

"I'm scared." I'm not sure I've ever said those words aloud before. My other phone beeps, letting me know my five minutes are up.

"I love you," he says. "We—*I'll* figure this out. I promise."

"Time's up."

"I know."

"...I love you back." I hit end before he can say anything else as the tears stream down my cheeks. I have to hold on to the counter to keep my knees from buckling. But they do anyway and I end up sliding to the floor. My cheeks are wet, but I've gone completely numb inside. The fight has gone out of me.

And I just don't know what to do anymore.

Chapter Twenty-Seven

I WAKE to the sound of someone knocking at my door. "Em?" Bolting straight up, I realize light is coming through the windows. "Em, if you don't open this door in three seconds I'm using my key, and I don't care if you're dressed or not."

My head is pounding and I force myself up as a key slides into the door and it opens to reveal Zara, dressed for work. As soon as she sees me she rushes forward, grabbing on to me and helping me to the couch. "What happened? Are you okay?"

"Fine," I say. "Just tired."

"Wow, that was convincing," she says sarcastically as I sit on the couch and she takes up a position beside me. "Are you hungover?"

"A hangover is more fun," I say.

She grabs a glass of water from the kitchen and hands it to me before sitting back down.

I drink it and feel slightly better once the glass is empty. Taking a few deep breaths, I tell her about my conversation with Liam last night. She listens intently, not saying anything until I'm finished.

"Three more. That's… not good."

"Nope."

"There has to be someone on the inside, orchestrating this," she says. "There's no other way. The FBI is as secure as *secure* gets. This doesn't just happen by accident. Did he give you the names—" She stops, correcting herself. "Stupid question, sorry." She hits her fist on the edge of the couch. "If I could just get into the master server and see what's going on, maybe I could figure out who is behind this."

"I think that's about seven tiers above your pay grade," I say.

"Well, so what?" she asks. "If we're going to be targeted anyway, why not go back and actually try to do something about it?"

"Go back? To DC?"

"Why not?" she asks.

"Because if whoever is after me finds out I'm there… and if Caruthers and Janice find out we've disobeyed a direct order—"

"What? They'll *fire* you?" she asks. "You were about to quit anyway."

"I was thinking more like *arrest* me. This feels more… dangerous. I'm not sure any of us are safe."

"All I know is this can't go on," she says. "In the meantime, you need to get ready. We need to get back to work."

I look over at her. "Wait, did something happen? Did Dent—"

She holds up her hand. "So far, no. But I *did* find something in all that video last night. Something I think you'll find interesting. And I want to bring Dent back in on it. To show her we can be trusted. And hopefully that way she'll be more inclined *not* to say anything to Strong."

"What did you find?" I ask.

"Oh, I think you'll be impressed," she says. "But first a shower because you smell like sweat and sadness. And in the meantime, I'll take care of breakfast. It's not Liam's five-star treatment, but it's as good as you're gonna get."

"Ok," I say, frowning and more than a little curious at what she could have uncovered. She certainly seems more like her old self this morning. I wonder if that's because she's really made some progress or if she's just putting on a show for me. Either way, I don't argue and I take a hasty shower, doing my best to wash the failure and disappointment of yesterday away.

When I come back into the living room, I feel better. Clean hair, even when it's still damp, will do wonders for your self-esteem. I square my shoulders as I head into the kitchen, where there is a steaming microwave burrito sitting on a paper plate beside a cup of coffee waiting for me. Zara's on the other side of the island, scrolling on her phone. She sets it down as soon as she sees me. "Much better."

"Yeah," I admit. "Thanks for checking on me. It was a rough night." The burrito is piping hot and I have to spit out the first bite for fear of burning my tongue. "How long did you microwave it?"

"Four minutes," she says. "That's how long I microwave mine."

"How do you have any tastebuds left?"

"You're just being a baby," she says and takes a bite before spitting it out herself and fanning her tongue. She puts her mouth under the faucet and runs water over her tongue for a moment. When she comes back up, she looks like a dog that's just finished a marathon at its water bowl. "Okay, I think we have different settings on our microwaves."

I can't help but burst out laughing and the darkness from last night recedes a little. "What's this marvelous evidence you found?" I take a tentative sip from the coffee and find it's just the perfect temperature. Though my tongue is still sensitive from the burrito.

"Here, let me show you," she says, wiping her mouth with a nearby towel. She heads back to the living room and opens her laptop. There's a video feed that's already been queued up. It looks exactly like the feed Lambert showed me on his computer, but this is a different truck and a different driver. Zara hits play and I get all three videos playing in sync. As far as I can tell there's nothing really remarkable about any of them.

"What—"

"Just wait."

A moment later the driver seems to hit some kind of pothole, because it's enough to jar the camera that's pointed towards him out of its housing. The other two cameras continue rolling as normal, but the one that was pointed towards him is now focused in on his dashboard. And it isn't an empty dashboard either. It's full of small toys and tchotchkes that line from one side to the other, all of them with one thing in common. They all feature a very famous mouse in some form or another.

"Remember the keychain?" Zara asks. "Tell me, does it look like something our driver friend here might keep as part of his collection?"

"Sure does," I say. "In fact, it looks like it would fit right in. Have you checked his schedule? Was he in the area the day Annabelle died?"

"He wasn't scheduled to work," she replies. "So he could have been anywhere."

Damn. She's really got something here. "Have you told anyone else yet?"

"And risk getting shut out of the investigation? Hell no. Plus, like I said, we need to bring Dent in on this. And now we go back to Lambert."

"Screw Lambert," I say. "We go after the driver directly. And then we find out if Lambert knew about it. The other driver could have been a smokescreen, a perfectly coordinated event made to look like he had nothing to do with it. If this is our guy… if he's killed all these women and Lambert's been covering for him…"

"…it would be enough to put him away forever," she says. "But only if the evidence is there."

"One thing at a time," I say, grabbing my blazer. "We gotta find this guy first. Do you have a name?"

"Oh yeah. You're gonna love this. According to the schedule it's our old friend Greyson Bauers. You know, the one with the bulging muscles?"

"You're kidding," I say, recalling our meeting with the man who told us they didn't even use cameras in their vehicles. I *knew* there was something off about that guy. "I thought he was front office."

"I guess he does more than one job around there," she replies.

"Let's get moving." I pour the coffee in a tumbler and we head out to the car. The sun hasn't been up long, but it's enough to warm the air. Out here it can get shockingly cold in the dark, but the frost on the ground is already beginning to melt and I can tell it's going to be another warm one.

By the time we get back to the office it's buzzing with activity. Avoiding Strong since we're still supposed to be off, we seek out Dent, who is in her office with Morrow, going over the specifics of the case.

"Morning," I say. Morrow barely gives me a glance while Dent glares at me under hooded eyes. She hands a file back to her partner.

Morrow glances at Dent tentatively but she nods. "It's okay. They're still helping on the case."

"Does Strong know this is still going on?" he asks. Morrow is a seasoned agent, probably not that far from retirement, given his age. But he comes across as even more by the book than Dent.

"I'm speaking with him later this afternoon," she says before turning to us. "What can I help you with?"

"We found something that may connect one of Lambert's drivers to the Witter case," Zara says. "Video evidence."

Morrow screws up his features. "From where?"

"Cloned from his computer last night," Zara says.

"Did you have a warrant for that?"

"Rick," Dent says, holding up a hand. "Where's this evidence?" Zara taps the laptop in her shoulder bag. "Let's see it."

She sets up the laptop and shows them the exact same video she showed me earlier.

"I don't get it," Morrow says.

"We found a keychain at the scene where Annabelle's body was dumped. It should still be logged in evidence. There wasn't enough of a fingerprint to pull a match to anything, but it was a very specific brand. One that looks a lot like what this driver seems to 'collect'."

Morrow quirks his mouth. "So you think because you found a Disney keychain at the scene, and because this driver happens to collect Disney paraphernalia that the two are connected? Do you know how many people buy that crap? It could have been a kid who missed trying to throw it in the dumpster." He scoffs. "You two have a lot to learn if you want to last in this job." He gets up, the file under his arm and heads out, leaving the three of us.

"Close the door," Dent says. I click it closed behind Morrow. "It's thin."

"But it's the first solid connection we've had," I say. "*And* the driver was off-duty the day Annabelle was killed. He wasn't in his truck. He'd be familiar with the location, driving for LGM. And he was probably familiar with Annabelle."

"What do you want to do?" she asks.

"Go after the driver. Greyson Bauers. We've had dealings

with him before, down in Roswell. But we have to track him down first."

"Which I can do," Zara says. "And I can find out if his driving schedule matches up with any of the other killings."

"We think Bauers is more than just a driver for Lambert," I say. "We still don't know where that thirty grand came from. Maybe Lambert hired Bauers to find out and things got out of control."

"Or, it's like my partner said and there's no connection whatsoever." Dent lowers her voice. "You don't know how much restraint it took for me not to march right into Strong's office this morning and expose the two of you."

"We appreciate that you didn't," I say. It's probably not best to mention that the situation is only getting worse. "We're close on this. I can feel it."

She sighs, turning to Zara. "How long will it take you to track down Bauers?"

"A couple of hours," she says. "I still have the schedules from Lambert's computer, so I should be able to figure out where he is and how long it's going to take to apprehend him."

Dent stands, looking over the case information spread across her desk before turning to me. "You wanted to speak to Andersen again?"

I nod. "I think keeping him in the loop might be beneficial. He knows more about the reservation victims than we do. He might have information on Bauers too."

"Ok," she says, pointing to Zara. "Find the driver. Meanwhile Dunn and I will go speak with Andersen. Maybe by the time we all come back together some of this will start to make sense."

"I'll get right on it," Zara says.

Dent pulls on her blazer and grabs her badge and weapon. "Use my desk. Keep the door closed, and the blinds drawn.

You're not supposed to be here, remember? It will be easier for you to work undisturbed in here without having to worry about Strong spotting you."

"Thanks," Zara says, smiling.

"Okay," Dent says to me. "Let's hit it."

Chapter Twenty-Eight

THE DRIVE OUT to the reservation takes us almost an hour. Most of the way Agent Dent is quiet and I don't bother rocking the boat by trying to make conversation. I can tell she's conflicted about this whole thing. Who can blame her? I'd be conflicted too. Not to mention this case is anything but straightforward. But I try to keep my focus on finding Suzanne and getting a killer off the streets. Better to think about that than the call with Liam last night, which I refuse to replay in my head because I know all it will do is drag me down into a depression I'll have to fight my way back out of. I can't let that happen, not when I'm in the middle of a case like this.

Working this case is probably the only thing that is keeping me sane. I *need* it, and I can't slow down.

"You're thinking pretty hard over there, Dunn," the woman beside me says. "Rough night?"

"You could say that," I admit. "I feel like I'm walking along a knife's edge. One wrong move and it's over."

"I don't know what you're dealing with, but I do know you can't keep this up long term. It will tear you apart. I've watched agents working undercover lose themselves and everything they love because the secrets they're required to keep wear them down. Whatever this is, don't let it go on a second longer than it has to."

"It's not that simple," I say. "I'm under orders."

She nods, knowingly. "I haven't known you very long. But I'm usually a pretty good judge of character. And I can tell you're a good person—a good agent. Someone who trusts their gut and who puts others first. It's the only reason I haven't already gone to Strong."

I wince. I've never been good at taking compliments because I'm never sure I deserve them. Still, it's nice to hear.

"But the one thing you're not, is a rule-follower." I turn, arching my eyebrow and she chuckles. "Didn't think I'd notice? You don't strike me as the kind of agent who lets orders get in your way. So why start now?"

I think back to what Zara said. About going back to DC unannounced. About trying to find out who is behind this breach. "Maybe you're right."

"Then again, what do I know?" she says. "I've been stuck in the same position for almost five years watching others pass me by."

"You don't want to be a field agent anymore?" I ask.

She shrugs. "I like the work. But this is a career for me. And there's only so much my body can take." She eyes me carefully. "I keep forgetting you're older than you look. But when you reach my age, you start thinking about finding other avenues. You see other, younger agents outperforming you in every way possible. And you start to wonder just how long you have left."

"But you can't be more than what, forty?" I ask.

"Forty-three," she admits. "But I'll take the compliment. I've got less than fifteen years left in this job. And I don't want to leave in the same position I started in."

I glance down. She's looking for a promotion—something

I freely gave up. "Have you applied to other offices?" I ask. "There has to be an opening somewhere."

"No," she admits. "I love it out here. New Mexico is my home now. I knew it the moment I stepped off the airplane six years ago. If I left, I'd be miserable somewhere else."

"So you're waiting for a position to open up," I say. "Which probably doesn't happen often out here."

"That's the long and short of it," she says, then motions ahead of us. "We're here." The yellow line on the middle of the road disappears as we pass the sign notifying us we're on Navajo territory. About a mile down the road we drive over a grate that's connected to a fence on either side. It's a cow grate, designed to keep the wildlife both in and out of the reservation without the need for a gate spanning the road that has to be opened every time someone drives through here. We pass a car going the other way who raises a hand and we wave back, the landscape opening before us.

"Pretty out here," I say, catching sight of a herd of wild horses grazing not far from the road.

"As pretty as it gets," she says. We head further down and with each turn we make, the road becomes less and less paved until we're driving on dirt. An occasional house sits back from the way and there was one grouping of about twenty houses a mile or so back, but other than that it's all open, undeveloped space out here.

We reach a T-intersection after crossing over a small bridge that goes over a dry riverbed. To the right is a school, which *is* gated off, but Dent turns right, where a small church sits atop a low hill ahead. We keep to the right, driving up and around the church, the gravel dirt road kicking up red dust behind us. It feels like we've left the world I know behind and have entered something else—a place untouched by humans. At least, it feels that way.

"Here," Dent says, pulling off the road and driving up to a small one-story house. It sits beside a large rocky outcropping that soars into the sky where two large birds circle high above. As I get out of the car, their calls are the only thing I can hear. Otherwise, it is completely silent. Above us, the blue sky goes on forever, wispy clouds pulled across it like cotton candy.

Our boots crunch the dirt as we walk up to the house, but before we can reach it, the door creaks open, revealing Andersen, dressed in a button-down shirt and slacks. "Morning," he says.

"Good morning," Dent replies. "I'm Special Agent Kelly Dent. I believe you know Special Agent Dunn." He nods as I give him a quick smile.

"Come to return my files?" he asks without a hint of emotion.

Dent seems thrown by the accusation, but given how our last encounter went, I'm not surprised. "Actually, we're here because we need your help," I say.

"I tried to give you my help," he replies. "And I was accused of stalking."

"I'm sorry about that," I tell him. "May we come in? We'd like to speak to you about the victims here on the reservation."

His face doesn't betray a hint of what he's thinking. If this guy plays poker I would hate to be sitting across from him. He motions with his head for us to follow him into the house.

Inside it's decorated tastefully. There are some woven tapestries on the walls and hand-made rugs on the floor. A TV sits in one corner, set to mute across from a small couch. The kitchen extends into a small eating area that looks out on the back of the property, which seems to go on forever. A washroom and bedroom are off to the side, though the door is open to both.

Andersen indicates we take a seat at the only table in the kitchen as he brings us two waters before taking a seat across from us.

"Were you the investigating officer on all five murder cases?" Dent asks, forgoing any further formalities.

"I investigated the first case," he replies. "After that, I was brought in on the others when they were discovered. Captain Munroe decided it was better if one officer handled them all."

"And from what I understand there are still two victims who are missing and haven't been discovered yet, is that correct?" Dent asks.

"Correct. But their method of disappearance is similar to how the other women were taken."

"So then you believe they were all kidnapped first, then murdered," Dent says.

Andersen's eye twitches, though it's barely noticeable. "Yes."

"I don't know if Agent Dunn told you, but we are looking at another kidnapping. Annabelle Witter's roommate went missing two days ago. We believe it's probably the same person who was responsible for killing Annabelle. And possibly, the women here on the reservation. Was there ever a white sprinter van observed in the area? One that didn't belong?"

"Not to my knowledge," Andersen says. "We didn't find out the girls had been kidnapped until days later. There weren't any witnesses."

"Other than their... *professions*... was there anything that the victims had in common?" Dent asks gently. "Did they all go to the same school? Or were any of them related? There... wasn't much in the file about their personal lives."

"I didn't know them all," he says. "Only three personally." I'm watching him carefully, and he remains guarded. I can't tell if that's because he thinks Zara and I betrayed him or if it's just how he is. "They were acquaintances, but I wouldn't call them friends."

"But they did know each other."

"Everyone knows each other here," he says.

"Right." Dent looks at me to jump in.

"Their ages ranged from nineteen to twenty-four," I say. "But from what you gave us, all the victims had different body types, different builds. Did you notice any other commonalities between them?"

"No," he says. "Otherwise, I would have put it in the file."

This is going nowhere fast.

"What about their online presence?" I ask. "Any commonalities there?"

"They were children," he says. "What do you want me to say? Children today are glued to their devices. Of course they had online presences."

"How did they advertise their services?" Dent asks.

Andersen's eyes flash, but again, it's so quick it's over almost before it began. "They didn't need to advertise. All they had to do was stick around the busy truck stops. Work came to them. The younger, the better." He says it with disgust. "Horrible thing to do to children."

"But these weren't children," I say. "They were all consenting adults."

"Last time I checked, Agent, prostitution is illegal in the State of New Mexico," he says. He seems to be growing more agitated.

"I didn't mean—I was just saying that they were all above the age of eighteen. Capable of making their own decisions."

"Could you make your own decisions at eighteen?" he asks. "Were you emotionally mature enough to decide that sleeping with men for money wasn't the only path for you?"

He's really starting to get worked up. "I know this can't be easy. You've been working this case for what, two years? That's a long time."

"It's a long time without any assistance," he says. "Despite repeated requests."

Dent narrows her eyes. "Wait, you submitted this to the Bureau?"

"Of course," he replies. "After the third disappearance we thought it would be prudent. But our requests went unanswered. All Albuquerque told us was it was a reservation problem and we should handle it ourselves." He leans forward. "But these girls weren't taken from here. They were taken out *there*, working *your* truck stops. Your city. And still, we heard nothing from you."

Dent exchanges a glance with me, but I'm at a loss. I didn't realize Andersen had already reached out to the FBI once. "I didn't see any record of a request for assistance, did you?"

"No, and I went through all the files," she says before turning back to Andersen. "I'm going to get to the bottom of this."

"It doesn't matter now," he says. "The fact remains we still have two missing girls. And now it appears you do too." He turns to stare out the window. "Though I expect it's already too late for all of them."

I don't like how ominous that sounds. According to the files, the victims from the reservation were usually found a week or so after they disappeared. The fact that two haven't shown up yet breaks that pattern. But if all of this was orchestrated by the same person, it might mean it's not too late for Suzanne.

"One more question," I say. "Do you know a man named Greyson Bauers?"

"I don't believe so," he says. "Who is he?"

"He works for Lambert. We think he may be connected in some way. But we're not sure. It's thin."

He turns to me, his face serious. "I've been trying to tell you from the beginning. Lambert is responsible for all of this. What will it take you to listen?" He stands. "How can you be so blind to what's right in front of you?" That's the second time he's accused me of not seeing the truth.

"We can't just use our gut feelings," Dent says. "We need *evidence*. And in this case, that is sorely lacking."

Andersen looks straight at me. "I never should have come to you for help."

Dent shoots me a look like she doesn't think we're going to get anything here. I'm inclined to agree. Andersen is angry and for good reason. But the fact of the matter is I just don't think we have enough information to establish that this is all being orchestrated by the same person.

"Please leave," Andersen says. "I no longer want you in my home."

We both get up and head back to the car without another word. Andersen doesn't exactly slam the door behind us. But I barely get across the threshold before it's closed.

"Well," Dent says as we get back to the car. "Any more bright ideas?"

Chapter Twenty-Nine

Zara sits in the darkened office, the only light coming from the computer, illuminating her face. She spent a solid four hours going through Lambert's information last night until she was too tired to keep her eyes open anymore. But there is a gold mine here. She's practically swimming in data. The remote cloner she installed on Emily's phone did its job better than she could have hoped and she pulled almost ten gigs worth of information.

The problem now is parsing through it all because half of it came through without any sort of organization. She attributes that to how the cloner worked and the fact that it was pulling data as fast as possible, not worrying about where to put it. It's a handy little device, one that Theo introduced her to. And she'd been saving it for a special occasion such as this.

She winces. Thoughts of Theo are *not* where she wants her head right now. She needs to focus on finding Greyson Bauers.

Running through the schedules takes a few minutes, but after some time she manages to decipher how they're set up and who is running on which routes when.

"Where are you?" she whispers to the darkness. All they need to do is pinpoint Bauers, then she can inform Em and go after the bastard. While the keychain isn't a slam dunk, it's *something*. And at this point she's happy to take anything she can get.

Finally, she narrows down the fields, running her cursor across the screen as she looks into Greyson Bauer's schedule. But when she hits the day in question, her eyes go wide. Her eyes fly to the clock at the bar running along the top of her laptop. "Shit!"

She slaps the computer shut and stuffs it back in her bag as she runs out of the room, headed down the hallway.

"Laidlaw?" A voice calls but she doesn't look back. She's sprinting for the exit and the parking lot. She tosses her laptop bag in the seat beside her as she calls Em's number. But it goes straight to voicemail.

"Em! I got a lock on Bauers. He's coming through Albuquerque *today*. I'm headed to intercept him. Call me as soon as you get this message. I'm going to try to track him down." She ends the call as her back wheels spin for a split second. She pulls out of the parking lot with a squeal of her tires, barreling down the road, swerving around the vehicles ahead of her, hitting the horn. Most move out of the way, but some are stubborn and she has to institute some of Em's unique driving techniques in order to get around them.

"Move!" she yells at a particularly stubborn truck ahead of her. Her phone automatically connected to the car when she got inside and shows her the shortest route to Bauers' supposed location. The schedule has him coming through Albuquerque on his way to Santa Fe up from Roswell, leaving at eight A.M. The clock on her dash says ten fifty, which means if he didn't run into any other traffic, he should be coming through very soon, if not already.

"Fuck you!" the driver of the truck yells loud enough for Zara to hear with the windows still up as she passes.

"Yeah, right back atcha!" She flips the guy the bird and hits the accelerator, heading for the interstate. She manages to get on I-25 headed north and drives until she passes over I-40. As soon as she's driven past the connecting ramp, she slows and pulls off to the shoulder, throwing on her flashers.

"Please, please don't have already come through," she says, checking her phone again as soon as she's stopped. No call yet from Em. That's strange. Usually she calls back quickly, and it's already been fifteen minutes. Maybe there isn't much service out where Andersen lives. Whatever the reason, this is up to her.

Five minutes pass. Then ten. Zara is seriously starting to worry she may have already missed him. She may have to end up driving to Santa Fe and intercept him at the delivery point. As she's considering the possibility, she sees a set of flashing lights in her rearview.

"Crap," she says, pulling out her badge so she'll be ready. The cop behind her looks like a state police unit and sure enough, he's wearing the trademark blue and gray uniform when he steps out. The cop adjusts his hat as he approaches, his hand on his weapon. Zara rolls down the window, holding her badge out.

"FBI," she calls out, and the man relaxes, though he still approaches with some caution inspecting her badge.

"I didn't receive a call you were out here," he says.

"It was a last-minute thing," Zara admits. "I'm tracking a suspect who—" As she's saying it she sees the logo blur by. The little green alien waving at her from the side of the tractor trailer. "Gotta go!" she yells and hits the accelerator.

"Hey!" the cop yells back but she's already picking up speed. The LGM truck is way ahead of her now and she's got to make up ground. She slams the accelerator to the floor and drives the car up to eighty, ninety, nearing a hundred trying to keep up. Traffic is staggered, and it's not easy to catch up to him. Finally, she sees the truck again ahead, driving in the center lane as it passes the slower cars on the right. Zara plows forward, catching up with the truck and pulling alongside the left. She lowers the window and holds up her badge, but her words are lost to the wind.

In the driver's seat sits Greyson Bauers. When he turns and notices Zara at first his expression is one of confusion, but then his eyes go wide with recognition. Instead of slowing down he pulls forward, trying to get away.

That son of a bitch, Zara thinks as she tries to match his speed. But as soon as she does, the truck swerves in her direction, running her on to the shoulder. She has to keep both hands on the wheel to keep from losing control of the car as bits of debris jump up and strike the grille and the windshield. She's practically hugging the barrier that splits the north and south lanes and Bauers' truck is still coming over. She hits the accelerator, but it's not enough. She can't get in front of him before he pancakes her against the concrete barrier. And if she hits the brake she won't be able to stop in time from being crushed by the trailer.

Panic sets in as Zara realizes she has no way out; she's about to be killed by this guy and there's nothing she can do about it.

But just as she braces for the worst, Bauers pulls back away and begins slowing down. She looks ahead of them and not one, but *two* State vehicles are ahead of him and one of them has an officer practically hanging out of the side of the car, a shotgun pointed directly at Bauers. Zara checks her six to see another state officer behind them, his lights flashing to help keep traffic off them. She pulls up and as the group of officers force Bauers to the right shoulder where he finally stops the truck, putting his hands up as the officer keeps the shotgun leveled at his head.

Zara parks in front of the car between them as the State officers yell at Bauers to get out of the vehicle. The car that was behind them continues directing traffic away from the right-hand lane to give them space.

"You looked like you needed a hand," the officer who

pulled up behind Zara says, coming up beside her as his colleagues get Bauers out of the truck and onto the ground. She gets a look into Bauers' cab, which is decorated full of Disney memorabilia.

"Thanks," she says. "I thought for a second there I'd bitten off more than I could chew."

"You did," he replies. "These trucks are no joke. I've seen the physics. It's not pretty when things go wrong. Never seen one try to intentionally run a car off the road before, though. I'm assuming he knows why you're after him."

"Oh, he knows alright," she replies. "I just need five minutes with him."

Half an hour later, Zara is staring at Bauers in an interrogation room, courtesy of the New Mexico State Police. Per her request, they held off officially booking him on attempted murder charges until she had a chance to speak with him. She's tried Emily's phone two more times, but still hasn't been able to get through.

She'd like to wait, but given that he almost just killed her, she's a little anxious to see what he has to say. She also hasn't been able to stop her heart from going a thousand miles per hour since the incident. It's bringing uncomfortable flashbacks of her time with that psychopath terrorist Simon.

"Okay," she says, pushing her emotions to the side as she enters the room. "We're only going to do this once. I ask a question; you give me the answer. And if you lie, I make your life a living hell."

"Psshh," Bauers says with a modicum of false bravado. "I'm not afraid of you."

"I don't care," Zara replies. "Tell me about the girls."

"What girls?" he asks.

"Okay." She walks closer and she catches him inching

back slightly. "You're already on the hook for attempted murder. That's a second-degree felony. Probably looking at nine years in prison." He doesn't seem perturbed, which doesn't surprise her. Given how quickly Lambert was able to secure his brother-in-law's release, he's probably feeling pretty confident. But this is no misdemeanor. He attempted to kill a federal officer. "Of course, there's the federal case. So you'd be looking at another twenty years if convicted. And don't worry, we can make sure those won't be served concurrently."

Bauers flinches, causing Zara to smile. "So if I have my math right, that's already almost thirty years. You're what, thirty-four? Which means you'll get out when you're in your sixties."

"I have the best lawyer," he protests.

"Yeah, I know," Zara replies, walking back around him. "But I haven't even gotten to the best part yet. See, we don't just have you on attempted murder. We have you on *actual* murder. Of six different women. That's *six* life sentences." She turns back to him. "Which means you never see daylight again."

"What murders?" he asks. "I didn't kill anyone."

"No? We have evidence to the contrary," Zara says. "But maybe if you cooperate, tell us where the other bodies are and where Suzanne Fray is located, the judge will knock some of that time down. Maybe you'll get to breathe free air again before you die."

"Ok, look. Maybe I know what you're talking about," Bauers says. "But *I* didn't kill anyone, okay?"

"Then how do you know what I'm talking about?" Zara asks, clasping her hands behind her back as she leans down to stare in the man's sweaty face.

"What's it worth to you?" he asks, but there's a tremble in his voice.

"The question is what's it worth to *you*?" she replies. "You're the one racking up time here. You tell me."

"Okay, okay," he says. "You're talking about the lot lizards, right? The five girls."

"Six," Zara corrects. "Maybe seven, depending on the location of Suzanne."

"I don't know who that is," he says. "But I do know about the others." He takes a deep breath. "It was my job to pick them up and… drop them off."

"And do what with them?" she demands.

"Nothing," he says. "I didn't do anything with them. I picked them up, then delivered them."

She's getting really frustrated by all the obfuscation. "*Where?*"

"To Karl," he admits.

"Karl Lambert," she confirms, and he nods. "Tell me how it works."

He sighs. "Karl would contact me and let me know he needed a special pickup. I would go meet the girls at the pickup location—"

"Wait a second," Zara says. "Girls? Plural?"

He nods. "Yeah, Anna was there to deliver the girl to me."

"Anna? Annabelle Witter?"

He nods again. "She'd escort each girl to us and get paid a finder's fee. She was kind of like a scout for Lambert."

That doesn't make sense. If she was working for Lambert, why would he kill her? Maybe it was like Emily thought—maybe she scammed him in some way? "Keep going," Zara says, motioning to Bauers.

"I'd pick the girl up, drive her down to Roswell," he says. "Drop her off at Karl's place. And that was it."

"That's not it," Zara replies. "What happened next?"

He holds up his hands. "Karl… he can be rough. But I was never there."

"But you knew what was happening." Zara is practically fuming.

"After the first one showed up on the news, yeah I knew. But Karl kept paying me and so I kept doing the job."

"And Annabelle, did she know?" Zara asks.

"She had to. She wasn't stupid. None of us were."

"How much did he pay you for this little service?" she asks.

"Ten grand."

"And Annabelle?"

"Six, I think."

Five girls at six thousand apiece. She wasn't skimming off the top after all. That was money she earned by delivering women into Lambert's waiting hands. She knew what was happening all along.

"Why did it stop?" she asks.

"No idea," he says. "I don't ask questions. I just drive my routes when I'm assigned."

"But it doesn't hurt you to have an extra fifty grand in your bank account, does it?" She can't even fathom her disgust. She glances at the camera in the room, recording all this before checking her phone again. Still no message from Em.

She turns back to Bauers. "So what happened with Annabelle?"

"Sorry?" he asks.

"Anna. Why did Lambert kill her?"

He screws up his features. "Annabelle's dead?"

"Don't you watch the news?" she asks.

"No," he says. "I've been running nonstop routes for Lambert. The day you and your partner came to the office I was preparing for another long haul. He's had me moving more in the past week than in the entire time I've worked for him." He pauses. "Anna is really dead?"

"Yeah, sport, she is," Zara says, unsure if she believes him. How could he not know? "I guess next you're going to tell me you don't know where Suzanne Fray is."

"I don't even know who that is," he says.

"She's Annabelle's roommate. And she was kidnapped two days ago in a white sprinter van. But I guess you don't know anything about that."

"Wait," he says. "White Sprinter van? Like the kinds the Indians use?"

Zara stops cold. "What?"

"Yeah, I got pulled over by one of those one time when I was out on their land. They're unmarked, right? Thought it was kinda odd, didn't have any lights or markings, but the guy was a cop."

"What guy?" she asks, her heart somehow managing to pick up the pace.

"Real serious guy. Made sure I got a ticket for a broken taillight," he says. "Wanted to know what I was doing on their land. I said I had a delivery but he wasn't having it. He escorted me back to the border and stayed there until I drove away."

"Tall, with no expression on his face?" she asks, and he nods. "And what were you delivering?" Frustration and urgency are beginning to overwhelm her.

"Okay, look, that's a separate issue," he says, trying to hold up his hands, but they're bound to the table.

"What were you delivering, *Greyson?* Let me guess, something that happens to be highly addictive and also very lucrative?" He averts his gaze.

"Son of a bitch," she says and heads back out to speak with the state cops. She can't believe this. Have they been looking in the wrong place this entire time? "I need a radio," she says.

"Sure," one of the officers says, showing her the supply locker. She grabs one and tunes it to the FBI frequency. Maybe her phone can't reach Emily, but this sure as hell will.

Chapter Thirty

"WHAT?" I demand, nearly crushing the police radio in my hand. "Are you serious?"

"That's what the man said," Zara replies. "Said he was pulled over by a white sprinter van, out on Navajo land."

Dent turns to me. "That's why our APB didn't pick them up. The truck we've been looking for is out here, outside our jurisdiction. Whoever received the call probably quietly buried it."

"Thanks, Z," I say. "Are you okay?" Listening to Zara explain what she went through to get Bauers was harrowing enough. I'm just glad she wasn't hurt.

"Yeah," she replies. "I'll be fine. Just a little shook up is all." Dent hits the brakes and puts the SUV in reverse, turning us around as we head back to Andersen's house. Though we're about thirty minutes out.

"Call Morrow at the office," Dent says. "He can help you finish up with Bauers. We don't want him out of our sight for a single second. If Lambert has people everywhere, there's no telling what will happen when he realizes Bauers is a snitch."

"You're thinking retaliation?" she asks.

"I think if he was bold enough to send someone after two

FBI agents, he won't hesitate to take care of Bauers. You need to keep a lid on this until we can go after him."

"Got it," Zara replies. "And Morrow is…okay?"

"I'd trust him with my life," she says. "He may be a little cantankerous, but he's a good agent. You can count on him."

"Ten-four," she replies. "I'll be back in touch if I find out anything else. Keep the radio close. Your phones aren't working; I've left like six messages."

"Be safe," I say.

"You too." I set the radio to the side as Dent speeds back towards the reservation. We're back on the paved road but won't be for long.

"Do you think Andersen knew?" she asks.

"I think he knows a lot more than he's telling us," I reply. "I don't like where this is headed."

"Me either," she says. "Something doesn't feel right."

Why would someone from the reservation go after Suzanne? That doesn't make much sense, unless Lambert has a man on the inside. Someone who has been thwarting this investigation from the beginning. Maybe that's why Andersen never could make much progress. He's been hamstrung since the beginning.

"So," Dent says as the landscape flies by on both sides. "Z?"

My stomach bottoms out. "What?"

"That's what you called her. Agent Laidlaw."

Oh my God. I did, and I didn't even realize it. I wasn't thinking; I was focused more on the fact that Zara had just barely survived a fatal car wreck and had broken this case wide open. "Oh."

"I'll just pretend it's another code name," Dent says. "Maybe she calls you 'A'. What do I know?"

Shit. How could I be so careless? That's the kind of mistake that could get both of us killed in the right circumstances. I'll have to let Zara know I screwed up. But I'm not about to tell her right in front of Agent Dent here. Maybe Zara realized I said it too, but if she did she was smart enough not to say anything else to draw attention to the fact.

I rub my temple, my teeth grinding together.

"Agent Dunn, it's okay," Dent says. "I know when to keep my mouth shut. You've proven you're trustworthy. I'm not going to go looking if that's what you're worried about."

"Sorry," I finally say. "It's just…"

"It's a lot," she replies. "Agent Laidlaw seems like a capable agent, but I can tell you two are close. As close as sisters—at least that's how it appears. So I get it. When it comes to family it's hard not to let your guard slip a little."

"It's just… I don't do that kind of thing," I say as she turns back on the dirt road. "That's not me."

"We all make mistakes." She doesn't look at me, but instead is staring ahead. I feel like there is more behind those words than she's willing to talk about. But I'm not about to start asking her about her past. Not now. That's a conversation we can save for later.

We take the rest of the ride in silence and make it back to Andersen's home faster than I expect. That's probably due to the fact Dent is pushing the SUV to its max on these dirt roads, kicking up all manner of rocks and debris behind us as she drives. But when we arrive at Andersen's place, his truck isn't there.

"Damnit," I say.

"I don't like this," Dent says. "Why would he suddenly leave?"

I jump out of the car and run up to the door, knocking as hard as I can, but there's no answer. I run to the side of the house, looking in the windows only to see the home is dark. He's not inside.

Back behind the home, I look out onto the landscape but there's no indication he drove off that way. No dust on the horizon anywhere. Returning to the SUV, I check the tracks in the dirt from where the truck was parked earlier. I manage to follow them out to the road but they're almost immediately lost to the rest of the tracks.

"Looks like he turned east, but I have no idea where he went after that," I say, getting back into the car.

"Do you think he could be involved?" Dent asks.

"I don't know. Maybe. He was pretty upset."

"And according to your partner, he would have had access to the vans." She turns the SUV around again and heads east, following Andersen's direction.

"You think he's working for Lambert in some capacity?" I ask. "I find that hard to believe. He *hates* that man."

"Or he's a great actor," Dent suggests. "I mean, isn't he the one who put this whole thing into motion when he delivered those files? Maybe they were designed to throw you and Agent Laidlaw off his trail."

I guess that's possible, but it doesn't make a lot of sense. Andersen has been working this case for years, following the trail of a killer. Why would he be working for the man he believes is behind it? And why would he offer up information if he's trying to cover for the man?

"We need to find his captain," I say. "I want to get someone else's perspective on this."

Dent taps the GPS on her dashboard, but it's spotty. The connection keeps going in and out. "I think I saw the courthouse on the way in. You remember the turn?"

"Yeah, it's only a few minutes back."

"Good," she says. "Because we need to get to the bottom of this right now."

WE PULL UP TO THE NATION COURT HOUSE WHICH SITS between what look like two houses; they've been marked as *Chapter Administration* on one side and *Remediation* on the other, though I'm not sure what that means in this context. The buildings are set adjacent to the only "suburb" I've seen out here; a collection of maybe fifteen houses set up along grid streets close to the buildings. Every other domicile I've seen has been way out on its own with a ton of land. But I suppose every settlement has its "downtown".

Dent and I get out of the truck, the sun really beating down on us now. Somehow it's hotter here than it was over at Andersen's place, where it was relatively cool. A row of trucks matching the one Andersen drives are parked out front of the courthouse. As we head inside, we're met by a pair of officers and a metal detector right inside the door.

I show one of the officers my badge. "We're here to see your captain." They wave us around the metal detector to a hallway that indicates the judiciary is down one end and the police services are located at the other. We follow the hallway to the right, coming upon a collection of small offices at the end. One of them has *Captain John Munroe* emblazoned on it. Inside sits a stout man, working at his desk.

Dent gives the door a quick knock, causing Captain Munroe to glance up. "Can I help you?"

"I'm Agent Dunn, this is Agent Dent," I say holding up my badge. "We're working with one of your officers, Wendell Andersen."

"FBI?" he asks. "I wasn't aware you were involved with one of our cases." He turns to his computer, typing for a moment. "Andersen didn't say anything about this."

"It's regarding the Witter case," I say. "The young woman that was found dead behind The Speedy Shop gas station last week."

Recognition dawns on his face. "Oh, right. From what he told me you'd taken that case off our hands. Is he still assisting?"

"Not exactly," Dent says. "Captain, do you keep white sprinter vans here on the reservation?"

He nods. "We use them for prisoner transports when we need them. They're lined with benches in the back. But honestly, we bought too many and they usually sit there, unused. People borrow them occasionally when they need to haul building materials, or if they're moving. We're happy to loan them out."

"Does anyone on the force have access to them?" I ask.

"Sure, they're parked out back. Do you need one?" he asks.

"No," Dent says, and pulls up an image on her phone, showing it to him. "Two days ago a white sprinter van was used to kidnap Suzanne Fray. Suzanne was Annabelle Witter's roommate."

His face darkens when he sees the video. "I don't understand. You think one of my vans did this?"

"We've just received information that someone matching Andersen's description has used your vans in the past for official police activity," she says. "And given his proximity to the case, we wanted to ask him about it. But unfortunately, he's nowhere to be found."

"What do you mean, '*official police activity*?'" Captain Munroe asks.

"He allegedly used the van to *escort* a drug dealer off reservation property," I say. "According to the drug dealer anyway. We're still investigating."

The captain sits back, his face twisted and disconcerted. "And you're sure it was Andersen?"

"He fit the dealer's description. We just spoke with him not more than an hour ago regarding the case, before we had this information and he nearly kicked us out of his house," I say. "When we went back to confront him, he was gone."

He sighs and shakes his head. "I've tried to help that man, but he seems to be sinking deeper and deeper into despair."

"Despair?" I ask. "From what?"

"The girls who've been left here on the reservation," he

says. "I thought he could handle it, but when his sister turned up—"

"Hold on," I say. "His sister was one of the victims?"

He nods. "Lucinda Melendez. Victim number three I believe. You didn't know?"

"He never said anything about that," Dent replies, pulling up the case files on her phone.

"I guess I'm not surprised. I tried to persuade him off the case, but he wouldn't hear of it. Said it was his responsibility to find out what happened to them. To bring justice to their families."

"Here it is," Dent says. "Melendez, L. Presumed abducted from Nine Mile Hill, body found on NW-43 on January sixteenth. Cause of death, strangulation. No evidence was found on the corpse, nor was there any at the dump site."

I recall seeing her picture, but Lucinda had to have been fifteen or twenty years younger than Andersen. "Big age gap."

"I guess technically she was only his half-sister, since his mother died a few years after he was born," Munroe says. "Still, he always watched over her. They were close."

"How is that not a conflict of interest?" I ask. "A man investigating the loss of his own sister?" Then again, am I really one to talk?

"Look around," Munroe says. "Resources are stretched thin here. We have a lot of land to cover and a lot of crimes to deal with. If someone is willing to take on a case, I don't argue. Andersen was adamant he could handle it."

"I'm not so sure about that," Dent replies.

"You think he's involved with all this somehow?" he asks us.

"It's looking more and more likely," I reply. "I'd have to get some forensics, but I'd be willing to bet it was one of your vans that took Suzanne Fray. We need to find Andersen and we need to find him right now."

The captain gets up and heads to an adjacent office.

"Julia, can you track down Andersen for me? I need to speak with him."

The woman sitting at the next desk over nods. "Sure thing, boss." She gets on her phone as Munroe comes back over to us.

"I'm sure we can get this all sorted out. Andersen is a good man. A good cop. He wouldn't be involved with this."

"Grief can make people do strange things," Dent says. "Including things they never thought themselves capable of." There it is again, the hint of something deeper with her. I don't know what's going on and I don't want to pry, but it's obvious Dent has felt that loss. Much like I have. Maybe we have more in common than I thought.

A moment later Julia comes in, quickly knocking on his door. "Can't raise him. He's not answering his phone, and he's not responding on the radio. You want me to run up to his house?"

"We just came from there," I say. "He's not home."

"Are all your vans accounted for?" Dent asks.

"Go check," he nods to Julia. "Actually, hang on. I'll check myself." He gets back up and we follow him through the courthouse to the back where there's a small parking lot. A smattering of trucks sit parked in the spaces, along with two white sprinter vans at the very edge. "Shit," he says.

"What?"

"One is missing. And that's Andersen's truck, right there."

Chapter Thirty-One

I PICK up the radio and call Zara, but it takes her a minute to answer. "Yeah?" She sounds out of breath.

"Are you okay?" I ask.

"Fine, what's going on?"

I exchange a quick look with Dent and decide not to pursue it. "We think Andersen may be our culprit. His sister was one of the victims and we've confirmed he's been using one of the white vans."

There's some rustling in the background I can't place. It sounds like she's in the woods. Though there aren't many woods around here, at least not until you get up into the mountains.

"Do you have him?" she asks.

"Not yet, the captain just put out a call for everyone to be on watch. He's got all the off-duty officers out here looking. But there's no telling where he could be. He might be fifty miles away by now. Did you get any more out of Bauers?"

"Working on it," she says, getting more out of breath. "Hopefully I'll have something for you soon."

"What are you *doing*?" I ask, my curiosity getting the better of me.

"Interrogating," she says, though I don't recall any time when Zara has interrogated so hard she's been out of breath.

"Is Agent Morrow with you?" Dent asks.

"Yep," she says. "Been a great help so far, thanks. Hey, I gotta run. We're… in the middle of something."

"Okay," I say, cautious. "I'll let you know if we have any further updates."

"Yep, me too," she says. "Good hunting." And with that she's gone.

"Is that… normal behavior for her?" Dent asks.

"Not really," I admit. "But she can take care of herself. We need to worry about Andersen."

"What are we supposed to do?" she asks. "It's like you said. He could be fifty miles away by now."

I reach into the back of the SUV, grabbing the files he provided, and turning to Lucinda's. Before I hadn't given it any special attention, but now that I know she's Andersen's sister, I want a closer look.

"I still don't understand why he would kidnap Suzanne," Dent says. "What's his endgame?"

"Maybe he thinks she knows something about Annabelle?" I suggest. "But why not just bring her in and ask her? Why take her somewhere?"

"Do you think she was in that house when we were there?" Dent says.

"No, that place was tiny." But then I remember some houses out here, especially the older ones, have basements that have been carved into the ground to keep things cool, such as stored foods and produce. It's possible Andersen's house had a crawlspace or even a basement that we didn't know about. "Shit."

She backs out of the space and speeds off towards the house again, kicking up so much debris a piece of rock hits the back window of the SUV, cracking it. It only adds to my anxiety. When we pull up to the house there's still no sign of Andersen. I draw my weapon and head to the front door again, this time not bothering to knock. "FBI! Stand clear!" It takes three solid kicks before I get the door open. Dent and I make our way through the house, finding it empty and with no basement access. I start pulling up rugs, looking for a compartment of any kind, but there's nothing.

"Dunn!" Dent yells from outside. I follow her out there to see a wooden platform sitting out in the middle of the dirt where it doesn't belong. There are piles of dirt to the side of it, indicating it's been moved recently. Dent and I have to work together to move it and as we do, we reveal an underground storage space, with a wooden ladder leading down about eight feet. The hole is empty as far as I can tell, but there's a bucket in one corner and a jug of water in the other. And it looks like a discarded sweatshirt on one side.

The same oversized sweatshirt Suzanne was wearing the day we went to see her.

"He's got her," I say, climbing back up the ladder. "She was being held in here." Dent gets on the radio to relay the information to the Captain but I stop her. "If Andersen is still out there, he'll be monitoring channels."

"Then he already knows we're looking for him," she argues.

"But right now we're just trying to find him. He doesn't know we found his secret. If he's still got Suzanne and learns we're hot on his trail, he might do something drastic."

"Then what do you suggest?"

I head back to the SUV and grab Lucinda's file again. "If Andersen took Suzanne, then he's probably responsible for Annabelle too. Which means he's trying to make a statement. He's on a mission. And he's being driven by grief."

"Okay, so?" she asks.

"Imagine if it were your sister who had been killed, what would you do?" I ask.

Something in her face darkens. "I don't have to imagine. I've lived it."

"I… I'm sorry," I say. "I didn't know."

"No one does," she replies. "I lost her when I was young. A *random* act of violence, they called it. But I don't believe that." She takes a deep breath, calming herself. "There is no truly *random* act of violence. Everyone does what they do for a reason."

"That's true," I say. "I lost my husband a few years ago. I thought it was—" I stop myself from telling her about Matt. Because the moment I tell her my husband was killed by an organization that had spread across the country like a disease, including in the FBI, she'll know exactly who I am. That wasn't exactly small-time news. And Emily Slate has built herself a reputation in the Bureau.

"—I thought it was because of something outside of my control," I finally say. "But it turns out it wasn't."

"You blame yourself," she says.

"Not anymore. I had to let that pain go. It was tearing me apart."

"Then you're smarter than me," she replies. "Because no matter what I do, I can't quit thinking that there was something else I could have done." She takes another deep breath, resetting herself. "That doesn't matter now. We need to find Andersen."

"What would you have done differently?" I ask.

"What?"

"What could you have done? To protect your sister?"

"Listen, Agent Dunn. I know you want to help," she says. "But I really don't want to talk about it."

I nod. "Do you want revenge? Do you want to hurt the person who took her from you?"

"Of course I do," she growls. "What does that have to do with—" she stops. "Andersen. You think he's trying to get revenge?"

"I think it's a good possibility," I say. "He believes Lambert is responsible for his sister—and the other women. And he can't get to Lambert. So maybe he tries to hurt him another way."

"But… kidnapping? Murder?" she asks. "Isn't that a stretch for a police officer?"

"Wait," I say, flipping back through the file on Lucinda. "It says here Lucinda was abducted from a rest stop off Trail 34." Pulling out my phone I see I only have one bar and it goes in and out. Still, I try opening the maps only for it to spin.

"So?" she asks.

"So don't the roads that share a border between the reservation and the public land have *two* names?" I go back into the information from Annabelle's death, which I've downloaded on my phone. One of the pages is a map where her body was found. And written along the side of Highway 17 in tiny print is *(Trail 34)*.

I turn my phone to Dent. "Look. Lucinda was abducted from the same place where Annabelle was dumped."

"It was in front of us this whole time," she replies.

I nod.

"Then you think Suzanne—"

"—may be where Lucinda's body was found," I say, looking at her file again. "It says here her body was discovered along Trail Road 4519."

"I don't think I know that road," she says. "Where is it?"

"Out in the middle of nowhere," I say, pulling out a paper map from the SUV's glove box. It takes me a minute to locate it. And when I do, I see 4519 is dead center of nothing, in the middle of Navajo territory. "This is where we need to go."

"Wait," she says, looking at the map. "I do know that area. It's where hundreds of Native People were killed during the Mexican-American War."

She pauses. "They call it The Passage."

Chapter Thirty-Two

Instead of potentially alerting Andersen by communicating over the radio, we decide it's best if we try to find and confront Andersen on our own. We don't want him to know we're coming but we also can't afford to wait. Whatever he's planning, he's already set in motion. Plus he knows people all over the area are already looking for him, though I'm not sure they'll be looking this far out. Trail Road 4519 is a long way from his home and the courthouse, putting it about as far out in the wilderness as one can get.

Out here there are no settlements, no service stations and nowhere to get water. If you don't bring it with you, you don't have it. And while I occasionally check our gas levels as Dent drives, more of my focus is on Suzanne. We were probably no more than fifteen or twenty feet from her in that hole and we had no idea. No wonder Andersen's behavior troubled me. Zara was right this entire time; he *is* a stalker. And he used those skills to kidnap and kill at least one woman, now maybe two. I just want to make sure we find him before it's too late.

"Dunn," Dent says, causing me to glance up. Ahead of us is a white sprinter van that's pulled off the side of the road. But I don't see any sign of Andersen or Suzanne.

"Careful," I say, removing my weapon from its holster. I keep it pointed at the floorboard and the safety on, but in case this is some kind of trap, we need to be ready.

Dent slows the SUV to a crawl as we approach, but there's nothing out here to hide behind. There are no rocks, no outcroppings—nothing. It's just wide open land, full of brush and little else. "Stop here," I say as we get within about ten feet of the van. I carefully open my door and slip out, making sure to use the door as a barrier in case Andersen has set himself up behind the van for an ambush. I crouch down, looking for feet that might be visible under the van, but there's nothing. I motion to Dent and she nods, opening her door slowly. Making my way around the SUV, I flip off the safety of my weapon, keeping my arms extended in front of me. I move carefully and with purpose, as silently as I can until I'm up against the side of the van. Dent is behind me and together we slowly work our way around the vehicle until we meet on the other side. The front of the cab is empty, but there could still be someone in the back.

I motion to the back of the van and she nods, the two of us heading there together. Once she's in position, I place my hand gently on the back handle and mouth the word *one.* She nods and I continue with *two* and finally opening the door on *three.* Dent tenses and I half expect a shot to go off, but she shakes her head. I glance around to the inside of the van, finding it empty.

"Damn," I say.

"Here," she points to the dirt beneath our feet. Two sets of tracks, leading out into the wilderness.

"How far do you think he took her?" I ask.

"If she's struggling or half conscious, not far," Dent replies, looking up. A hawk flies overhead, circles once, then continues on. "C'mon."

"Right behind you." We follow the footprints, avoiding the larger brush bushes and what few rocks we see. I half expect to come upon a snake or something worse, but there's nothing. Finally I see two forms in the distance, barely shadows against the bright reflection of the desert. "I see them."

Dent removes her weapon again as we pick up the pace. As we get closer I can see one of the forms standing, while the other is in a lying position, leaned up against a rock. For a moment I think we're too late, until we're close enough that I can see Suzanne's face. She's staring up at Andersen, breathing hard. Her hands and feet have been bound with thick rope and the skin around her tank top is red in places from sunburn.

"It's over, Andersen!" I yell, training my weapon on him. "Give this up, now." He holds his weapon in his hand, pointed at Suzanne.

Suzanne turns at the sound of my voice and cries out but Andersen doesn't move. He doesn't look at us, nor does he make a move to drop his weapon. We're less than twenty feet away, I can drop him if I need to.

"I'm not going to tell you again," I order. "Drop your weapon and place your hands on your head!"

He says something but it's so soft I don't catch it. Creeping forward, I keep all my attention on him, not even daring to blink. As I get into a better position, I see he's not actually pointing the gun at Suzanne, but instead it seems to be pointed at the ground.

"Andersen, you have three seconds before I drop you where you stand," Dent says.

"I was wondering if you'd catch up," he replies. "We've been here for almost half an hour."

I exchange a quick glance with Dent, both of us mirror images of each other with our weapons on him. Finally, he turns his head to look at me. "I couldn't make myself do it again."

"Do what?" I demand.

"Kill someone," he admits. "I think I knew I couldn't do it

when I let her survive that first night. Then when you came by and told me you hadn't made any progress, I thought it would be enough. I thought that would give me the strength to do it. But I still can't."

"Please," Suzanne cries "Help me."

"Put the gun down, Andersen, then we can talk all you want," I say.

But it's like he doesn't hear me. "With Anna I convinced myself that her death would serve the greater good. That it would be the final straw that would convince everyone that Lambert needed to be stopped. And even though I gave you everything you needed; you still couldn't get the job done."

"You planted the keychain, didn't you?" I ask. "That driver you pulled over. You thought it would connect back to Lambert."

He turns to face me fully. "They've been bringing drugs here for years," he says. "Under the guise of anything and everything. The trucks bring them in, hook up with the dealers and the dealers poison our community. And when our children are poisoned, they lose themselves. They will do anything to stay poisoned. Including sell everything they own until there's nothing left. Except for one thing."

"Is that what happened to Lucinda?" I ask. "She got into prostitution because she was a drug addict?"

"Lambert didn't just take my sister," he says. "He poisoned her against me first."

"Against *you*?" I ask.

"Against all of us," he says. "She wouldn't listen to reason. I couldn't bring her home. That's when I discovered Anna." He glances back at Suzanne, who has been trying to scoot away, but freezes as soon as his attention is back on her. "Tell them. Tell them what your friend did to my sister."

"I don't know what you're talking about," Suzanne says. "I don't know what any of this is about."

"We know about Anna's relationship with Lambert," I say to Andersen. "We know she found girls on the street for him."

He turns back to me. "He likes girls from the reservation. Says he likes their silky black hair. Their smooth complexions. He says they are the sweetest fruit." His hand tightens on the weapon and I lock my gun on his chest.

"Don't do it," I say. "Put the gun down. Right now."

"I tried to reason with her," he says. "For weeks I tried to get her to help me infiltrate his operation. To put a stop to it." He's looking past us, into the distance. "But she refused. Said she wasn't interested. Even when I told her what he was doing to some of those girls. That some were ending up dead. She didn't care.

"I thought… if I had to take a life to make things better… she was the best option. After all, she looked like you."

I narrow my gaze. "Like me?" Annabelle Witter was a short-haired blonde about two inches shorter than I am. "We don't look anything alike."

"Yes, you do," he says. "Dead white girls land on the front page. Dead native girls get a byline on page twenty."

"You killed Annabelle because you thought if we connected her death to Lambert we would take him down?"

"I told myself the ends justified the means. This one time. That and she had to pay for what she did to my sister," he says. "But it made no difference. Lambert still walks free. And my sister is still buried. There is no honor in killing. I have broken my oath."

He's beginning to unravel. "Andersen, whatever you have done or haven't done doesn't matter right now. All that matters is we get Suzanne to safety. Agreed?"

He turns to Suzanne again. "She never told you about me?"

"I have no idea what you're talking about," Suzanne cries. "I never even met you until two days ago!"

"Just let her go!" I call out. "This doesn't have to end badly."

"I learned I wasn't going to hurt her the moment I hesitated in pulling this trigger," he finally replies. "I've discovered I couldn't do something like that twice."

"Then put the weapon down!" Dent yells.

"I'm glad you're here, Agent Dunn. And you too, Agent Dent. Now you can take Suzanne back to safety. And hopefully she can put this behind her." In one fluid movement the gun is at his head and he's pulled the trigger as I prepare to squeeze off a shot. There was no hesitation—no second-guessing. There was nothing I could do.

Suzanne screams as the boom echoes into the distance while Andersen remains motionless for a beat, then falls to the ground. Dent and I rush up, kicking the gun away as she checks his vitals. "It was a clean shot, he's gone," she says as I work to undo Suzanne's restraints. Tears are streaming down her face as she thanks me over and over.

"He… he kept apologizing to me," she says through the tears. "I couldn't figure out why he wouldn't just let me go."

I look over to the motionless body of Wendell Andersen. All of this could have been avoided if he hadn't tried to do it all alone.

I guess he needed to prove something to himself. Or maybe…*disprove* something.

Chapter Thirty-Three

Several hours later I'm sitting back in the Albuquerque field office, waiting to learn my fate. Dent and I stayed on the scene until Munroe and his men arrived with an ambulance for Suzanne Fray. I haven't heard any updates, but from what I managed to catch, she was mostly just malnourished and dehydrated from staying in that hole for two days. Apparently Andersen grabbed her and drove her out to his place, keeping her there until we showed up.

As for Andersen, Hendricks arrived and pronounced him dead on the scene before zipping him into a black bag and ironically loading him into the same white sprinter van he used to transport Suzanne.

I've been thinking about why he didn't just use his truck to move her around, but given there were only two seats and she would have had to have been right beside him, possibly punching or kicking at him, my guess is he wanted to make sure he could move her without any fuss. Plus, he knew the cameras were working at her and Annabelle's apartment and wouldn't have wanted his truck to show up anywhere. The white sprinter van was innocuous enough that he could use it to spy on her schedule before abducting her from Loyola's.

As I'm sitting there, wondering how Andersen's family is going to deal with *another* death, I spot Zara sauntering in and my eyes go wide. She's covered in dirt from head to toe, her suit ripped and torn in two different places and she's bleeding from the mouth, holding a napkin to the wound. Her face is slightly red as well. It looks like she's been in a brawl.

"Hey," she says, plopping down into the chair beside me. "How's it going?"

"What the hell happened to you?" I ask.

She dabs the napkin against her mouth again. "You know how you said you didn't want Lambert to get to Bauers?"

"Yeah."

"Well, you were right. He sent someone to shut him up."

"What does that have to do with you looking like you just fought off a cougar?"

A moment later Agent Morrow comes in, looking slightly less worse for wear, though one of the sleeves of his suit has been suitably torn.

"Laidlaw," he says, nodding.

"Morrow," she replies, giving him a wink. She turns to me once he's out of earshot. "You know he's actually a pretty good agent, once you get past all the pretentiousness."

"Would you please just tell me what the hell happened already?"

"Calm your tits," Zara says. "I'm getting there. Okay, so we figured someone might try coming after Bauers and as soon as we had him processed in the system, sure enough, an attempt was made on his life."

"In the precinct?"

"Well, not *in* exactly. We figured we'd try to sweeten the pot a little."

"*We* as in who? You and Morrow?"

She nods. "Yep. So after processing him we made a big show of getting—"

The door beside me opens, revealing Strong, his face

somewhat flushed. He glares down at me. "Dunn. Get in here." As soon as he sees Zara his lip curls. "You too."

Agent Dent is standing to the side of the office, her arms crossed. She watches us as we come in and take the only two seats across from SSA Strong. Strong glances at Zara again. "You're going to explain yourself."

"Yes, sir. See, I was—"

"In a minute," he replies, turning his attention back to me. "Agent Dent has told me you and Agent Laidlaw were operating under her authority. That even though you had been removed from the Witter case, she insisted you provide your —" He glances at her a moment with trepidation. "—expertise to the case. Is that correct?"

"Yes, sir," I reply.

"And it was in the course of this cooperation that you were able to determine Officer Andersen was responsible for killing Annabelle Witter and kidnapping Suzanne Fray." I nod. "She has also informed me that Officer Andersen believed a man named Karl Lambert was responsible for killing the five women missing from the reservation. And that this was some convoluted plan to bring more attention to the subject in order to apprehend Lambert."

"That seems to have been his goal, sir," I say.

"Tell me this, Agent Dunn. Why would an Agent of Dent's experience want two fresh agents straight out of training to assist in a complex and multi-layered case such as this? What sense does that make?"

I don't bother looking at Dent. I know that would just give the game away. She hasn't ratted us out, at least I don't think she has. Which means we're still safe here. "I can only assume she wanted a fresh perspective, sir. I've heard sometimes seasoned agents can get in a circular pattern of thinking. Maybe she thought two agents who'd only recently been assigned might offer something different."

He sits back. "Something different. You know, something

has been off about the two of you ever since you've arrived. Normally people don't transfer into this office with standing orders. But you two did. I was told not to put you on any significant or high-profile cases. I assumed this was because you were too inexperienced to work them effectively." He takes a deep breath, working his jaw. "So you are either extraordinarily lucky, or you are not what has been presented to me."

I swallow, shooting a quick glance at Zara.

"Well?" he asks. "Care to explain?"

"I'd have to go with extraordinarily lucky, sir," I say.

He slams his fist on the table. "Don't give me that bullshit, Dunn. I'm not an idiot. I want to know what's going on, right now."

"Respectfully, sir," I say. "I don't know. We are here because we're following orders. I assume you are as well."

He nets his hands together. "I don't like it. I don't like not knowing what's happening in my own office."

"I'm not sure anyone does," Zara says.

"And you," he says, turning his attention to her. "What the hell did you get into?"

"Oh," she says, looking at her suit. "Agent Morrow and I managed to apprehend a *second* operative of Karl Lambert's. One who is willing to testify that he was ordered to kill Greyson Bauers to silence him regarding his work for Lambert."

"Wait, wait," Strong says, holding up a hand. "A second operative? Who?"

"Officer Ridout," she says, then gives me a quick smirk. "He was the officer originally assigned to the Witter case by Albuquerque. In fact, he and Officer Andersen argued about it."

Strong rests his chin on one hand, his face twisted in consternation. "Do you mind telling me how you did that?"

"Sure," Zara pipes. "We had an inclination that Lambert

might send someone to shut Bauers up, considering he was handing us everything on a silver plate in there. You can speak with Agent Morrow for the details. He's coordinating with Chief Ramirez right now. Let me tell you, she was not happy to learn one of her officers had been bought by Lambert." Zara turns to Dent. "That's a good partner you have there."

"Thanks," she replies.

"So we figured we'd stage a 'prisoner transfer' to get Bauers out in the open, hoping someone might come after him. Once we finished processing him at ABQ West, we decided to have him moved to Central and made a lot of noise about it. I remember Andersen telling us he thought Lambert had people on the inside, keeping his record clean. And wouldn't you know who showed up when we tried to transfer Bauers? Ridout."

"How did he know?" Strong asks.

"I assume he saw it come across once the processing was completed. We didn't *know* it would be someone from the force, but I had a suspicion. Which was why Morrow and I stayed out of sight while the West department handled the transfer."

"Then how was Ridout involved?" Dent asks.

"That's the best part. He shows up just as Bauers is being placed in the van, showing them he has a court order to take over the transfer, signed by a Judge Sloane." She shoots another glance at me. "I knew if he got in that van we'd never see Bauers again, so I did the only thing I could. I bum-rushed him."

"You did what?" I ask.

"Ran right into him," she replies. "And started beating the crap out of him. And let me tell you, it felt really good to deliver a few solid punches to a traitor." She gives me a knowing look. I'm wondering if it was Ridout's face she was seeing as she was beating him up… or Theo's. "Of course, there was a lot of confusion, the west officers got involved, Morrow lost a sleeve of his coat and everyone walked away with bloody noses. But I was finally able to explain and get Ridout arrested for presenting a false court order. And as soon as he was in the interrogation room, he folded like a cheap suit."

Strong is rubbing his temple. "You mean to tell me you instigated a brawl to apprehend this man?"

"Sure did," Zara replies. It's hard not to laugh at the cheerfulness in her voice. "He's signed an affidavit with his willingness to cooperate with this office and its investigation. I figure between him and Bauers, we have Lambert dead to rights."

Strong looks at me. "Did you know about this?"

"No, sir," I say. "Wait, when I called you on the radio, was that why you were out of breath?"

"Maybe," she says innocently.

"See, this is what I'm talking about," Strong says, pointing at the two of us. "That's not something someone with a year of work under her belt would do."

"It is if she's desperate enough," Zara replies. "Bauers is our one chance to nail Lambert. I couldn't let him get away."

"And you were willing to risk getting shot to do that," he says.

I lean forward. "Sir, trust me. Agent Laidlaw has good instincts. Agent Dent and I met with Karl Lambert. He is not the sort of person you want out there on the streets."

"I've heard of his reputation," Strong sighs. "Very well. If you think we have enough to go after him, I'll speak with the DA tomorrow. Dent, you ready to handle another one?"

"Not a problem," she replies.

"Are you going to want these two back on your team again?"

She shrugs, giving us a smile. "Couldn't hurt."

Strong lets out a long breath. "Why do I feel like this is going to come back and bite me in the ass?"

"Don't worry sir," Zara says. "We don't bite. We just nibble."

Chapter 34

ONE WEEK LATER

"*Cheers!*"

We clink our glasses, causing beer and alcohol to spill all over the wooden floor. Though no one really seems to care and we all take a drink anyway. My poison of choice is two fingers of bourbon and after the week I've had, I need it.

It turned out using Bauers and Ridout against Lambert wasn't as clear-cut and easy as we had originally hoped. While both men were more than cooperative, somehow Lambert got wind of what was happening and decided to try fleeing the country. He might have actually made it too, had it not been for Zara and Agent Morrow's quick thinking—blocking off what appeared on the satellite to be little more than a dirt path but actually turned out to be an underground road Lambert had constructed years earlier which completely circumvented the Mexican border. Zara's cleverness and a little help from the US Border Patrol meant we managed to collapse the tunnel before he could get very far and we managed to apprehend not only Lambert, but over half his operation.

The whole case has turned into a huge, nationwide news

story. But thanks to Agent Dent and SSA Strong, our names and faces have been kept away from any media. Zara and I have been happy to work in the background, doing our part without being front and center for a change. Not only that, but not being at the head of the case has given me more time to reflect. I finally think I'm understanding why people love this place. There's a simple beauty to this city that can't be found anywhere else. It's very freeing.

Agent Dent claps me on the back, clinking her glass with mine again. We both empty them. "Dunn, I don't really care who you are or where you come from, but you are one hell of an agent."

Zara appears at my side, grabbing my other shoulder. "I've been telling her that for years."

"Years? Really?" Dent says. We pause a beat before all three of us break out into laughter. Most of the office is in attendance, including Morrow and the brothers, the latter of which get really rowdy at social events, despite their calm demeanors in the office.

Thankfully Strong has backed off any more incriminating questions and decided that he doesn't want to get into another hornet's nest. Especially after he found out Lambert claimed to have dirt on him, despite the two men never meeting. Which then resulted in Strong marching straight into Lambert's cell and decking him. The DA called it excessive work stress while Lambert's oversized lawyer is trying to get the case thrown out because of it.

But there's no way that would ever happen; there's too much evidence. Quezada was right, Lambert kept video of everything. And a raid three days ago of his place of business uncovered video of him having sex with each of the five women from the reservation, including Lucinda. Given the time stamps on the videos and Bauers' testimony, it places Lambert with each of the women hours before their respective times of death. Bauers also provided the locations of the last two women. Apparently, he was ordered to take them as far out into the desert as possible, so no one would ever find them. Lambert felt like things were getting too hot after the first three.

And then there's the whole drug empire. Cases and cases of it which had been shipped up from the Cartels down south. Homeland Security and the CIA are working in conjunction with our office to trace the drugs to a specific Cartel in hopes of preventing any more from coming into the country—at least via Lambert's method.

As I look around at all the smiling, happy faces, I'm reminded of all the people I've left back in DC. It's hard to be here and celebrate with them, but at the same time, I feel like I'm beginning to build a new family here, and that in itself feels like a betrayal.

"Stop scowling so hard, you're gonna ruin someone's night," Zara says, coming back over after doing a round of shots with the brothers. In her hand is a pink drink with an umbrella perched on top.

"Sorry," I say. "Just thinking."

"Missing Liam?" I nod. "Your dogs?" I nod again. "Nadia? Elliott? Caruthers?"

"Ok, let's not get—"

"Your creaky old chair that you never want to get fixed? The smell of the dingy city in the middle of August, when, for some reason, all the sewer pipes open up and flood the streets with the smell of vomit?"

"You've made your point," I say. "And no, I don't miss that stuff. But it's hard, you know?"

"I know. I'm in it with you," she says, handing me the drink.

"What's this?"

"I dunno. Sunset something. It'll make you think you're

back in the islands." I take a tentative sip. She's right. This is very close to something I tried when I was down in St. Solomon. "See, all you need is a little distraction."

I take a few more sips. I've only had one other conversation with Liam since everything went down with Andersen. There haven't been any further developments back home, but he assured me he and the team are still working on it during their every waking minute. I asked him about Theo but he said he hadn't been able to get in contact with him since everything went down. I haven't told Zara yet; I don't want her to fall back into her funk. She's been doing so much better after she beat the crap out of Ridout. I think it was like an exorcism for her. At least, that's how she likes to describe it when she's telling the story.

Finally, I find a booth to sit down for a minute and take the opportunity to munch on some of the chips that have been brought to the table. The FBI have taken over the entire restaurant, with Strong treating us to a night out, which is actually really nice. I don't recall Caruthers or even Janice ever doing anything like this before.

But as I sit and watch my new friends laugh and joke with each other, reveling in the knowledge that a huge criminal network is off the streets and we've managed to prevent any further killings, I let my shoulders relax and just sit and enjoy the atmosphere. Maybe this place isn't so bad—I could even learn to like it here. And I might as well, because there's no telling how long this assignment is going to last.

"Em—I mean *Claire*," Zara says, running up to me, grabbing both hands. "Gotta dance."

"I don't dance, you know that," I say, keeping my butt in the seat.

"Yeah, but you're undercover," she whispers. "Your alter ego is a dancer. Well, not a *stripper* but you know what I mean. We're doing it. Can't say no."

I groan, but allow myself to be pulled up and over closer to the bar where some of the agents and administrative personnel are already having the times of their lives. Even Strong is busting a move out on the dance floor, though I'm not sure if I'd call what he's doing *dancing*. More like *shaking about in a semi-controlled manner.* At any rate, I allow myself to relax and just move with the music. And soon enough, I find I'm actually having fun.

"See?" Zara yells over the music. "Told you."

"You were right."

"Now if I can just get some video," she says, pulling out her phone. But I grab it before she can open the device. "Hey!"

"One thing at a time," I say. "Baby steps."

"Ugh, fine," she says and I hand the phone back to her. She takes it and is ready to open it again when I see her face fall.

"What is it?" I ask. She looks around and shoves the phone back in her pocket. We leave our drinks on the bar and head outside into the dark night. "What's going on? You're worrying me."

"It's a text from Theo," Zara says.

"How does he have that number? We're supposed to be completely off grid."

"I am," she says. "No one has this number, especially him. Not even Caruthers. But that's not all. He says there's a problem back home."

"What kind of problem?" I ask.

"It's Janice—he says she's dead."

The End?

To be continued....

Want to read more about Emily?

A CHILLING MESSAGE FROM THE CAPITOL DRAGS EMILY SLATE out of safety and back into the storm, to confront her greatest threat yet.

After receiving a devastating call, Emily and Zara are forced to return to D.C. to confront the conspiracy that has splintered the FBI and put their lives at risk.

But the city of magnificent intentions hides more than just political secrets. Two agents, sidelined like Emily, are found dead under suspicious circumstances, signaling the sinister forces at work are escalating their plan.

With the FBI under direct attack, the rules no longer apply. Stripped of her badge's protection, Emily finds herself outside the law for the first time, racing against a shadowy adversary with more than just her career on the line.

Navigating a labyrinth of lies without her standard arsenal, Emily must rely on her wits and Zara's unshakeable loyalty. They are all that stand between the FBI and its complete destruction. As the body count rises and the web of deceit tightens, Emily faces a chilling question: How do you catch a traitor in an organization built on trust?

Learn more in *Fire in the Sky*, book 17 in the Emily Slate Mystery Thriller series.

To get your copy of *Fire in the Sky*, CLICK HERE or scan the code below with your phone.

New Series Alert!
Dark Secrets Await…

I HOPE YOU ENJOYED *FIRE IN THE SKY*! WHILE YOU WAIT FOR the next installment in Emily's story, I hope you'll take a chance on my new series which introduces Detective Ivy Bishop. And as a loyal Emily Slate reader, I think you're going to love it!

Detective Ivy Bishop is celebrating her recent promotion with the Oakhurst, Oregon Police Department when she receives her first big case: a headless body that's washed up on a nearby beach.

Jumping into action with her new partner, Ivy is determined to show she has what it takes to make it as a detective. But she's harboring a dark secret, one that happened when she was young and continues to haunt her until this day.

Little does Ivy know this is no ordinary case, and will tear open old wounds, and lead her to question everything she ever knew about her past.

Interested in learning more about Ivy? CLICK HERE to snag your copy of HER DARK SECRET!

Now Available

I'm so excited for you to meet Ivy and join along in her adventures!

CLICK HERE or scan the code below to get yours now!

The Emily Slate FBI Mystery Series

Free Prequel - Her Last Shot (Emily Slate Bonus Story)

His Perfect Crime - (Emily Slate Series Book One)

The Collection Girls - (Emily Slate Series Book Two)

Smoke and Ashes - (Emily Slate Series Book Three)

Her Final Words - (Emily Slate Series Book Four)

Can't Miss Her - (Emily Slate Series Book Five)

The Lost Daughter - (Emily Slate Series Book Six)

The Secret Seven - (Emily Slate Series Book Seven)

A Liar's Grave - (Emily Slate Series Book Eight)

Oh What Fun - (Emily Slate Holiday Special)

The Girl in the Wall - (Emily Slate Series Book Nine)

His Final Act - (Emily Slate Series Book Ten)

The Vanishing Eyes - (Emily Slate Series Book Eleven)

Edge of the Woods - (Emily Slate Series Book Twelve)

Ties That Bind - (Emily Slate Series Book Thirteen)

The Missing Bones - (Emily Slate Series Book Fourteen)

Blood in the Sand - (Emily Slate Series Book Fifteen)

The Passage - (Emily Slate Series Book Sixteen)

Coming soon!

Fire in the Sky - (Emily Slate Series Book Seventeen)

The Killing Jar - (Emily Slate Series Book Eighteen)

A Deadly Promise - (Emily Slate Series Book Nineteen)

Solitaire's Song - (Emily Slate Series Book Twenty)

The Ivy Bishop Mystery Thriller Series

Free Prequel - Bishop's Edge (Ivy Bishop Bonus Story)

Her Dark Secret - (Ivy Bishop Series Book One)

The Girl Without A Clue - (Ivy Bishop Series Book Two)

The Buried Faces - (Ivy Bishop Series Book Three)

Coming Soon!

Her Hidden Lies - (Ivy Bishop Series Book Four)

A Note from Alex

Hi there!

Yes, I know—that was quite the cliffhanger! But Emily is about to face her toughest challenge yet, and I don't want you to miss a moment of it.

Much of this book was inspired by a trip I took to Albuquerque last year. The city captured my heart in ways I hadn't anticipated, and I hope you felt a bit of its unique charm through my writing.

So, what's next for Emily? How will she handle this latest tragedy? There's only one way to find out. Rest assured, there are plenty more stories to come.

Whether you've recently discovered Emily or have been here from the start, thank you for reading. You make this journey possible, and I am deeply grateful.

Sincerely,

Alex

P.S. If you haven't already, please consider leaving a review or recommending this series to a fellow book lover. Your support is crucial for continuing Emily's adventures. Thank you, as always!

Made in United States
Cleveland, OH
08 June 2025

17589417R00156